LESS THAN
a Lady

LESS THAN a *Lady*

USA TODAY BESTSELLING AUTHOR

EVA DEVON

Entangled Publishing, LLC
2614 South Timberline Road
Suite 109
Fort Collins, CO 80525
Visit our website at www.entangledpublishing.com.

Select Historical is an imprint of Entangled Publishing, LLC.

Edited by Robin Haseltine
Cover design by LJ Anderson
Cover art by RNC

ISBN 978-1-68281-099-6

Manufactured in the United States of America

First Edition December 2015

This book is for the love of a jolly good time and all those wonderful romantic adventure stories that came before and lifted my heart.
And always, this is for my son. You are the reason why.

Chapter One

Lord Darcy Blake, the third Earl of Chase, was not pleased. Not pleased with his mother, his servants, his country, his mistress, nor, at this moment, his king. But particularly, he was not pleased to be standing in an obscure hall of an obscure wing of Hampton Court Palace wearing a petticoat.

Bloody hell, if he'd known ten years ago, when he'd brought Charles back over from France, that he'd be wearing pink ruffles in a barely lit drawing room, he would have left the damn monarch to the Frogs. And if he had to stand another interminable moment in anyone or anything's presence save a flask of spirits he was damn well going to tell the world to sod off.

Still, needs must. Kings called. And Chase men always

answered... *Always*.

"You make a rather unattractive woman, Chase," drawled Scott Winters, otherwise known to all his compatriots as the Earl of Ice.

Darcy narrowed his eyes, looked over his shoulder, and leveled his brother-in-arms with a ball-crushing stare. "Indeed? I thought you'd toss my skirts up at once."

Winters laughed and pulled a flask from the full folds of his coat. Leaning back in the gilt chair just a few feet away, he angled his head to the side. "I believe you are confusing me with Rochester, Old Chap."

"That walking bag of the French curse?" Darcy turned towards the long mirror propped against the pale painted wall. He looked like an idiot. "This is preposterous."

The pink skirt hung from his narrow hips, but stopped a good several inches above his ankles, revealing his large silver boot buckles. The damn pink bodice wouldn't even lace up in the back, and his shoulders seemed to explode out of the puffed sleeves.

A smile twitched at Winters's lips. "Come now old man...pardon. Old girl. You look quite charming."

Darcy snorted. God's teeth, if ever he saw a woman such as himself, he'd turn tail and run. After his cock had withered in horror. Women were not meant to be built like soldiers. What in God's name was Charles thinking? "This is madness—"

The door at the far end of the room swung open. The king strode into the room, dogs yapping at his buckle booted feet. His long red coat swung about his tall frame as he walked, and his black wig shone dully in the dim candlelight. Charles's eyes, on the other hand, glowed sharply.

Winters stood.

Darcy stepped forward and they both inclined their heads to the king, then waited. The Spaniels darted about the room sniffing and licking. After a moment, they glanced at the king, circled up together, and plunked themselves into a giant circle of fur before the fire.

Although decadent as Bacchus, Charles bore a cunning intellect that inspired respect in the hearts of men. Not many kings forced into exile ever claimed their thrones, but Charles had grasped his with a bold fist and wild nature.

The king narrowed his eyes. "Madness, Chase? What could elicit such censure from your person?"

"Your Majesty, 'tis simply that I look nothing like a woman," Darcy protested.

The king glanced Darcy up and down, his face expressionless save a glint of amusement in his eyes. "How true. And yet it amuses Us."

Darcy cleared his throat while Winters coughed back a laugh. Gesturing to the too short gown then his face, which he knew bore his father's rough stamp, he attempted reason. "This will never fool Warrington."

Charles nodded as he crossed to stand before the great hearth blazing with fire. "It's not meant to."

"But Your Majesty—"

"Chase." The king cut him short with a gesture of his hand. "We are not best pleased with you."

Oh why had he bedded Richmond's daughter? Why, oh Heavenly God, why? "What I mean to say, Sire, is that there must be better suited men...if not *women* to fulfill your purpose."

The king looked back over his shoulder as he rested his

hand on the marble mantle. "This is why We are king and you are earl. We have placed you in a frock for reasons of twofold."

Chase held his breath, praying the king would divulge such reasons.

Winters laughed; a vastly irritating, self-satisfied sound. "Please do say we're to parade him in St. James's Park. I think he could turn a lovely trick."

"Your silence at this moment, Winters, would be golden." Darcy focused his attention on his king.

Charles smiled. A beatific, disgustingly amused smile. "As fascinating as Winters's suggestion is, Our needs are far more practical. You are to play Beatrice in a court performance."

"I beg your pardon, but there are countless young men who have portrayed women as a profession. Would it not be better to use their talents?"

The king narrowed his eyes to dark slits then looked from Winters to Darcy. "Since your friend, here, shall be aiding you by keeping an eye on the suspected conspirator Warrington while you learn the ways of a woman, We will be plain." Charles smiled tightly. "We would hire an actor if We merely needed a moment's entertainment, but We need something far more dangerous. You may have to prove a rose with thorns, Chase."

The king pushed away from the hearth and eyed his ringed fingers. "Whispers are growing about a Puritan revolt against any traces of Catholicism in Our Court. We believe Warrington is somehow involved. And if so, We want no one to know that one of the members of Our cabinet may find himself at the bottom of the Thames, courtesy of king and country at Our command."

"But his family was killed by the roundheads," Darcy supplied.

The king stared back, his dark eyes cold. "Yes. They were, but he has been associating with the radical Protestant element as of late. Unfortunately, Warrington is quite vocal in his disapproval of Our lack of an heir and the possibility of Our brother James's succession. We think he may be planning to seize the crown and give it to my bastard Monmouth when We are dead. The poor boy is easily led and We worry traitors will appeal to his vanity and secret longing to be Our heir."

Warrington was an ass, but he was a good soldier and had so far proved himself capable in the House of Lords. Still, his father had been a rabid Protestant, though loyal to the Catholic-sympathetic crown.

Both Charles's mother and brother James were Catholics. A dangerous thing in this land which hated Papists as much as they hated the plague. "I do not see my role in any of this."

One of Charles's spaniels trotted by his beribboned feet and he bent down, lifting the panting creature in his arms. "We have arranged a meeting with Amelia Fox this evening after her performance at the Peacock."

"The actress?" asked Darcy.

"No, the Duchess of Kent," quipped Winters.

Darcy threw Winters a withering stare.

Stroking the long eared dog, the king went on, "She is the other reason why We have specifically chosen you. Mrs. Fox and her brother Edward are the children of one of Cromwell's most noted generals. We fear they are both working for Warrington."

Darcy looked from the king to Winters, not entirely sure he was following this. "So, I am to train with a possible traitor to catch a traitor?"

"Your intelligence is commendable, Lord Chase," said the king. "But yes. With your talent for swaying the ladies, you will surmise along the way whether Mrs. Fox is indeed assisting Warrington. And your guise is that of a pupil. The court play is necessary to support your association with her.

If you discover the lady has played the traitor, London will lose one of its most charming jewels. But then again, one does not shine when one plots against the king."

"Of course, Majesty," said Darcy firmly. Charles could not afford to be merciful with traitors, not when his own father had been beheaded.

The king patted his little dog and then set it down. He raised a dark brow. "You are familiar with Mrs. Fox, of course."

"I have read of her, though I have not seen her perform," Darcy admitted. The rags published rave reviews of her performances and half the men at court had written odes to her eyes, hair, voice…her ears.

"She is a woman of singular talent." Despite his suspicions, admiration warmed the king's voice, and Darcy wondered just what kind of talent the woman had.

The king was notorious for his custom of making actresses into mistresses. But if she were a potential traitor, Darcy doubted even this liberal king would take her to his bed

Darcy fought back a sigh of resignation. He had no wish to involve himself with the female version of himself. Actors never stopped acting. He'd learned that long ago. Everyone had performed in entertainments on the continent to keep the exiled king amused. Darcy had proven himself quite the young thespian.

"Could I not introduce myself to Mrs. Fox as an admirer?" Darcy asked, desperate to be free of skirts. Surely, the king would not truly burden him with such an indignity.

Charles stared back blankly. "If you knew anything of Mrs. Fox you would know she is particularly suspicious of admirers and is reported for her selectivity. Even with your talents, We doubt you would make much ground with her."

Darcy inclined his head.

"And besides"—the king smiled, a toothy, slightly frightening smile, as if savoring the words he was about to say—"We want you to act like a woman." His voice tensed, and Darcy knew the king was thinking of Darcy's affair with Richmond's daughter...and countless other wives of the men at Court. "A ladylike, delicate flower."

Darcy winced, realizing that not only was this a mission, but a punishment for overstepping in the boudoir. "And Mrs. Fox will teach me to wilt."

The king's smile broadened. "You have no idea, Chase. No idea, at all. You will do as she says. And you will get close to her." With that, the king turned and strode from the room, his dogs running on short legs, their nails clacking on the wood floor.

"Well, blow me six ways from Sunday," muttered Winters.

Darcy frowned. "I'd rather not."

"Hell, I'd rather you not, old man." Winters strode forward and clapped him on the back. "Never fear. At least you'll be spending the evening with a real and very beautiful woman."

Darcy nodded. True. Very true. And actresses were generally exceptionally friendly even if they were selective. And God knew he needed a friend right now.

Still, he disliked the whole situation, not just the skirts bit. He wasn't at all fond of the idea of spying on a woman. Somehow it seemed to go against everything he'd ever been taught about the nature of a relationship between gentlemen and ladies. Yet, Charles needed him.

Winters took a swallow from his flask then placed it back in his coat. "Shall we to Southwark?"

Extending his hands out from his sides, as Darcy couldn't bring himself to touch the frothy pink monstrosity, he sighed. "Indeed, but first get me out of this frock."

Winters paused. "I never once thought to hear these words from you."

Darcy grasped the waistband of his skirts and yanked at the ribbons. "Sod off. Just bloody well sod off."

Chapter Two

The Thames stank. Reeked. Wafted with odious and nefarious smells. Darcy took in shallow breaths, slowly adjusting to the pungent aroma. He refused to look over the sides of his family barge, lest he get an eye full of raw sewage.

God's teeth, piss smelled like roses compared to the mixture of different physics in the air. But the great river way was not to be overly disparaged. 'Twas the lifeblood of London, and thusly of the nation.

Even so, one needed to cross the damn cesspit to reach the more liberal pleasures of city life. Darcy narrowed his eyes as they neared the bank in his family barge. Resting his gloved hand on the hilt of his rapier, he gazed at the approaching dockside.

Southwark was a fantastical mix of pleasure and crime. One best approached it prepared for a damn good fight. The sun had yet to set, but come the night, one could get their throat slit as quickly as they could get their cock tickled.

Winters approached from the back of the barge, balancing easily on the rocking wood. He drew in a loud inhalation. Then sighed. "Ah London, how I loathe her. Or do I mean love?"

Darcy shrugged. "Oh, I'm sure you love her. One must be forgiving of the tired old girl."

The barge slid up to the slime covered stone wall and shuddered to rest. Darcy looked up at the high, narrow steps that had been responsible for the tumble and neck adjustment of many drunk men.

Winters clapped him on the back. "Ready to gaze upon your instructor?"

Darcy glowered at Winters. "I am avoiding any possible thought of me in a frock. You know that."

Winters's lips twitched as he pulled on his feathered hat. "I do beg your pardon."

Darcy nodded. "Right then. Let's go."

They climbed the slippery steps and came up to the top of the bank. Darcy smiled. The narrow street was filled. Packed with every walk of life. Lords and ladies come for a bit of underbelly pleasure, hawkers, actors, acrobats, and even a bishop or two. God, he loved London.

As they stepped from the stone bank side to the street, his boots squelched into deep mud. Quickly, they moved into the thick crowd of bodies outside the theaters, bear-baiting lodges, and houses of wild women.

The dull roar of people behind the high walls of the bear baiting pits warred with the multitudes selling their wares and generally living the life of those who could only afford to live day to day. And so lived every moment with fire.

A fire that most noble men would never know. Darcy

trailed his eyes over the people. Their worn, animated faces filled his vision and for a moment he felt genuine hope. They were all so alive. And he could never complain when he had so much. He shook his head. Ennui was for morons. Life was full and he was damn well going to seize every moment he had. Even if all his moments were technically owned by his king.

"You have clearly become a most boring fellow, Chase, to have missed Mrs. Fox's performances." Winters flung the edge of his bottle green cloak over his shoulder. He let his hand rest on the hilt of his rapier as they strode deeper into Southwark. "She has tantalized my attentions many a time and inspired a dozen cock-stands if one."

Darcy shook his head. "Actors. I still do not understand the public's obsession with watching other's lives."

"Have you even seen women on stage since the king's decree?"

Darcy frowned. "I suppose I have not."

Winters laughed. "Then that is where your misunderstanding lies, my friend."

"We shall see."

A crowd lingered in front of the two-story Peacock Theater. It was a relatively new building. Unlike the theaters from the previous era, it was entirely indoors. Its smooth, square structure beckoned with bright posters and playbills.

Darcy had seen it all at some point or the other in his travels on the continent, but it had been years since he'd been to a public theater. And he suddenly realized he'd missed it.

People from high and low class shoved to gain entrance into the building. Darcy smiled at the mayhem. "What play do we see tonight?"

"The Scottish Play." Winters pressed forward and crossed through the double doors of the theater.

"Don't be a superstitious idiot. Call it what it is." Darcy followed and discreetly pulled a few coins from his purse, avoiding the watchful eyes of cut purses.

"Fine then," conceded Winters. "*Macbeth*," he whispered so no one would overhear.

Darcy passed a shilling over to the ticket collector. The old man pointed a gnarled finger to the stairs on the right. Nodding in thanks, Darcy headed up the stairs with Winters in tow.

He stopped at the top of the long hall that had doors leading to the plain rows of onlookers. He peered up at the lettering above the doors. He hadn't picked a box. Actually, he hated sitting with those who came to be seen and not to watch the performance. A box really served no other purpose, often times having a poor view of the stage. Spotting the door coinciding with his ticket, he stepped in. "And I suppose Mrs. Fox plays the noble Lady MacDuff," he said over his shoulder.

"Good God no." Winters shuffled into the narrow pew-like seats. After checking it for leftover crumbs or spilt wine from the last occupant, he threw himself down. He glanced around, spotted the wine seller, and snapped his gloved fingers. "She's Lady Macbeth, of course."

Darcy arched a brow in surprise then adjusted his sword as he sat. "Interesting. Well, at least it's not *Hamlet*. God knows my arse wouldn't survive that play."

Winters scowled in mock scorn. "Is that all you can say about such a splendid work of literature? Your arse must be very sensitive."

"A pox on you," retorted Darcy. "I have respect for literature, just not hard wood seats and four hour plays."

A boy carrying a wine jug half his size shuffled up to them and poured out the red liquid into plain tankards. Winters nodded and handed the boy a few pennies, then waved him off.

Taking a long swallow of the acrid, yet extremely potent wine, Darcy leaned back and eyed the celestial bodies painted on the backdrop behind the proscenium arch. The stage was raised about four feet off the ground, with a series of lanterns at its ledge. They threw shadows and light over the wood planked floor.

Winters lifted his hat from his head and placed it in his lap. The feathers shivered, and the great diamond buckle at the front glimmered in the candlelight. "When *was* the last time you were at the theater, old man?"

"Oh, I don't know. Ages." He'd been involved in court dramas, basic debaucheries glorified with costume. He'd done his own kind of acting with the ladies of the court. All in all, he'd had little time for the London companies.

The buzz of the audience died down. A man stepped out from the wings and onto the stage. All eyes focused on him. His eyes were heavily lined with grease paint, and the flames from the stage candles flickered eerily over his face as he pounded the tip of his staff against the floor. "Lords and ladies, we give you 'The Scottish Play.'"

The crowd hummed into a silence so thick a person could cut it with a knife. Macbeth and Banquo made quick work of the first scene and then the witches arrived with a crash of thunder. The crowd shrieked in delight at the women with their long, wild hair and their barely covered bodies.

Darcy stared, surprised at the truth of the performance. But it was not until the prophesy of Macbeth's ominous reign was laid that he began to feel shivers of anticipation. What would Amelia Fox be like? Would she master the part? Could a woman?

The stage emptied, and it was time for her to enter.

A tall woman strode on stage, a letter in her delicate hand. There was nothing delicate about her appearance. She radiated presence and power. Her long black hair tumbled down her back in thick curls. The shift she wore was thin, allowing the flickering candlelight at the foot of the stage to toss shadows in the gentle curve between her hips and her long, slender legs. As she glanced at the letter, her face glowed with excitement, her very expression lighting the theater. The passion blazing in her gaze filled the room with palpable tension. And suddenly, Darcy felt himself responding to her allure.

He shifted as the muscles in his lower stomach tightened. He took a quick swig of wine.

"'They met me in the day of success; and I have learned by the perfectest report they have more in them than mortal knowledge.'" Her voice hummed through the air with a sultry melody. She spun in a circle, clutching the letter. The movement sent her shift floating around her legs, baring her calves and giving the audience a glimpse of her slender thighs.

The sight sent a shot of pure lust to his cock. Darcy couldn't move. Nor could he tear his gaze from her. She was the most erotic creature he'd ever laid eyes upon. After a moment, he realized he had no idea what she was saying, he simply was captivated by her presence. A presence that dominated the entire space around him.

"I told you she was awe-inspiring," whispered Winters.

Darcy gave a sharp shake of his head, strangely annoyed that Winters, or anyone else for that matter, was sharing this experience. And all he could do was watch as she gracefully moved across the stage. Her corset cinched in her waist and molded her breasts into perfect peaks meant to show off a woman's most delectable attribute. And hers were as awe-inspiring as her talent.

Swallowing, Darcy shrugged down in his seat, trying to ease the growing pressure between his thighs. This was going to be an intensely long and uncomfortable two hours if he kept responding to her like this. There was nothing to be done, but sit back and wait for his chance to make her acquaintance. After all, a woman's pleasure was his own personal talent.

Amelia wiped the last of the smudged grease paint from her face. "The face crème, if you please, Ned."

"Wait your turn." Ned Kynaston's firm lips twisted into a smile as he rubbed the crème into his own face. "Good lord, what prima donnas these female actresses have become."

Tsking, Amelia stood up from her chair and reached across the small table to grab the pot from him. "I learned from the best. *You*."

He laughed and nodded. "Someone had to play the girls' parts. I couldn't play both…" He tilted his head to the side, his dark eyes widening with consideration. "Well, I suppose

I could."

Amelia rolled her eyes. Ned was a genius as man or woman, but now he limited himself strictly to man. At the king's decree. His limitation, however, was her freedom. Luckily, the actor didn't seem to bear much of a grudge, given his intense amount of talent in any role he played.

She pulled the top off the small jar. "Your duel with Macbeth tonight was quite good."

Ned smiled cheekily, then hid it with a thick coat of modesty. "Did you truly think so, pet? I thought it a touch too limp wristed."

"Amelia!" The higher voice of the gossip and writer Samuel Pepys cut through the din of actors and audience members filtering in from the attending room. Pepys rushed forward, his dark brown wig flapping about his shoulders and slightly chubby face. He smiled with the enthusiasm of a puppy as he reached out for her hand.

She gave it to him and smiled. Even if he was a lascivious letch who loved to watch the girls undress, he was witty beyond measure and always good at lifting dreary spirits. "A pleasure, sir. Have you not already come twice this week?"

He pouted and stroked her hand gently. "Thrice, madam. Who would not, if only to watch your mad scene?"

Amelia bit back a laugh and drew back her hand. She hated the mad scene. Every night she sat in the back wings rubbing her hands raw, desperately driving herself into a frantic terror. And every night it worked. One night she was going to run screaming off the stage and then they'd cart her away with the genuinely mad people.

And then where would she be? Her brother would argue she belonged in his home and by his side preaching to the masses. But what else would a minister say?

Mr. Pepys smiled hesitantly. "I have come to invite you to a court mask in four weeks time. I know you are very popular and wanted to ask you most early so that you had not already promised the day to someone else. May I have the honor of escorting you?"

A court mask? She loved the pageantry of such events, for the music and color was always superb. The company, on the other hand, often delved into Bacchanalian revelry. But it was an opportunity to meet important people that she could not miss. If she had her way, she was going to exceed Elizabeth Barry and become the most powerful actress in London. "Mr. Pepys, you do me great honor. Of course I shall go with you. But tonight, we shall not be able to chat long."

His enthusiastic face dimmed. "Indeed? Then I shall not waste a moment of our time together."

Ned smirked at Amelia. "And what of our time together, dearest scribbler?" With great show of ambivalence, he began combing his jet black hair back from his perfect face.

Pepys's face glowed with excitement at being the focus point of two of London's premier actors. "Oh, my dear sir, we are to sup tonight, are we not?"

Clear to form, Ned's smile turned puckish. "We're certainly on, Pepys. You owe me money." He gave a pointed look at Amelia, his lips parting in a devilish grin and then he looked back to Pepys. "You sir, have lost our bet."

Amelia narrowed her eyes at the two men. Oh, this did not bode well.

Pepys's eyebrows popped up into the curling folds of his wig, and he placed a hand on his pressed linen cravat. "How marvelous. A bet I am happy to lose."

She placed her hands on her hips, and glared at Ned. "What bet, you cheap rate, pub side actor?"

Ned's mouth dropped open in mock horror. "Silence your filthy mouth. I have only ever been in one pub side play, and I was not a cheap rate. I got one and six, I'll have you know."

She crossed up behind Ned and tried a different tack. Gently, she placed her hands on his shoulders and began massaging the surprisingly tight muscles. He kept staring into his mirror, his gaze fixed on her reflection, and she stared at him in the mirror, their faces just inches apart. "Now my love, what have you bet upon?"

Ned shook his head and pouted his lips. "You'll be angry."

Scowling, Amelia smacked his shoulder. "Out with it, you prima donna."

Dropping his jaw in mock shock, Ned fluttered his lashes innocently. "Would you listen to her temper?"

"Most stirring," said Pepys, quietly approaching as if he hoped not to disturb their tiff.

"I'll give you a piece of my temper." Amelia gently grabbed a hold of his shirt and twisted it, arching her brow. "Now tell."

"Not the shirt. Not the shirt." He waved at her hand. "'Tis silk, woman."

Amelia laughed a half groan and released him. "You are incorrigible."

"True." Ned turned himself out so he could be seen from the best angles. He wiggled his dark brows at her. "You are seeing a *man*."

Amelia gaped at him. How had the overzealous, melodramatic, board trotter found that out? "You spied on me?" she hissed, wishing beyond all things that Pepys was gone. For the man was notorious for writing everything down. And the fact that the Earl of Chase was visiting her could *not* be written down. After being so careful not to link her name to any man, noble or low, she was not about to be labeled a rakehell's mistress.

"Spied is such a cruel and vulgar word. Accidentally overhead is much more preferable."

"*Spied*," she ground out.

"Ah, so this is why we cannot chat long," said Pepys as he clapped his hands together with pleasure at his deduction. "Well, it is certainly time you allowed yourself some male company, aside from the friendships of your fellow actors, and my humble self."

Amelia drew in a calming breath. "Mr. Pepys, though I enjoy your concern, it is not your concern. Nor yours, Ned."

Ned smiled apologetically, sensing that he had touched a sensitive point. "My dear, sometimes I get carried—"

Clearing her throat, Amelia forced a smile to her lips. But how to avoid the topic of Lord Chase? "And sadly, Mr. Pepys owes you nothing. I meet tomorrow with a new playwright, who has written a work for me." She hurried to her dressing table, picked up her brush, and began stroking her hair. "And now I must ready myself to go home."

Ned stood and pulled on a striped sapphire waistcoat. "Indeed? What is his name?"

Amelia kept brushing her hair, smoothing the thick, black curls into ringlets. What name could she give? "I'm sorry?"

Mr. Pepys leaned forward. "The playwright, my dear?"

She glanced over her shoulder at Pepys, not daring to look Ned in the eye. He would sense her lie like the best pointer in Kent. "William something or other. I can't recall his last name."

Ned snorted. "Something or other? Really, my pet." Picking up his large, feathered hat and embroidered coat, Ned shook his head. "Tonight we shall not press you, but I will find out your amour's name." He strode up behind her and leaned in, placing a quick kiss on her cheek. "You saucy little secret keeper." He righted himself and gestured sweepingly towards the door. "Song, wine, women…and perhaps a few others, Pepys! Let us find some."

Ned strode out of the room as if making an entrance onto the stage, and Pepys shuffled behind him, his face alight with anticipation at the night's debauchery.

As soon as they left the room, Amelia let out a sigh. At last. A few moments to prepare herself. She was actually supposed to teach a nobleman to act. If the idea weren't so appalling, and it wasn't an order from the king, she'd find it hysterical. And of all things, the man was supposed to learn to be a woman. Preposterous!

Yet, she would be one hundred pounds richer, and the king had directly told her that she could reject any advance the lord might make on her person. She'd heard about the Earl of Chase and had a bad feeling she'd be instructing him to behave like a gentleman more often than a lady.

Amelia stared at herself in the mirror then laughed. Perhaps a corset would keep the man in his place. Supposedly, it kept a woman in hers.

Chapter Three

"No, I will not have supper with you this night, my lord." Amelia hurried towards her carriage, a trail of men behind her. It was silly really, their admiration of her.

"But madam, I am overcome by your moving performance," protested Lord Styne as he waddled beside her, waving a handkerchief from his white powdered hand for emphasis.

Keeping her focus on the small carriage just across the narrow alleyway, Amelia hugged her cloak tighter and shook her head as she rushed. "My lord, I suggest you take a good draught and rest."

She had far too much on her mind to banter pleasantly with her admirers, but they would try. All of them determined to find a way into her good graces and bed. When she reached her carriage, she stopped and turned to the small pack of men. A quick smile and wave, and hopefully she could be on her way.

But a man in a peacock green hat loaded down with so

many feathers a full flock must have been sacrificed, waved a small box in her direction. "Please, Mrs. Fox, take this token as an offering of my esteem and a promise for supper some night soon."

Amelia fought a snort. Indeed. Giving her a jewel meant he expected to bed her. In the end, they were all the same. They saw her as an object to obtain. She shook her head at the disappointed lord then threw a desperate look at her wiry young footman, Tom.

He jumped down from the back of the coach and hurried round to the door. He pulled it open, and unfolded the carriage step. Amelia gathered her skirts and stepped up into the coach. "Alas sir, I cannot," she said over her shoulder. She sat and arranged her skirts while Tom shut the door.

Now safely ensconced, she leaned out the window and blew them a kiss. One always had to keep her public in a state of perpetual anticipation. "Goodnight to you all."

The carriage rattled down the narrow alley, leaving her admirers mumbling and roaming off. Amelia leaned back and let the darkness of the London streets calm her. In a few minutes, they would cross London Bridge and she'd be home in no time at all. Tonight, she needed her sleep. For tomorrow, she'd have a pampered lord to put in a petticoat.

Things were going marvelously for her, and if she succeeded with Chase, perhaps the king would bestow his protection on her...without asking for favors in return. Amelia glanced out the window as they crossed the madcap bridge with buildings that seemed ever to grow upward. One day they surely would fall right into the Thames.

She could not help wondering what Lord Chase was like.

The rumors were notorious. Though she found such gossip fascinating, she had no wish to have her name publicly linked with his. It was hard enough to be an actress in society, let alone a mistress or both.

No, she'd have to keep their names from ever being coupled. If not, she'd either have to become what the public assumed, for no man would believe her protestation of innocence, or she would have to give up the stage. That was something she would never do. She'd given up too much already to tread the boards.

As they reached St. James's Park, the sky grew darker, oil lamps far and few between. The still night of the vast park always seemed such a bizarre contradiction to the rowdy noise of Southwark. Though she loved the beauty of the fields and the stars, the place was rife with highwaymen, because of the ill light, but it was the only way home.

She would never forget her brother on his way from Michelmass last fall—

"Stand and deliver!" A strong voice ordered from just outside the coach.

Oh, bloody hell, no. Amelia covered her eyes with her hand and grimaced. She just wanted to go home to bed. Still, one had to expect these things. She'd experienced far worse in the slums of Southwark than a mask happy bandit.

Taking a calming breath, Amelia started for her dagger before the inevitable occurred. She only hoped Tom and her coachman, John, didn't do anything bumble-headed.

There was a series of whimpers and *oomph's*. Indication that her two servants were disarmed by the likely experienced thief. She winced. She wasn't terrified. These thieves didn't want to murder. They wanted money. And had a tendency to leave their quarry largely unruffled. Still, her stomach twisted in apprehension as she waited for her coach door to swing open.

Before she could get to the blade tucked well beneath her skirts, the door swung open. Light from the carriage lanterns spilled onto the floor and a black gloved hand reached inside. "Please descend from the coach, madam."

Amelia gaped. He sounded like a gentleman. "Have you killed my men, sir?"

A tasking sound whispered through the dark. "Certainly not. I abhor blood. I have merely brained them. They are sleeping the sleep of the innocent at present. Now, do step down."

She worried her lower lip. If her men were incapacitated she was going to have to be exceedingly wary. "If you insist, sir."

"I do."

She took the strong hand and let it guide her down until she could see the man attached. He stood bathed in the warm glow of the coach lanterns. She glanced to the side, spotting her men lying on the grass, their chests rising, no telltale signs of blood on their persons.

Slowly, relieved no one had yet been harmed, she gathered her nerves and looked back to the highwayman.

A black mask covered the top half of his face. Interesting.

Amelia eyed him. Had he read some sort of manual on how a highwayman should dress? It seemed so. He stood a good six foot. His strong limbs were clothed in black from his long dark cloak and coat, to his folded leather riding boots. It was a stage convention that for some reason struck her as funny. Or perhaps it was his mask and red plumed hat that amused her. He looked quite the dashing villain.

The mask did not hide a strong jaw and russet brown hair. His lips broke into a smile as his eyes, barely visible in the holes of the mask, roamed over her breasts, paused at her necklace, then moved back to her face.

Now that she felt the man wasn't going to accost her with any particular violence, given his demeanor, she allowed a twinge of deep annoyance to rattle through her. Why did men always go up from the breasts instead of down from the face? She supposed it was something ingrained. It did make one feel like a mare at market. "I know you are not mute, sir highwayman, and yet you say nothing."

He smiled, a sparkling, devil's grin. "What can I say? I am transfixed by your beauty." He lifted her hand to his lips then gently kissed it. As he lowered it, he whispered, "But your necklace madam, it would inspire poetry from Dryden, himself." He cocked his head to the side, and subtly flicked out his right hand, which she suddenly noticed held a rapier. Its silver blade glinted in the moonlight, and he held it at a distance, but with warning. "Since I am so endeared of it, will you *gift* it to me?"

She eyed the blade, fairly certain that he would not use it, but not quite bold enough to take the risk. "It would be a pleasure." Damn. Damn. Damn. Why had she chosen to wear this necklace tonight? Though it was only a small diamond cross, it had been a present from Ned, and she'd never hear the end of this. She reached up to untie the velvet string, only to find that her dresser had tied it too tightly. She dropped her hands. "I am unable to remove it."

"Then let me be of assistance." He stepped forward, his eyes lingering on her lips. "It would be my pleasure."

"How noble of you," she retorted. Could the night grow

more difficult? Would he have to cut the necklace from her throat? Highwaymen had become so common it was almost as simple a nuisance as going to have a tooth worked upon.

As he stepped forward and pressed his thigh against her skirts, she realized that yes the evening could grow vastly more difficult. She fought a groan. Somehow she couldn't quite see this fellow trying to force himself on her. He was simply too glib. "I don't suppose that is a pistol, sir?"

He trailed his gloved hand along her collarbone. "Do you wish me to alleviate your curiosity?"

Amelia resisted the urge to roll her eyes. The gentleman highwayman was obviously quite taken with himself. She had to get a hold of her dagger. Well, it looked as if she'd be doing a bit of acting tonight, and he'd be getting far more than he'd expected. Only, as soon as she got her hands on her blade, it would be she who did the pricking, not he.

"**B**loody hell," growled Darcy. Mrs. Fox's carriage wasn't being held up by a highwayman. It simply wasn't. Darcy gripped his horse's reigns and glanced over at Winters. "Doth mine eyes deceive me?"

Winters cocked a brow and adjusted his reins to one hand as he slipped a pistol from his coat. "It depends. If you see a horse and a man in a mask with a damned ridiculous hat… I'd say your vision is admirable."

Darcy blew out a breath. "Right."

"I don't suppose we could just risk that the highwayman will only ravage her jewels?"

Ravage? God's teeth, the highwayman would have to be

dead below the waist not to be attracted to Mrs. Fox, and the very idea of a man forcefully putting his hands on her skin boiled his blood. "It depends on which jewels you have in mind, Winters."

Darcy reached to his waist and pulled out his rapier. Its steel hissed along its scabbard and winked in the dim evening light. "Shall we save the damsel?"

Winters nodded, his jaw setting into a hard line.

Simultaneously, they urged their horses on and raced across the field. The wind tugged at Darcy's hat and cloak, but he kept his focus on the man standing close — too close — to Mrs. Fox. This was supposed to have been simple. Merely a ride through the park, keeping an eye on the woman. But no. She'd had to go and get burgled.

He cut across the field and right up to Mrs. Fox's carriage, just in time to notice that the actress's cloak was flung back over her shoulders, exposing the swells of her breasts. And she was sliding her wine red skirts up her thighs. "What the blazes!" He pulled his horse to a quick stop and jumped from the horse's back.

The highwayman whipped around.

Mrs. Fox's hands reached into her skirts, and Darcy pinned his gaze to the jeweled dagger strapped to her thigh. His eyes widened at the expanse of pale flesh, just a few inches from the apex of her legs encompassed by the red garter. She grabbed the blade and dropped her skirts.

Winters jumped down beside Darcy and pointed his pistol at the highwayman. He probably would have shot at the thief, but Mrs. Fox stood just behind the bastard.

As the highwayman lifted his rapier, Mrs. Fox slashed her dagger across his sword arm. The highwayman roared then grabbed the dagger from her hand without so much as mussing her hair. "You vicious wench!"

A sharp sense that he knew that voice caused Darcy to hesitate. Nonetheless, he lifted his rapier. "Back away from the woman," he ordered, calmly, like he'd kill the man over breakfast without spilling his ale.

Winters pulled the hammer back on his pistol and the sound of metal on metal cut through the air. The highwayman froze then very slowly turned towards them, his free hand extended in the universal sign of supplication. He did however keep a firm grip on his rapier. "My lords, clearly we have a misunder—"

"Save it," said Winters, his voice as cool as his name.

Darcy looked to the woman. He didn't know her and she was naught but a mission, but the idea that she could have been hurt or abused forced his heart to a fast beat. Mrs. Fox stood with her back pressed to the coach, her cloak still thrown over her shoulders. Her breasts rose and fell in sharp breaths and her deep green eyes flashed with passion and anger, just like they had on the stage. To Darcy's surprise, he didn't sense much fear. Instead he saw a barely concealed hot anger as she held herself tensed, apparently ready to fight any of the men.

Wise girl not to trust a soul. Wise girl to feel anger at being so taken upon.

Darcy stepped forward, staying clear out of Scott's line of sight. "Are you well, madam?"

She gave a tight nod, clearly focused on the highwayman only a few feet in front of her.

"My lords, you can see the woman is unharmed." The highwayman looked over his shoulder at her, a pained expression tightening his lips into a strained smile. "I'll return the jewels if need be."

Darcy tore his gaze from Mrs. Fox and focused on the highwayman. The sound of that voice bothered him. He stretched his arm out till it was perfectly straight and pointed the tip of his rapier at the thief. "Take off your mask."

The highwayman shifted on his booted feet. "I beg your pardon?"

"The mask, man." Scott gestured with his pistol at the highwayman's face. "Take it off."

Even with the mask, one could see his eyes widen with alarm. The thief shook his head, the red and black feathers on his hat waving wildly. "No."

The sound of another pistol being cocked cut through the air. "I have no wish to kill you," said Mrs. Fox matter-of-factly.

Darcy and Winters swung their gaze to Mrs. Fox, who'd somehow produced a pistol.

"You'll do it." She tilted her head to the side, her curling black hair falling gracefully over her neck. "Or I'll gift you with a rather large hole in your left buttocks."

The highwayman tensed then frantically patted the small of his back. "Bloody hell woman, you lifted my spare pistol! Who the blazes are you?"

She re-cocked the pistol. "Mrs. Amelia Fox. Thieving is your talent. Sleight of hand is one of mine." She sauntered to his side, keeping a safe distance. "Drop your sword."

The highwayman looked down at his blade as if surprised that he was still holding it. He cleared his throat. "Certainly. After all what good is it, you with my pistol and all?" He laughed hollowly then quickly dropped his rapier. It fell with a thud to the grass.

"Well?" prodded Mrs. Fox.

The highwayman stared at them innocently. "Yes?"

Winters blew out a breath. "Oh for god sake, Chase, let me just blow a hole through his head. That should whip the mask off quick enough."

Darcy cocked his head as if weighing the option. He stared at the highwayman and asked, "What do you say? Or do you like the idea of bearing a whole in your head and arse?"

The highwayman flashed a quick glance at Winters then Mrs. Fox. He smiled tightly and lifted his free hand to the leather mask. He inched it up so that it revealed a little more of his face, but kept his eyes and nose bathed in shadows. "There."

Darcy strode forward and pressed the tip of his rapier into the thick folds of the man's black doublet. "You test our patience."

"Hey now! You'll tear the wool. I'm not made of money," protested the highwayman.

"What? Stealing not what it should be?"

"I have a great many bills, my lord," insisted the highwayman.

Darcy glared at the infuriating thief. He squinted trying to make out the barely visible features. He moved back and sliced one of the buttons off the man's doublet. "Take it off," he ordered.

"Yes, yes, all right," he groused. Sighing like a martyr, the man whipped his hat and mask off in one motion. His long brown hair tumbled to his shoulders.

Darcy narrowed his eyes as he caught the sharp profile of the thief. "Tony!" Darcy exclaimed, incredulous that the young duke was in St. James's Park. Thieving no less.

Tony winced, then tentatively, like a boy expecting a good set down from his mother, turned back to face Darcy. He cleared his throat and brushed back the hair that had fallen into his eyes. "Winters." He nodded a greeting towards Scott, then turned his attention back to Darcy. "Chase, old man, it's been ages."

Darcy gaped at the young lord. Anthony Pendrake, ninth Duke of Haverston, had last waved goodbye to them as they'd escaped transportation from the Tower jail to the Tyburn hanging tree ten years ago. "Ages, you whelp? What the devil are you doing robbing helpless women?" he demanded.

"I am not entirely helpless," cut in Mrs. Fox. She lowered Tony's pistol. Propping one hand at her waist, she eyed the men skeptically. Clearly, not harrowed by the night's wild escapade.

Tony laughed, a slightly pained sound. "I concede that point to you, madam."

Darcy slid his rapier back into its guard, and Winters re-cocked his pistol. How was he to tell the king that he had made contact with Mrs. Fox a full day before he was supposed to? On top of that, he was going to have to come up with an excuse for Winters's and his sudden appearance on the scene.

Darcy glared at Tony, not sure whether he should punch him or grab him to his chest. They'd survived a year of hellish torture together. But the man had put him in a damn tight spot. "You still haven't answered my question. What are you doing turning highwayman?"

Winters smiled, a dry amused grin. "Clearly, he loves the

costume."

Tony shot a scowl at Winters, adjusting his hat in his gloved hands. The red feathers brushed his long black coat. After a moment, he shrugged, taking on an air of boredom. "Oh, I'm filled with ennui, you know. Since the king was restored to the throne there's no amusement save whor—" Tony cut a quick glance Mrs. Fox, then cleared his throat. "Courting women."

He was lying through his perfect white teeth. Even so, Darcy was not about to interrogate the former spy in the middle of St. James's Park with a potential traitor standing by. "You will come and visit me. Tomorrow."

"I—"

"*Tomorrow*."

Tony nodded, with a suspicious amount of contrition.

Winters strode forward and clapped Tony on his shoulder, sneaking a quick look from Darcy to Mrs. Fox. "Come along Haverston. Let's catch up on old times. We'll have a drink and then perhaps later, we can do a bit of *courting*."

Before Tony could protest, Winters grabbed the duke's shoulder and literally dragged the young lord to his horse. "Mind the hat, mind the hat," Tony groused.

As Winters mounted up, he said, "We must have a serious talk about your choice in wardrobe, Your Grace."

"Stuff it," retorted Tony.

"Oh, and Tony," Darcy called.

Tony hesitated. "Yes?"

"The jewels," Darcy reminded.

Tony shifted on his boots, glancing from Mrs. Fox, to Darcy, to Winters then sighed. He yanked the necklace from under his cloak. "If I must."

"Return it to the lady," Darcy ordered.

Tony gave a wry smile then tossed it to Mrs. Fox, who caught it easily in her palm.

"Just a lark," the young duke said lightly. "I do hope you'll forgive me."

She snorted. "Just the once, mind you."

"I'd never dare challenge a lady such as yourself again." Tony gave her a quick bow then turned to Winters.

Darcy waited for the duke to mount up in a rather undignified but necessary arrangement behind Winters. As soon as they'd rode off, and the sound of their bickering faded into the park, Darcy turned his full attention onto Mrs. Fox.

No immediate danger at hand, he could truly look at her.

Her long dark hair framed her face in thick curls that brushed the tops of her breasts and draped down her back. In the dim moonlight, her skin appeared paler than marble and her green eyes shone almost black in the darkness.

As she stared back at him, their eyes met, and her sensual pink lips opened, exposing just a hint of her velvet tongue.

Darcy's breath hitched in his throat at the sight of her mouth opening.

She quickly broke their gaze, tucked the necklace into a pocket, then fiddled with the pistol in her other hand. Frowning, she eyed the small barrel. "You know, I don't believe it's even primed."

"Let's not find out." Darcy crossed to her quickly and slipped it from her grasp. Their gloved fingers barely caressed, but she tensed at their contact. Well, well, she was as entranced by him as he her.

Tucking the pistol into his breeches, he looked down at

her.

Once again she smiled, her eyes crinkling with confusion. "You, sir, are staring." She lifted her hands and patted her face and hair. "Am I mussed?"

Mussed? Her hair was a bit tousled and her cheeks glowed. "You were not frightened at all?" he asked, surprised by his own curiosity.

She blinked. "I'd have to have been a fool, and I should like to think I am not, to not have felt some alarm." She shrugged, her breasts pressing tightly together. "But one must expect such things this late in the park."

"Very brave and practical of you," he said softly. Darcy was having trouble not letting his eyes wander to her breasts and so he focused on her mouth... Which seemed to be as equally dangerous, because now he was considering how it might feel beneath his.

"My servants—"

"Are unharmed and we shall tend to them but first."

"Do you wish repayment?"

He didn't reply immediately and the silence between them grew, slowly, crackling with awareness. She looked up at him, her own glance flicking to his lips.

He smiled hungrily at her. "I have an idea. Perhaps a kiss?"

Despite the small reservation that he shouldn't dally with a suspect, he found himself moving towards her. She stepped backwards, still gazing into his eyes. As he returned her stare, he didn't think either of them would ever be able to look away.

Finally he stood close enough for his thighs to touch the folds of her wide skirts. Her eyes widened and she thrust her hand out. Like it was a guardian at the gate. "You may kiss my hand."

Darcy took it and pressed a soft kiss into her palm then guided her hand to rest on his shoulder. She drew in a soft breath, clearly shocked.

"Thank you, madam. But..." He caressed his fingers along her cheek, cupping it. Leaning down, he halted a mere inch from her mouth, and whispered, "This is more what I had in mind."

Chapter Four

Good lord, what was she doing?

She was bloody well standing in St. James' Park with a damn handsome man—who had also saved her from a highwayman, even if the two had turned out to be acquaintances. That's what she was doing.

Heat spread from the center of her body at his nearness. His presence was tempting. And she was seldom tempted. She parted her lips to tell him no, and just in that moment, his lips descended over hers.

Her protest died a hasty death as his warm lips moved over hers, caressing her. At first, she didn't kiss him back, hardly believing she was kissing a stranger, but at last she gasped at the sensual feel of it.

He growled low in his throat. Circling her waist with his hands, he lifted her onto her tiptoes. The strange seduction of it sent a shudder of desire through her.

As she pulled back for a little breath of air, it occurred

to her that they were not alone.

The footman. And the coachman. Their stirrings punctured the night air. She felt a wave of immediate relief that they had regained consciousness and were shuffling in the grass to stand.

The slightly dizzy feeling that had lightened her head vanished, and Amelia jolted back, whacking her rump against the coach door. She pushed at her rescuer's shoulders. She might be a public exhibitionist but not when it came to being kissed *off* stage. "Stop."

He hesitated a moment, then pulled back, his broad chest lifting in deep breaths. The sight of his dark eyes, warm with desire for her, was shocking. He looked as if he could eat her right then. And for a brief second, she delighted in the fact that he wanted her.

Even so, she'd have to send him on his way. It didn't matter if she had enjoyed his kiss and the way he looked at her. She'd made a vow a long time ago that she would not allow herself the pleasures of a lover. She wouldn't be the harlot her father insisted all actresses became.

After a moment, he straightened to his full height. "Allow me to escort you home."

Amelia gave him an apologetic smile. "You don't have to be quite the gentleman."

He arched a dark brow at her. "Gentleman? If I was a gentleman you'd already be safe and alone in your bed." His eyes searched her face, as if somehow he could read her thoughts, then he stepped back and offered her his arm.

Letting out a sigh, Amelia took it and allowed him to move her away from the coach door and open it. As he handed her in, she said, "It really isn't necessary, though I appreciate your thought." Then again, the idea of getting to know her strange rescuer was dangerously appealing.

The leather of his glove slid teasingly against her fingers as he pulled his hand free. "Alas, madam, I am a man born to duty." His lips twisted in an ironic smile. "Consequently, I must obey it."

He released her hand and strode to his horse. Amelia settled against the seat, waiting while he tied his stallion to the rear of her coach.

His deep voice rumbled through the air as he talked with her coachman.

Oh lord, she was such a fool. It was very likely that her servants had seen her kissing this man. And with her luck, the servants would spread the gossip like warm butter. Amelia rubbed her hand over her forehead, wishing for the complications of the night to desist.

The carriage leaned to the left as he pulled himself inside, and the light from her small lantern swung with the movement. He lowered himself to the seat opposite hers and folded his arms over his broad chest. He sat silently for a few moments then said, "A trifle awkward is this not?

She laughed, glad to relieve the tension between them. "Yes. Yes it is."

"Well perhaps we might talk a little."

"I suppose that might not be unbearable," she teased. In truth, she wanted him to know as little as possible about her. Though, he had heard her name when she had so blithely proclaimed it to Tony the Highwayman.

He inclined his head. "I shall endeavor to prove perfectly affable."

Oh, she felt fairly certain of his affability, and thusly, the sooner she said adieu the better.

The coach jolted forward and they sat silently for a moment in the blue light of evening. Shadows played over the hard planes of his face and the dark blue fabric of his simple, yet elegantly stitched coat. Darcy kept his eyes on her and eventually folded his gloved hands over his lap. "You are Amelia Fox?"

She nodded, but said nothing, having no wish to encourage him to believe she would receive him at some later time.

"What an honor to come to the aid of someone with such repute." He smiled, a slow smile.

Amelia resisted the urge to roll her eyes. The man was clearly aristocracy. He breathed it from his beautiful voice to the inherent self-importance that seemed to come second nature to him. Aristocracy might note someone such as herself as famous, but they did not respect her. Really, in many ways she was little more than a monkey they could order to perform. But she wouldn't complain. She made a great deal of money entertaining her betters. "My *repute* wouldn't have done much without your honor and assistance."

He laughed. "Actually, you seemed to have the situation well in hand. I think if my friend and I had not arrived, you would have gotten the better of Tony."

She smiled grudgingly. "He was rather easy to distract."

Darcy's eyes glittered with amusement. "Men usually are."

Amelia laughed ruefully. Usually, she was not good with men, but she was having no trouble conversing easily with him. "Well it did not take a great deal of skill to direct his attention elsewhere."

He lifted a hand and shook his head. "Do not disparage

yourself, madam. I only have the deepest admiration for your skills." He leaned back, almost lazily, against the seat. "Your ability to fend for yourself is most heartening. Men cannot always be knights on white horses."

"How true. I find often that they are usually the fire breathing dragons."

He narrowed his eyes ever so slightly, clearly surprised by her comment. "Well, given tonight's events, I'm sure you could douse any man's steam."

"Including yours?" she parried, not able to keep a smile from her face. He truly seemed to admire her independence. Which was not something she was used to in men.

"I have my own ways to ward off enterprising and fierce maidens."

Amelia laughed. "A useful skill, I'm sure."

The coach slowed to a stop, and much to Amelia's surprise, she realized they were in front of her townhouse. The footman's steps clattered on the cobblestone as he scurried to open the door.

"Alas," he said, "Our journey seems at an end." He climbed out of the coach then held out his gloved hand. She took it. The heat of him warmed her hand, even through their gloves. She bit her lip to hide its affect as she rushed out of the coach.

She peered up at the houses on either side of hers. It was not quite late enough for the razor tongued gossips in her square to be in bed, and she had no wish to be seen emerging from a coach with a man. Even so, she smiled at her witty companion. "Thank you. You have been most kind."

The humor slipped from his face as he looked down at her. "No. I have not." He held her hand for a moment longer than he should have then brought it to his lips. As he kissed her palm, he kept his eyes on her. He stepped back and headed to the rear of the coach. He untied his stallion and guided the animal into the street. He mounted up then swept off his hat, inclining his head to her. "A true and surprising pleasure, Mrs. Fox."

With a flick of his reigns, he rode off into the dark London streets.

Gone as quickly as he had come.

Amelia stood on her front step, staring. A part of her truly hoped to see him again. But that would be very bad. For though she liked him, she liked him in a way that would not suit a simple friendship. So, it was best to end it before it began. Besides, she could only take so many nights like this one. Blowing out a breath, Amelia swept up the stairs, deliberately avoiding her footman's impertinent and questioning stare.

A smile played at her lips. Her friend Kynaston was never going to believe this. After all, she barely could.

Today was going to be bloody awful.

Not only was she to meet with the Earl of Chase, she had her brother to contend with. A brother who seemed on the verge of doing something very dangerous and dimwitted. For, he was running about, making assignations with her at inns in Southwark, of all places, in broad daylight, as if they were in some sort of caper. On top of that, he was making insinuations about her morals... Though after last night— No, she would not think on that.

Amelia folded her hands together, digging her fingers through the leather of her forest green gloves as she and her brother sat at a table hidden between two wooden beams and the door to the kitchen of The George Inn. "Edward, you are being a toad. Not to mention an idiot."

"You must not be an actress. Father would be ashamed." He glowered at her from under his black vicar's hat. "It will only get you in a great deal of trouble, spiritually and temporally."

"Will it indeed?" she drawled. It was so difficult to take her brother seriously. At five and twenty, he still maintained his boyish good looks with dimples in his cheeks and their mother's corn blond hair.

Though not five years ago, Edward had railed against their father and his Puritan strictness, Amelia knew full well that her brother meant what he said.

"I know exactly what Father would have thought." She hesitated, trying not to think of the worn woman her mother had been. She'd been so beaten down by their father's unforgiving beliefs and zealot ways. No wonder she'd left her children and harsh husband. "He hated all women."

Her brother didn't bother to deny their father's beliefs. Instead, he blushed red, a bright color the dim early morning light could not hide. "I'm sorry," he said gently. "You know I don't mean to be like him."

Yet, after Richard Allworthy's death, Edward was trying to make the man love him from the grave by following in the bastard's footsteps.

Neither of them could escape their father, though he'd been dead these past five years. Not even changing their last name to avoid being linked to his political maneuvering had freed them. Not that anything so symbolic ever could.

"I know you don't mean to be." Amelia reached her hand out across the table, and he took it, just as they had done when they were little. When there had been no one to comfort them but each other. "But these new friends of yours. They worry me."

"Whatever you may think, they are good men."

She gripped his hand and leveled him with a hard stare. "They are extremists."

His eyes widened and he glanced right to left, almost as if he expected a king's man to nab him that very moment. But there was no one in the dining hall at this mid morning hour. "Shh. The truth is, I asked to see you here because I do not think I shall be able to see you for some months."

For the first time since the Royals had ridden back into London, Amelia felt the old fear sink into her stomach. She'd grown up with plots and plans and generals marching through her house. She drew back her hand. "I do not like the sound of this," she said, her voice low. "What are you doing?"

Edward glanced at the fire flickering in the hearth across the room. "It is best you don't know."

She shook her head and glared at her brother. She hated secrets. "Please don't—"

His face hardened. "You cannot stop me."

Amelia fisted her palms on the table. "No, I cannot," she hissed. "But I can reason with you."

"Reason?" he demanded. He leaned forward, pressing the wide black cuffs of his sleeves into the rough wood table. "Do you think we live in an age of reason? You have seen the debauchery first hand—"

Groaning, Amelia pulled back from her brother. Yes, she'd seen the debauchery, but she'd also seen the glorious scientific discoveries so valued by the men of this new era. Discoveries that never would have been allowed to take place under Cromwell's reign.

Under that crazed Puritan's order, she'd not been allowed to even walk the streets without proof of some sort that she was out for a purpose and not just to enjoy the air. She could still recall narrowly avoiding the stocks on more than one occasion.

For goodness sake, she'd be willing to put up with a great deal of debauchery to walk in the park on Sunday again without being told she'd burn in hell, nor be punished publicly for it. Amelia drew in a calming breath. "Edward, these words are not yours. Whose are they?"

Immediately, his light green eyes shuttered and he leaned back. "You know I love you, but you don't share my beliefs."

Amelia snorted. She couldn't help it. *He* didn't share his own beliefs. Something or someone in the last year had changed him from the young man in love with life she had always known to this pale reflection of their father. "Do you forget that you wished a place at court? That you had plans to travel the world and make discoveries in the mysteries of science?" As she spoke her voice grew louder, as if trying to siphon out some of the anger beginning to boil inside her. "Will you give that up?"

His eyes widened and he lifted his hands, shushing her. "Please. Do not talk so loud. I have no wish to draw attention."

"Or be seen with an actress?" she snapped.

The silence that lingered between them cut her right to the heart, and Amelia locked eyes with her brother. He truly was ashamed of her. Just like their Father. "Fine. I should not wish to sully your position in heaven or upon this earth." She stood and gathered her skirts. "Good-day."

As she strode from the sparsely populated dining room, his footsteps thudded behind her, but she didn't look back. How had he come to judge people so harshly? He himself had been harshly judged all his life and had loathed it.

She rushed out into the sunlight, her heart heavy. Disoriented by the sudden turn of the morning, Amelia stopped in the yard surrounded on three sides by the inn's rooms. The mud was thick, and her leather boots sunk into the horse pawed earth. And to think she had come here to help him. Well, he didn't want her help. Not an actress's help. She grimaced and kept walking, her eyes stinging with tears of anger and frustration.

"Wait! Amelia, please!" Her brother pleaded.

Closing her eyes, she counted to five. She would not have a shouting match with him over this. If he could not accept her for whom she was, there was nothing to be done. He was still her brother, and she would always love him.

He stumbled to a halt beside her, the wide skirt tails of his black coat flapping about his legs like crows wings. "I am sorry. Understand that I must do what I must."

So, he did not truly feel sorry for his hard judgments. He simply wished her not to be angry with him. He'd never been able to stand that. Not since he'd been a boy in swaddling. Biting back her angry retort, Amelia glared at him. "And I must do what I must. I have an appointment at the palace."

"Th-the palace?" His skin paled and he reached out to

her, grabbing her elbow with his gloved hand. He smiled hesitantly. "Indeed?"

She narrowed her eyes. Why was he shaken? He was trying to hide it with the smile, one that had always gotten him sweets and later the favors of many pretty wenches. But she could sense his worry. "Yes. The palace."

He dropped his hand back to his side and nodded. "I see. Yes. Well." He cleared his throat, and his smile disappeared. "Do be careful."

"Careful?" Why on earth need she be careful? She'd done nothing but earn the king's favor. And they long since shucked the danger that came along with their father's name when they had chosen Fox.

"The palace is a dangerous place."

For even a king had lost his head at a palace. The unspoken words hung between them.

"I know, Edward." Any anger she'd felt dissipated, and suddenly it was she who was shaken. Her stomach tightened and she wanted to grab hold of her brother and demand to know what he was up to.

But she didn't, for he would not tell her. Richard Allworthy had raised determined children, if nothing else. "Here I-I brought this for you. I know you are making no money now, not having a parish." She pulled out the little envelope filled with gold guineas that she had intended to give him. He looked so thin now, and most probably he wasn't eating properly at his boarding house.

Edward swallowed, his blue eyes shining with shame and gratitude. "I don't know what to say," he whispered.

"Don't say anything. Take it." She shoved the money into his hand then grabbed his shoulders and gave him a quick hard hug. "You must not simply vanish. Come and see me."

He slipped the envelope in his pocket and rested his hands on her back. "I will if I can."

Amelia slipped out of his embrace and forced a smile. Though she half feared he would scowl, she said, "Good. Come and see a play. It would do you good."

Edward laughed, his old charm lighting his eyes. "Perhaps God shall forgive me one transgression... If it is Shakespeare. None of this new, sensationalist rubbish."

"Then we have a bargain." With that, she strode to her coach just across the yard. As she climbed in, she resisted the urge to look back. For if she did, she would be giving validity to the thought that she might never see her brother again.

She did not know if she could take that.

For she and her brother had both watched their mother vanish into the night without a trace.

Heavy drops of rain fell from the sky, splattering on Darcy's summer cape, but he didn't feel the chill. No, he was consumed by the urgency between brother and sister. He moved farther back into the shadows of the inn.

At this distance, he couldn't hear a word, but the air was tense around Mrs. Fox and her brother Edward. He'd followed them out from the dining room, away from his hiding place and up the narrow servants stair that had also been too distant to hear anything.

A light breeze whipped Mrs. Fox's thick skirts against her legs and her brother stood, gesturing for her to listen to him. She held back before she allowed herself to relax. Even from this distance, Darcy witnessed the brilliance of her smile. His breath hitched in his throat. God the woman was glorious. He hadn't been able to push her from his mind and had lost a damn full night of sleep over her passionate green eyes and saucy tongue. Oh, the things he wanted to do with that tongue.

He snapped out of his lustful thoughts as she handed her brother a small envelope. He took it and she threw her arms around him, hugging the young vicar.

Darcy narrowed his eyes, waiting patiently.

After a few more words, she turned and headed for her coach. She climbed in and then rattled off toward the theater.

Darcy wiped a gloved hand over his mouth. Why would brother and sister meet clandestinely?

Edward Fox stood in the center of the inn's yard rubbing his hands. The man looked damn distressed. And no wonder, considering he'd been spotted with known Puritan conspirators.

The vicar headed out into the busy street, weaving his way amongst the people of Southwark.

Darcy followed him into the sunlight and quietly strode out into the bustling way, remaining unseen by his mark.

Fox stopped in front of a rickety two story, white plastered shop. A sign with the mark of a printing press swung over the door. He glanced right and left then slipped inside.

Resisting the urge to laugh at the man's cloak-and-dagger theatrics, Darcy walked up to the thick glass windows and stared inside at the books and folios on racks. Fox could learn a good deal in subtlety from his sister.

What a spy she would make…or perhaps she already was.

After a moment, Darcy pushed open the heavy oak door and stepped into the cool dimness of the shop. The low, dark wood ceiling hung ominously over head. Rope laced its way back and forth between the walls. Parchments hung drying and the acrid smell of ink permeated the air.

The clerk and Mr. Fox stood by the long oak counter holding a quiet conversation. The clerk's eyes flicked over in Chase's direction. "I'll be with you in a moment, sir."

Darcy nodded then angled himself so he appeared to be studying the books kept in locked cage bookcases. But he kept the two men in the perimeter of his vision.

Fox leaned in and handed the clerk a small package. The same package that Mrs. Fox had passed to her brother. Darcy felt a sinking sensation.

This did not bode well for Mrs. Fox. Granted, she might just be a caring sister. But if she was handing her brother things that he was passing to an underground Puritan bookshop, it was a very bad sign for the lady's innocence.

Under her bright colors and acting at the playhouse, no one would ever expect a woman who walked the boards to be a rebel for God.

Until now.

The thought should have brought him pleasure, for it brought him a step closer to success. But all he could think of was Mrs. Fox and the way she had given Tony what for. He would have to harden his admiration for the actress. It was time to begin the interrogation… Using whatever means necessary.

The first traces of dawn light spilled over the street and bathed the front door of Mrs. Fox's house. He stared at the expensive edifice that cradled the scandalous woman in comfort while he skulked in the gloom and tugged his hat farther down to hide his visage. A bitter note filled his heart.

He'd been staring at the building since Lord Chase left the actress on the doorstep over an hour ago.

His life should have been so different… But wishes were not horses. No. Only action mattered.

It was all going according to plan. The king had believed the lies that he had spun, that he was a traitor, when nothing could be farther from the truth. All the right people were falling into the right places.

That alone should have given him some form of satisfaction. Yet, it did not.

Nothing would ever be repayment enough for the betrayal that had so brutally altered his life. Still, he would persevere. One day soon those who had used him and taken everything he'd ever loved would understand what pain and loss meant.

Turning at last, he slipped into the darker shadows and headed towards the older part of the city, no thought to meet his bed this night. Someday he would sleep again. Maybe when he no longer heard the screams of his father, his mother, his sister, and infant brother. Yes, then he'd sleep. But that wouldn't be for a very long time. Until then, he'd have to wait. For his revenge.

Chapter Five

"So, what happened with Tony?" Darcy lifted his rapier, preparing to advance along the narrow strip laid down in the wide hall at the palace often used for dueling practice. His boots slid easily along the highly polished wood floor.

Winters shrugged off his wine red coat and doublet and readied to engage opposite Darcy. "Ah. That."

They slowly advanced towards each other, their eyes never looking away. Darcy loved it. He and Winters had perfected the art of not showing their thoughts, and it made sword play damn difficult and exciting. For one never knew when a blade would suddenly sing forward towards your gullet. When finally within reach, Darcy thrust, and Winters parried, the two blades clashing.

Darcy quickly made several thrusts, forcing Scott to give ground. "Did you discover how he's slipped into thievery?"

Winters didn't even blink as he brought his blade to

block every strike. "He gave me the slip as we were courting a few wenches."

Darcy laughed. Winters lunged, and Darcy quickly stepped back, parrying across his body to deflect the sharp thrust. "Getting soft are we?"

Moving as if in a dance, they both retreated, mirroring each other's footsteps as they looked for a weak point.

Winters narrowed his cold blue eyes and held his left hand out behind him, balancing easily. "Not soft enough, apparently. The damn rascal wasn't as distracted by my charms as he was by Mrs. Fox's."

Darcy fought a scowl at the very mention of her name. Suddenly, Winters's blade was an inch from his chest. Darcy froze, damn well keeping this practice match from turning into the real thing.

Winters's eyes widened in the barest hint of surprise as he lowered his rapier. "What was that about?"

"Nothing." If he could call lusting after a suspect nothing.

"That was quite the nothing."

"Forget it." Darcy shook his head. He was not going to tell Winters that he'd kissed Amelia Fox last night then had a merry little chat with her on the way home. Which gave him pause, but for some reason, he balked at the idea of sharing the experience. "En garde."

Winters narrowed his eyes then shrugged. "If you say so."

They resumed dueling positions and this time, Darcy waited for Winters to strike first. As soon as their blades clanged, Darcy threw himself at the man with single minded intensity. He let fly his blade as though it had a life of its own, and Winters ran backwards, barely able to keep up with the speed of Darcy's thrusts.

Darcy backed off and threw Winters a cocky smile. "Out of shape are we?"

"Mmm." Winters tugged at his linen shirt, pulling the laced neckline away from his throat. He strode forward, his rapier extended. And then he began his strike, this time, his own blade flashing like lightening.

"What happened to Mrs. Fox after I left?" A devilish smile curled Winters's lips. "Did the actress raise her curtain?"

Darcy stumbled and was suddenly down on one knee. He tumbled backwards, over his shoulder, then back up on to his feet. God's teeth, what was wrong with him? "Pardon?" he said, coolly.

Winters stopped. "What in blazes is ailing you, man?"

Darcy looked away and thrust his free hand though his hair. He bloody well wasn't going to admit that a bit of skirt, granted a very intriguing bit of skirt, had him so preoccupied.

"That's it. You bedded her. How—"

"No," growled Darcy. "I did not." For some reason the idea of having this conversation did not sit well with him.

"Why ever not? She's handsome beyond compare, and she's an actress to boot." Scott walked over to his coat and belt then holstered his rapier. "Granted, she is potentially a traitor, but bedding her would only make it easier for you to obtain the truth."

Darcy hesitated. "What?"

Winter's brows lifted in surprise. "So, you *didn't* bed her yet." He pulled his doublet and coat on. "You should consider it."

Should Darcy obtain his own desire while obtaining the information the king wished? The idea certainly had its appeal. But it might be dangerous. Seducing a suspect only worked if one could easily control one's own desire. His desire for Mrs. Fox was particularly strong.

Not only that, Mrs. Fox had ended their heated kiss with a suddenness that belied womanly arts. She'd been downright maidenly in her hasty retreat.

Darcy drew in a breath. That was hardly possible. A woman in the theater was at the mercy of the men who came backstage, the other actors, and the heads of the company. The very idea that she could still be in possession of her virginity was laughable.

"You have your first lesson with her this morning, do you not?"

Darcy blinked and glanced towards Winters. "Yes. In less than an hour's time, as a matter of fact."

"Did you tell her your name last night?"

"No," he replied. Strangely, she had not inquired it of him.

"Do you not think she will find it suspicious that you were so handily on the scene last night?"

Darcy shook his head. He'd often found that as much honesty as possible in a lie was best. "I shall simply tell her I attended her play last night and was riding home."

Winters crossed his arms over his chest, disbelieving the simplicity of his answer.

"I do live near St. James Park," he pointed out.

"So you do," agreed Winters dryly. "And perhaps she will believe you. I guarantee she will not be pleased that you and her rescuer are one and the same."

Darcy wasn't going to argue with that. Not after the kiss they'd shared.

His friend yanked on his coat. "Well, I am after Warrington and will see what I can learn over a friendly pint."

"I do feel you have obtained the more dignified end of our mission."

"Oh, I don't know. Hours in Mrs. Fox's company? Sounds delightful to me."

"I'll be wearing skirts," Darcy gritted.

"You have to take the punishment for your crimes." A self satisfied smile curled the corners of Winters's lip and his cold eyes shone with amusement. "*I* didn't bed Richmond's daughter, now did I? You did that all by yourself."

Darcy scowled. "But only because you were bedding Glouster's wife."

"I can't be in two places at once, old man." Winters turned on his heel and headed towards the open, gilt double doors at the end of the hall. "Good luck charming the actress." He paused and called over his shoulder. "If you need assistance, do feel free to call on my vast expertise."

"Keep walking, you peacock."

Winters laughed, stopped, and threw his cloak over his shoulder as he glanced back. "Cock, I suppose is the correct word in this case." He strode out into the meandering mazes of the palace, leaving Darcy to himself.

The one thing he didn't need was more experience if he chose to seduce Mrs. Fox. What he needed was a level head, and not the head south of his belt, to make certain he could bed her and keep the upper hand. But surely, in the end, she was no different than all the other women who had paraded through his bed? Once he had her, she wouldn't affect his judgment in the least.

Drat! Why couldn't she get the blasted man out of her head!

Amelia checked her appearance in the mirror, as tall as herself and framed in golden cherubs, for the third time in as many minutes. She looked appropriately plain, having chosen a simple dark blue gown with no lace to decorate the low cut bodice. She glanced at her lips. Last night they'd swollen from her rescuer's kisses. This morning they were untouched by rouge. Unthinkingly, she caressed her bottom lip with the tips of her fingers.

If she had any luck, she would never set eyes on the lord again, and thusly never be tempted to stray from her path of a manless life.

Scowling at her own reflection, she dropped her hand to her side. She would not be controlled by her temptations.

Sighing, she turned from the mirror and looked to the closed door, twice as high as a man. Lord Chase was late. Something she did not appreciate. As an actress, if she was late to rehearsals she could be fined by the company. It was a matter of respect. Perhaps, she could create punishments for her new pupil if he made a habit of keeping her waiting. Amelia smiled to herself. She quite liked the idea of chastising the notorious lord.

The door at the end of the room swung open. The *click*, *click*, *click* of spaniel feet echoed through the hallway, and a horde of at least ten dogs trotted into the drawing room.

"Madam!" called the king as he strode into the room, his hands wide in greeting.

Amelia nearly sputtered. The king! She flushed at the honor, but before she could drop into a curtsy he was before her.

Gold brocade spilled from his shoulders and draped from his outstretched arms as he strode right up to her and heartily clasped her shoulders. "Do forgive Our lateness." He leaned in to kiss her cheek. His elaborate wig, which fell in cascading black curls to his waist, brushed her shoulders.

For a moment she feared she'd be smothered in his voluminous silks and lace, but even so, she could not help feeling a moment of awe at being so close to the Merry Monarch.

Though his young reign had inspired a rather mad and eccentric dress in gentlemen, he was a force that belied his billowing silk britches and beribboned shoes.

After he pressed a kiss to her cheek, Amelia dropped into a deep curtsy. "Majesty, it is an honor to await you."

He clapped his jeweled hands together. "Well said. Well said." He turned towards the door. "Chase! Come man!" The king glanced back at her, a surprisingly devilish grin tilting up his mustache. "We've just been lecturing the rascal about gentlemanly conduct."

The Earl of Chase strode into the room.

"Is that not so?" prompted the king.

Amelia's mouth dropped open and she very nearly pointed at the earl, resisting the urge to yell *you*, like some character she might play on stage.

"Certainly, Your Majesty," assured Lord Chase, his voice as intoxicating as a rich burgundy.

Gracious, the man was handsome, his dark hair thick and lush. In answer, her fingers curled, remembering the softness of its folds. Oh, and his arms. Even now, under his dark green coat, his muscles flexed deliciously. Amelia's breath shortened and her cheeks warmed. Blinking, she shook her head. She could not allow herself to go on thinking like this.

Lord Chase smiled knowingly, as if he could read the sins flitting through her mind. He swept a deep bow, his cloak swirling about his tall frame and the black feathered hat in his hand. As he straightened to his full and intimidating height, his dark eyes swept over her body with a hot urgency that sent a jolt of pleasure to her stomach. Amelia swallowed. Surely, the king could sense the banked lust in his lord's gaze.

Amelia stared back at Lord Chase, and she realized he didn't seem at all shocked to see her this morning. Strange. She shook the thought away, distracted by the dire prospect of her task.

The king glanced from Chase to her, his eyes twinkling like the diamonds decorating his waistcoat. He wagged a finger at Amelia. "Now, We trust you to turn the earl into a most pleasing woman, Mrs. Fox."

Amelia laughed, and she fought a wince at the ever so slightly shrill tone. "It shall certainly be a challenge." She would do her very best, despite his manly stature. She threw Lord Chase a cutting stare. "Before I am done, Majesty, he shall be unsexed."

The earl coughed.

The king let out a hearty laugh. "If you can do that, there shall be many a grateful husband and father in this court."

Amelia arched a brow and said pleasantly, "And no doubt, the young maids."

The king frowned and crossed over to the earl. "Not so sure about that." King Charles clapped him on the back then squeezed his shoulder until Amelia could have sworn the earl winced. "He does seem to please the ladies, if not their guardians."

"I will take that as a compliment, Your Majesty," said the earl. "A man should always strive to please the ladies."

Amelia narrowed her eyes. She'd like to see him try to please her. She'd give him a nasty piece of her mind.

"Quite," said the king, his eyes narrowing. "But in this you must become the lady, and then We shall see."

A decidedly rueful look darkened the earl's brow, but he inclined his head towards the king. "I am ever eager to prove useful."

Charles released Lord Chase. "You see, Mrs. Fox, Our dear friend, Mrs. Gwynn, shall not be happy 'til she sees his lordship in skirts in one of our musicales."

"Anything for Mistress Gwynn," said Amelia. She'd never met the king's mistress. But she'd seen her on the stage and had the deepest admiration for her as one actress to another.

"Well then, We shall leave you to it." With that the king swept from the room, taking his dogs with him.

Amelia sank into another curtsy as she watched him depart. When the clicking of little dogs' feet had vanished down the hall, she half wished she could sink so far into the floor she'd never be seen again.

Folding her hands, Amelia glared at her new pupil. If she could call the blasted devil a pupil. "Well, sir, I should begin with a few rules."

He tilted his head to the side, and his long black hair fell over his shoulder. "Please. My ears are all yours."

"I wish for us to maintain a purely professional

relationship."

He pulled at the tie of his cloak, slowly letting the chord come undone. "That is unfortunate."

"Your disappointment is noted."

The rich black fabric slid from his shoulders, and he swept it over his arm. "Mrs. Fox, I am delighted to be your student and shall devote myself to you for hours on end."

"Your devotion is also noted," she said dryly. "Would you care to air any other feelings before we work, my lord?"

"Only that I am *completely* at your disposal," his lips curled wolfishly.

Slowly, she sauntered towards him, pinning him with a warning glare. "You shall maintain a professional attitude or I shall make certain that when next you sing, it is an octave higher than before."

Deep, rolling laughter burst from his lips and it was a delightful, shiver inducing sound. "Hold madam, hold." He dropped his hat and cloak upon a nearby chair, then turned fully to face her. He crossed his arms over his broad chest, and the rich green fabric strained slightly against his muscles. "That is, indeed, a serious threat." He glanced down at her through hooded lashes. "I do believe you mean it."

Amelia stared at him for just a moment longer than she should before she wrenched her gaze away. "I do." She stepped back and cleared her throat. "Now, shall we to our lesson?"

He hesitated, his brows drawing together questioningly. "You do not wish to discuss last night at all?" He unfolded his arms and drew off his gloves. "I had quite a pleasing time."

"My lord, though I found you amusing and enjoyed your

company, given the circumstances, I have chosen to put last evening's events from my mind. I suggest you do the same."

He dropped his black gloves by his hat and cloak, as if deliberately prolonging the silence. The air crackled with tension and Amelia took in several shallow breaths, her corset feeling unusually tight.

And then, very softly, he whispered, "I think not."

Chapter Six

Darcy had no idea what he was doing as he stared down at the mouth he'd quickly grown to desire too much. Whatever he was doing, his cock liked it. Very much indeed. Because it was becoming damn difficult to keep it from hardening.

As a matter of fact, he had a deep suspicion, that in all actuality, the head below his waist had seized control of his brain the moment he spotted her again.

Last night, he'd enjoyed her kiss as much as he'd enjoyed her wit. And he wanted to experience both again. And preferably in that order.

But this was a guarded inquisition. And he damn well couldn't let his desires dictate his procedure.

So, instead of tilting her head back and taking her mouth with his, he stepped away and did his best to nonchalantly cross to the delicate writing desk in the corner of the room. Several books were stacked on it. All Shakespeare. He turned his back to her then, discretely as possible, he readjusted the heavy and hardening weight in his breeches.

Drawing in a slow breath that did nothing to tame the need pounding straight to his groin, he turned back to Mrs. Fox. "So, mistress of mine, where shall we begin?"

She stared blankly at him, her green eyes wide and dazed. Darcy could hardly believe it, but it was as if the woman had never experienced desire. Hell, he couldn't blame her, *he'd* never quite experienced desire like this before.

She folded her hands before her then quickly strode to the desk. The blue folds of her skirts swished as she walked. The fabric was rich yet plain, without a trace of embroidery or lace. It was as Puritan as one could get without wearing black. Which made him wonder, if somewhere in her heart, she harbored the doctrine of her father and brother. If she did, she might very well be aiding the king's enemies.

However, in complete contradiction to Puritanical law, she did not cover her breasts, neither did she deck herself with lace at the bodice. The lack seemed to emphasize the perfect swells rather than detract from them. A sight that would lead the most sainted man astray.

If the other women of the court ever saw how perfect Mrs. Fox could look without all the lace and beading they so loved, they would tear the woman to shreds... If the men did not kill each other in attempt to claim her as a mistress first. Darcy scowled. The very idea of one of the powdered and frilly lords of Charles's court touching her flesh filled him with a sudden sense of possessiveness.

"My lord." Her voice sliced through his contemplation of her body, and he noticed the book in her outstretched hand. "I think we shall begin with the britches parts."

He blinked. "I beg your pardon."

"The parts in which a girl pretends to be man. Since Shakespeare wrote these parts for *boys*, they might be easier for you to understand."

"Ah." And it was about to begin. He really was about to pretend to be a woman. For king and country, he reminded himself. For king and country. He cleared his throat, not particularly thrilled to put on a frock in front of this beautiful woman. "Do you not think we should perhaps begin with physicality?"

"Your eagerness is appreciated, however, every actor must begin at the beginning not somewhere in the middle." She very carefully opened the leather book, as if it was made of glass. "You shall read Viola. I shall read Olivia." She handed him the script. "Here."

Darcy took the book from her and for the briefest moment, their fingertips touched. She pulled her hand away, and he pretended not to notice the tingling response that spread down his hand.

She smiled tightly then stepped back. "No physical gestures please. We shall simply hold the conversation that is between them."

Nodding, Darcy quickly scanned the page. He knew the scene well… At about twelve, his mother had insisted he play the part. He'd been the darling of the Dutch Court that year, but only the king and a few other nobles that had lived with His Majesty in exile knew that. Thank God.

She nodded at him. "You may begin."

Darcy looked up from the script, already knowing the lines.

She stood before him, her hands folded, clearly knowing

the lines herself. "*Stay*," she began. "*I prithee tell me what thou thinkst of me.*"

Darcy easily responded, "*That you are not what you think you are.*" The words flowed from him, memorized, and their irony did not escape him. Was she not pretending to be the person before him? Was she a traitor?

"*If I think so, I think the same of you*," she bantered, Shakespeare's words tripping lightly from her tongue.

Darcy stared at her, her green eyes warming his body with their clear passion for the text. "*Then you think right, I am not what I am.*" Good god, the words really were fitting. Neither he nor she were themselves. Each was hiding behind layers of lies.

She tilted her head to the side and smiled. "*I would you were as I would have you be.*"

"*Would it be better madam, than I am? I wish it might for now I am your fool.*" Darcy's voice trailed off. If he was not careful, he would prove her fool, for her love for her work was compelling. It made him wish to love it as much as she. For he had not known such passion for something outside of one's country and one's king.

When she did not continue he folded his arms over his chest, waiting for her critique.

Awe softened her face and she smiled. Her face shone with such purity and pleasure that for a moment, he feared he would never breathe again. What would it be like for her to look at him like that as a man and not an actor?

Darcy shoved the thought from his mind. He was here to find out if she was a traitor. Nothing else.

Mrs. Fox shook her head, a rueful smile on her soft lips. "Though I do not wish to admit it, my lord, you have a natural talent for acting. You must have had some experience in the past."

He hesitated. His childhood had been strange and complex, but if telling her would make her feel closer to him, then all the better. "When I was a child I performed for the nobles of the court."

"Perhaps then, you do not truly need my assistance."

Darcy laughed and closed the book. "Madam, I may understand the inner nature of Shakespeare's characters, but I do not know how to conform my adult form to that of a woman. I left behind theatricals when my voice changed. And since, my life has been swords, horses, and politics."

"Hmm. Yes, there is nothing womanly about you," she agreed.

"Mark Mrs. Fox, I must move and speak as a woman does. Mrs. Gwynn will be satisfied with nothing less."

She frowned. "It is very odd that she should wish one so manly to be so feminine. Surely, there are betters suited?"

Her words echoed his when he'd first heard of this strange mission, but of course his skills were needed to spy upon Mrs. Fox. "Perhaps that is the point. I think it will amuse herself and the king to see me out of my usual role."

"Well then, my lord, we shall not disappoint them." Her eyes sparked with a wicked glint and she crossed to the tall windows and a large rectangular box resting on a gilt, high back chair. "I have a present for you."

Suspicion tugged at Darcy's gut. She looked damned pleased to give him this gift. She pulled the red silk bow on the velvet box then lifted the lid. The rustle of fabric filled the air as she swept a massive pink skirt from the box.

"Oh, balls," he growled.

"No," she laughed. "No balls."

Damnation, he'd very happily think on a woman's slit, especially if it was hers. But he inclined his head and gave her a little bow. "I am at your mercy."

"Yes. Yes, you are." She frowned, nibbling at her lower lip. "I think you shall have to remove your jacket and waistcoat or the skirt will not fit about your waist."

"I shall remove whatever you command," he teased as he shrugged out of his coat then began to slowly unbutton his waistcoat. He worked each fasten deliberately, keeping his eyes trained on her face.

She held the skirt to her chest and looked slightly askance, but he felt her gaze on him from the corner of her eye as he stripped to his linen shirt and breeches. "Is there anything else you would like me to remove?"

She sharply shook her head. "No, but you must allow me to have your sword."

Darcy smiled, relishing the thought of her hands on his sword. "You wish to take my sword?" He shouldn't tease her thusly, but he couldn't help it. As an actress she'd heard far worse on the stage, but alone in this room, the words seemed far more evocative. "You see, it is rather large. I think you might need both hands."

"Your wit, sir, is anything but novel." She arched a dark brow. "Since your *sword* is so precious to you, it will give me great pleasure to take it from you."

"*Touché*. You may have my blade, but I'd rather like to keep my sword."

"So I thought." She reached out, palm open. "Now, hand the rapier over."

Blowing out a breath, Darcy unbuckled the ornately

jeweled belt from his waist and did as she requested. Surprisingly, she swept up the sheathed sword in one hand, keeping the heavy pink skirts in the other.

She was a great deal stronger than her slender form suggested. Gently, she placed the blade down on one of the brocade fainting couches.

Flicking out the skirt, she grinned. "Arms up, my lord."

Gods, she was enjoying this too much. Then again, he couldn't blame her for her delight in having the upper hand. Darcy lifted his arms, the silk of his linen shirt, easily accommodating the movement. Her soft scent of lavender and roses surrounded him and he closed his eyes for a brief moment, savoring it.

She lifted the skirt to put it over his head, then frowned. She reached up on tiptoe, but could not reach over his head. She tottered forward and her breasts brushed his chest. Quickly, she jumped back as if she had touched a hot stove.

"I am too short," she murmured. "You shall have to do it."

Darcy remained silent as he took the skirt from her. These brief touches should not be affecting him so powerfully. Hell, he'd been involved in court orgies. This innocent, fully clothed stuff should leave him cold.

Instead, it had him wanting to open the windows and yank off his clothes to cool his heated skin. Making short work of it, he yanked the massive piece of fabric over his head.

Without the full underskirt, it fell over his hips and actually brushed his booted feet.

Mrs. Fox made great show of circling him and studying the pink, lace bedecked folds. "This shall be your rehearsal skirt, and as soon as you move easily in this, you shall progress to a full frock."

"Huzzah, a full frock," he quipped. "My dreams at last have come true."

Amelia tried to focus on the girlish pink color swathing the earl's lower body, but it did no good. The man would look male in a bonnet...which did not bode well for her task. Nor did it bode well for the tingling sensation in her stomach.

As she stood, taking in the muscular form of the earl, every fiber of her body screamed for her to request the king find a different actress. But she wanted the king's favor.

For her entire life, she had never let her desires get the better of her, and she would not begin now. Not even for a man who with a single look could cause her breath to hitch.

This was business.

As matter-of-factly as possible, she circled to his back and took the laces of the skirt and pulled them tight. He jolted and she bit back a laugh. If he did not like the skirt's tight lacings, how would he feel about a corset? She tied the strings and let her fingers rest for a moment at his waist. 'Twas bigger than a fashionable woman's. But not with fat. No, the flesh under her fingertips, covered only with a thin linen shirt, was hard and warm. She gave him a little shove. "Right then. Walk about the room, if you please."

He glanced back over his shoulder, a pained smirk turning his lips. "Aye, aye, madam." Lord Chase then proceeded to stride in a circle, his boots kicking out the skirts as he covered the ground quickly.

Amelia folded her arms under her breasts and fought a bemused frown. It was very bad. Very, very bad. "Stop," she called.

Turning to her, he widened his eyes innocently. "How was that?"

She tried to keep her face blank, and she dug her fingers into her arms to keep from laughing. He looked so ridiculous standing in the middle of the room in his skirts, asking how his walk was. She cleared her throat. "I think perhaps, you should take smaller steps." Amelia looked to his boots. "Much smaller."

He glanced down at his large feet and wiggled them. Their buckles glinted in the afternoon light. "Hmm. Could it be the shoes?"

"Here. Watch me." She crossed to him, her steps small, and she added a subtle sway to her hips. "You see, a woman takes very little steps. In fact, a truly graceful woman looks as if she floats."

"Floats?" he echoed. "Hmm." He drew in a deep breath then blew it out. "Shall I try again?"

"Yes."

He took several small steps forward, and this time managed to look like he was bobbing up and down, his skirts swishing like a bell. Turning back to her, he said with a surprising amount of hope. "Better?"

Amelia bit her lower lip. She nodded "Yes." This was going to be a very interesting process.

Lord Chase frowned and glanced at his backside. "I do believe my skirts"—he glanced at her, obviously flinching at the words that had just come from his mouth—"are coming undone."

Amelia hurried over to him and grabbed the ties at the back of his waist. What tactic should she try? She stroked her hands along the waistband, smoothing it, and suddenly she stilled. His body was so hard and strong beneath her fingertips. Amelia held her breath, realizing that he, too, had gone still when she touched him.

"I-I think that is enough for today." Her voice sounded strained, even to her own ears.

With a slow smile, he said, "Until tomorrow, Mrs. Fox." He stepped away from her, trailing his hand in a sensual caress along her waist.

He picked up his rapier and coat then strode from the room, skirt and all.

Amelia stood stock still, staring after his vanished form. And a thought suddenly struck her. Had she given the lesson today, or had he?

Chapter Seven

Somehow she had survived three weeks of lessons. Three weeks of being in this outrageous and seductive man's presence. Three weeks of forcing herself to act as prim and proper as her brother would have her be. It had been thrilling torture. And everyday something terrible had happened. She'd grown to like him just a little bit more and more. And not only did she like the man who had a jolly wit and adventurous spirit, her body quite liked him, too.

It was dangerous.

For with every meeting, a little voice in her head whispered that perhaps she should give up her principles and yield to her growing desire and curiosity for Darcy Blake, Earl of Chase.

"Mrs. Fox?" the earl prompted from across the ornate hall.

She nearly jumped then cleared her throat.

"One moment," she said hastily, desperate to buy a little

time to recover. "Your *lesson* is caught in its box."

After a groan, he teased lightly, "I believe you delight in making me dance to your tune."

She did. For he did it with such good humor. But even so, his presence sent her reeling.

It was powerful and puzzling, his effect on her. No man had ever shaken her so or made her think about flinging herself headlong into the abyss of sin. She had the unfortunate feeling it was because she *did* like him. He wasn't like the other men who drooled over her and shunted baubles in front of her face.

She dug her hands into the box and caressed the silk panels with her hands. A grin pulled at her lips. The corset was Ned's, borrowed without the fastidious actor's knowledge. But no doubt he would love to know how Lord Chase handled the contraption. In fact, she was curious herself. She whipped around and presented it. "Shall we, my lord?"

A pained expression flitted over his strong face. But then he nodded with the resignation of a man being led to the gallows. "Indeed."

As Amelia widened the laces and let him slip the garment over his head and shoulders, she folded her arms under her breasts, enjoying the bizarre image of such a big man in the silly device. At last, he wiggled into it, pulling the bottom edge to his hips.

Moving behind him, Amelia tugged the crisscrossed laces, preparing it. He growled at the discomfort and she couldn't stop herself from smiling. "Oh, hush, you great lion, I haven't even started."

She gave a hard tug to the strings, cinching his muscled waist in. She gave another tug, pulling it tighter.

"Christ!" he hissed as the air whooshed out of lungs. "That is most unpleasant," he wheezed.

Amelia tied off the strings tightly then circled round the front to look at him. He stood with his shoulders tense and his body stiff as a ramrod. His waist looked bizarrely small under his broad shoulders as the boning dug into his narrow hips. But nothing matched the surly indignation stamped on his masculine face.

He waddled a few steps forward and frowned.

Amelia burst out laughing. He looked so distraught. So completely alarmed.

His face creased in a mock expression of indignation. "Are you amused at my expense, madam?"

She nodded vigorously.

"I think 'tis time for a lighthearted game. I'm going to capture you and throttle you for enjoying my pain."

And to his word, he suddenly darted forward.

Shocked, Amelia's eyes widened she ran several steps back. The man was about to find out how limiting women's clothes could be. He couldn't move very well in the corset and she evaded him easily until suddenly he stopped, perplexed. "God's teeth, woman, how do you breathe?"

Amelia placed a hand to her waist, laughing so hard her eyes watered. "You don't," she gasped back.

He arched a brow at her. "Come here and get this thing off me."

"I think we should try a curtsy, don't you?"

The earl scowled. "If I curtsy I think I shall topple."

"Where has that sense of adventure gone I admire so much?"

"It eloped with my pride," he grumped, then he smiled a

slow smile. "You admire me do you?"

"I supposed a tad. I admire you as much as I could any man."

He laughed. "Praise indeed."

Lord Chase glanced down at himself. "Horrifying, but shall I try it?"

"A curtsy?"

She pressed her lips together and nodded.

His face grew serious and he squatted.

A laugh burst from her lips. "Oh dear."

"That bad, eh?" He attempted to tug at the corset then stood straight. A pained expression crossed his face as he tried to draw in a deep breath. Trapped by the boning, his shoulders expanded then contracted. "Truly, how do you breathe?"

She pursed her lips in mock pity. "Poor lord." She crossed to him and placed her hand on his middle. Instantly, she felt the tingle of laying hands on him. Weeks together should have dimmed that. If anything the sensation had grown. Despite this, she forced herself to demonstrate.

"Don't even bother trying to breathe from here." She patted his stomach. "You must take shallow breaths. From your chest. Like this."

She drew in several small breaths, using only her ribcage.

The earl stared at her breasts as they pressed together. "Most fascinating. Please do keep demonstrating."

She huffed. "You are quite terrible."

"As you might say, I am a man."

"A common excuse."

"And a true one." His gaze upon her bosom hadn't wavered. "You keep breathing, I'm taking this damn thing off."

She wagged her finger at him. "Oh no. You've got a good half hour to go."

"Surely, we could do something more pleasant."

"Such as?"

A devilish smile warmed his beautiful face. "You could teach me to kiss."

"I highly doubt you need any further instruction."

"Teach me to kiss…like a woman."

Her insides rioted as she was suddenly tempted to take him up on his offer. She hadn't forgotten how glorious his kiss had been and he was offering her the perfect excuse to feel his lips upon hers again. She could do it. It would be so easy.

But therein was the difficulty. She wasn't prepared for this. She had to think. She had to decide if a slide into sin was worth the price, for she was sliding.

Abruptly, she raced around him. "I have forgotten an appointment."

"I thought you were enjoying having me in a corset."

"All pleasures must come to an end," she said briskly tugging on his laces.

As soon as he'd helped her tug the corset free, he turned and looked down into her face. "Ah. But Mrs. Fox, our pleasure has not even begun."

Her heart slammed against her ribs and she clutched the corset to her front like armor. She couldn't even form a reply as his words settled deep in her mind. She couldn't allow him to be right. Could she?

Before the traitorous thought could be truly considered, Amelia bobbed a quick, terribly performed curtsy and raced from the room. She knew she was in trouble. Today, he had crossed her line. He had gone beyond their relationship as teacher and student. Even if he had done it subtly. But that was not the problem.

The problem was that she had liked it. Liked it very much indeed.

"Tell me again why I dragged myself out of Lady Anne's bed to come to the playhouse?"

Darcy glared at Winters. "You adore the theater."

"Not as much as Lady Anne's clever tongue."

"Fine then." Darcy folded his arms over his chest, standing amidst a crowd of men waiting for admittance into the dressing rooms of the Peacock theater. "You're here because we are trying to elucidate Mrs. Fox's guilt."

"I beg your pardon." Winters poked his finger into Darcy's plain lace cravat. "*You* are elucidating it." He then retracted his finger and pointed it at himself. "*I* am making friends with Lord W. You watch her, and I watch him. Are you confused on this matter or…" He shrugged, a self sacrificing sigh slipping out his lips. "Perhaps you need me to hold your hand."

"You try to hold my hand and I'll pull your gullet through your nostrils."

Winters grinned. "My, aren't we testy."

Yes. Yes he was, but damned if he was going to admit it.

"I take it Mrs. Fox's skirts have proven iron clad."

Darcy felt the odd urge to grumble, but instead he said firmly, "God man, it's only been a few weeks. Give a fellow a chance."

"I recall a time when you could have had the most devoted maid's skirts up in a few hours. Clearly, you are slipping into your dotage."

"Sod off." Darcy gritted his teeth. He'd been walking around as hard as a mason's stone since this afternoon.

He wanted Mrs. Fox.

Which was why he was standing here, convincing Winters and himself that he was just furthering the mission, and not his advance into the lady's bed.

Darcy glowered at a young dandy dressed in powder blue, his highly curled blond wig tied with matching silver bows. He looked like a bloody cake in all his lace and sparkling jewels. Hell, pretty much all the men standing in the small retiring area looked like cakes. Just different hues of the same rainbow. Winters and he stood out like great black vultures in the gilt plumage. "Damn it, they can't all be here to see her," he protested.

Winters laughed and adjusted his rapier, keeping it from tripping a man in a particularly high pair of heeled shoes. "Don't bet your balls on it."

A short man came through the door at the end of the hall. "Pardon, my lords, but Mrs. Fox and Mr. Kynaston will receive a few of you now."

"Finally," growled Darcy.

"My, aren't we the eager little lord," drawled Winters.

"Bugger off." He'd pushed her too far today. It had felt right and for one moment, he'd been certain she was going to take him up on his suggestion and, indeed, give him a kissing lesson. Instead, she'd turned all prickles and left him without a word. He needed to see her.

Yes, damn it. *Need.*

Over the passing weeks, Mrs. Fox had proven elusive and difficult to read but what he had discovered? She was a kind, witty, and slightly wounded soul. He longed to make her smile. And today, he'd ultimately failed.

Ignoring the cries of protest, Darcy and Winters barged to the front. "We're here to see Mrs. Fox," declared Darcy, hoping his tone alone would get him through the door.

The short, wrinkled man looked up at him through milky blue eyes. "Of course you are, but so is every man jack of you." The servant held out a wrinkled hand and rubbed his fingers together.

Who knew bribery ran such a hardy life in the theater? Darcy grabbed his leather coin purse and fished out several schillings. "Don't admit anyone else," he ordered, lowering his voice.

Passing the coins discretely into the man's calloused palm, he brushed by him.

Winters followed him through the curtained door.

The dim candlelight flickered against the dark wood and the wine red curtains draped along the walls. A single table and chairs pushed up against the wall with two mirrors on it dominated the room, but it was Mrs. Fox standing next to the plank table that caught his attention.

Darcy's heart pounded at the sight of Mrs. Fox in an emerald green gown. Her corset cinched in her slender waist, pushing up her breasts into two mouthwatering pillows. God, how he'd longed to touch her breasts this afternoon. He'd been as foolish as a boy.

Tonight, her long dark hair was piled atop her head with a few curls draping down over her shoulder and brushing her left breast.

She was beautiful. Every bit of her, and that beauty seemed to have sent his wits packing.

She stared back at him. After a moment, she propped her hands on the hips of her wide skirts and narrowed her eyes.

Winters slapped Darcy on the back, "The lady and I barely met, and that was weeks ago. Introduce me, man."

Darcy blinked, and forced himself to look away from her. She was in a fine temper. Clearly not happy with how their lesson had ended. "Lord Winters, this is Mrs. Fox."

Winters strode forward, his hand outstretched, and he took her pale hand in his. Much to Darcy's annoyance, the man lingered over it before gently pressing his lips to her fingers.

"Didn't you have an appointment with Lady Anne?" snapped Darcy.

Winters's eyes paused at Mrs. Fox's breasts and his lips parted into a wolf's grin. "Who could think of another lady in Mrs. Fox's presence?"

Darcy snorted. "Leave your two-penny lines for the dolts outside."

"Oh, I don't know," chimed Mrs. Fox, her lips parting in an amused smile. "His words sound as if he's learned them from an all too familiar school. *Your* school, Lord Chase."

"A palpable hit, madam," said Winters as he released her hand and propped his on his rapier.

The curtains in the corner of the room swished open. A tall, trim man strode forward in purple, gold, and white glory. "Amelia, my pet, whoever are you conversing with? Introduce me."

Ned Kynaston.

Hell, even Darcy knew the most famous actor of his day. He'd had his sketch in the Fleet Street sheets often enough.

Amelia gestured to her fellow actor. "Mr. Kynaston, may I present the Earl of Winters and the Earl of Chase."

Kynaston inclined his dark head and smiled. His eyes narrowed as he focused on Darcy. He looked from Darcy to Amelia then back to Darcy again. Twirling his lace cuffed wrist, he said, "A true pleasure."

Indeed. What did Kynaston know about Mrs. Fox and his meetings? From the way he glanced back and forth, clearly he knew something.

After a moment of silence, Kynaston strode towards Winters. Once again, he looked at Amelia, his eyes sparkling with some unknown amusement.

Mrs. Fox cocked her head to the side, as if warning him.

Whatever warning, Kynaston ignored it, turned to Winters and said, "My Lord, I do believe you and I are the awkward wheels here." He leaned in towards Winters as if they were conspirators, and Darcy and Mrs. Fox couldn't hear. "Perhaps you and I should pair off," he whispered loud enough for half of London to hear.

Winters frowned for a moment then nodded. "Certainly, Mr. Kynaston. Always a pleasure to meet a new talent."

"Ah!" Kynaston beamed, fluffing his cravat. "Are you a man who enjoys *talents*, sir?"

Winters drew in a deep breath then arched a blond brow. "Indeed, sir, but only of the usual variety."

Kynaston tsked. "Pity." He grabbed up his pink hat, decked with white feathers, from the rack at the end of the room. "Still, I think you shall prove most interesting."

Trailing his eyes from Winters to Darcy, the actor looked Darcy up and down. Darcy almost laughed; the man was sizing him up like a stallion… Something that had not been attempted by a man since his last visit to the French court. Kynaston let out a quick sigh of pleasure then pointed his gloved hand at Darcy. "Lord Chase, you must take very, very good care of my dear friend, Amelia."

Well, at least the actor had not been perusing him for his own desires. Darcy nodded. "Have no fears, sir. Her pleasure is my utmost concern."

Winters rolled his eyes and coughed.

Kynaston's brows rose and he patted Winters on the back. "Dear, dear. The only thing for that cough, my lord, is a good dose of spirits. Let us go."

Winters shot Darcy a you'll-owe-me-more-than-you-could-possibly-wish glare and followed the actor out.

Mrs. Fox sauntered forward, her hands once again propped firmly on her hips. She tilted her head to the side, in mock question. "Come for another lesson?"

"I confess not."

"A pity. I do think you are very much in the need of a lesson in feminine modesty."

"How so?"

She tsked. "Do you not recall my rules?"

"Very well."

"Then obviously, you feel they are beneath you, and therefore modesty would become you."

Darcy blinked innocently. "Which rule do you speak of?"

She snorted. "I believe I strictly stated our relationship should be only a business one."

"So you did."

She gestured to her dressing room. "And yet you asked me to kiss you today. And worse, you have sought me out. You are here."

"So I am."

"If you are not here for a lesson, you cannot be here for business."

"Your logic is most stimulating."

Her gaze narrowed. "I wish no compliments from you. Only your absence."

Darcy frowned. This was not going as planned. "Surely I can come watch a play, and speak to you afterwards?"

She hesitated, though her eyes still shone with suspicion. "You came to the play?"

"Mac—"

She held up her hand. "No! You must not say it."

"I do beg your pardon. I never would have taken you for the superstitious type."

She smoothed her hands down the front of her skirts. "In general I am not, but there are traditions that I respect. I have no wish to summon old ghosts."

"A common cry of any man. The Scottish play is one of my favorites, and I must say you are the most magnificent Lady M that I have ever seen."

A pink blush tinged her cheeks. Her pleasure at his compliment was genuine, not feigned as so many actors did. Folding her hands before her, she asked, "You truly came to see the play? I find that hard to believe."

"You are my acting teacher, and I merely wished to witness your talent for myself. It was a wonderful performance."

"Then, I am glad you came. The theater is a great haven

for many people. Perhaps you shall find that to be the case."

Actually, he acted enough without the benefit of the playhouse. For instance, right now. He could not ignore the slight bitterness in his mouth at lying to her. But duty to his country superseded any guilt he felt. "It is possible. I have always had a great passion for it. Surely you and I can be friends?"

Mrs. Fox arched a dark brow at him and he knew what little ground he'd taken slipped from his fingers. But that was hardly going to stop him. He'd simply try a new tack.

Striding toward the rack on the wall, hung with cloaks and velvet hats, she reached for a rich blue cloak. She plucked it off and whipped towards him. "In truth, I think you wish to be more than just a friend. To that, I say no."

Darcy stepped towards her, smiling as innocently as a debauched man could. "Do you not think we could discuss Mac—" He stopped before he could say the accursed name, but sensed the curiosity in her as she glanced at him.

This had to be the best course to get in her confidence. He'd chip away at her resistance with what she loved. Underhanded, but necessary. "The Scottish play?"

She shook her head, her brows drawing together. "I—"

"Did you know my father procured an original Folio?" he cut in before she could naysay him. "'Tis in my family library."

Her hands slipped to her sides, the cloak still in her grasp, but forgotten. "Truly? So many were hidden away during Crom—" She swallowed and drew in a slow breath. "During the last twenty years."

It was clear she loved the theater. Could a Puritan spy actually have such a love for Shakespeare and plays? He could understand it if it was a guise, but the undiluted admiration in her eyes at his owning a Folio was not pretense. He'd stake his life on it.

"Would you like to see it?" he asked.

She bit her lower lip and glanced away. Several emotions flitted across her face, each disappearing before he could identify them. At last, she looked up. "Yes."

Truly? Was she actually giving in? "Good."

"Can you bring it tomorrow?"

"It is very valuable, and I should not like to risk harm coming to it."

"I understand." The regret in her voice turned it low and melodious.

He drew in a breath, wondering if his approach was a wise one. But he'd come too far now to venture back. "You could still see it."

"How?"

"Come to my library."

Her spine snapped straight. "Your home, you mean?"

Darcy sighed. The woman did seem to be puritanical in her suspicion of his motives. Which, given the circumstances was extremely prudent. "Yes, my home. But my mother shall be there. You needn't fear seduction, madam."

Her lips twitched and suddenly, she laughed, an enchantingly infectious sound. "Forgive me, but you live with your *mother*?"

He laughed at what seemed a very odd thing to her. "No. No, not at all. If I still lived with my mother, I should have killed myself long ago. Or perhaps she would have done it for me." Not bloody likely, given that he was the only heir to the Chase holdings. "She lives in the family house on the river. I live here in town."

"I see. An agreeable situation for you both."

Darcy inclined his head. "You have no idea."

She grinned ruefully, and Darcy wondered if perhaps her relationship with her parents had been a precarious one. If she was somehow simultaneously a rebel and a Puritan reformer, her brother had to be spitting nails at her acting. "Tomorrow morning then? Before our lesson?"

"Your mother won't mind?" Suddenly all her boldness faded. "I-I'm accepted in certain circles but—"

"My mother will adore it." His mother would hate it more than she had hated his father. Which was saying a great deal. Though she had acted and let her son act, it had never been outside of court. Anything beyond the palace walls was vulgar, low, and immoral. A true hypocrite was his mother. "She is a devotee of the theater herself."

Mrs. Fox smiled. "Then yes."

"I shall send my coach for you."

"I look forward to it."

"So do I." And he did. He would begin asking a few subtle questions about religion and politics and see how she danced to his tune. He swept her a bow. "Good night." He turned on his booted heel and headed out through the curtain.

Darcy stopped in the outer waiting room and drew in a long breath. God's teeth, he was leaving her to be stormed by her admirers. He was a firm believer, as many of Charles's men were, that women should have a great deal of freedom. But right now, he damn well wanted to stay with her and not gallantly leave her to herself. That, however, was clearly not her wish.

He would have to take his time with her.

For sometimes to get ahead, one had to wait and watch and look for the weakest point to attack.

Chapter Eight

"You will not have an actress in this house." The solid tone of Lady Adelaide Blake, dowager Countess of Chase, hummed through the small breakfast parlor like the big bells of Westminster.

Darcy pressed his fingers to his temple and looked up from his porcelain plate filled with sausages, cheese, and bread. "Mother, it is a simple request. Mrs. Fox is perfectly respectable."

"Ha. Respectable indeed." Lady Chase leaned forward, pressing her delicate wrist against the table. Leveling him with the look that had turned many a Parliamentarian into a bowl of quivering mush, she said very calmly, "I will not."

Darcy dropped his hand from his temple and picked up his knife and fork. "The king receives her, Mother. Certainly you can."

She adjusted in her chair, shifting her dark green skirts. "The king receives a great many women he should not. And

I might add that while he receives them at court, he is also receiving them in his bed." She pursed her lips, then took a sip of her exotic tea to calm herself.

His mother was never anything if not calm. Sharp as a battle axe, but calm. She had good cause for disliking women who provided intellectual and physical comfort, virtually taking the place of wife. His father had believed with utter certainty that wives were meant for breeding and little else.

"Mother, you know I would not ask such a favor of you unless it was of great import."

She gazed out the tall windows that looked out onto the park. Morning light filtered in, shining in her blond and silver hair. She turned back to him and arched a brow. "I should have known you never would have breakfasted with me unless you had a motive."

"That is hardly true." Darcy cut a piece of sausage and frowned at the delicately painted plate. Had he so ignored her? Yes. Yes, he had. But she never made their meetings easy. He put the fork down, no longer hungry.

Just as he took a long drink of over-sugared tea, she asked, "Do you wish to make this woman your mistress?"

He choked on the hot liquid and quickly set his cup down. Blinking furiously as tears stung his eyes, he grabbed for his napkin.

"I am no fool," she continued as if he hadn't just turned into a fountain. "You do not have female friends, and I doubt you are changing your colors now."

It was true.

He'd tried, but inevitably either he or the woman he attempted friendship with developed an attraction. Which could be damned awkward. After many attempts, he'd just given the whole thing up and resigned himself to having only male friends.

Carefully, Darcy placed his knife and fork on the rim of his plate. He wiped his mouth with the napkin and looked his mother in the eye. "I want it, but if you must know, Mrs. Fox will have none of it. She is a most curious woman."

His mother tilted her silver and gold head to the side. Her diamond ear bobs twinkled in the light. "If that is the case, then why are you bringing her here?"

He snapped his napkin back onto his lap. "Hope springs eternal." Though he could hardly countenance that he was saying this to his mother, he couldn't bloody tell her the truth. Yes, he could hear it now. *Pardon Mother, but I'm questioning a potential spy and wish to bed her as well. I thought I'd give her a glance at Father's prized Shakespeare to lure her in.*

"There is something you are not telling me, and I do not like it. While I don't care for the idea of an actress in my home, I will not have you use her for some strange gains."

Darcy widened his eyes innocently. "Whatever can you mean?"

His mother waved her hand at him, the lace about her elbow flitting like a flurry of snow. "Don't take that innocent tone of voice with me, young man. It didn't work when you were clinging to your nanny's skirts, and it won't work now."

What would she say if he told her he was about to be in skirts again? She'd explode through the roof. "I have already invited her. Shall I turn her away from the door?"

"That is your affair. If I do not wish to see her then I won't."

He could order her to receive Mrs. Fox, and technically,

she would have no choice. But his father had ordered her about until the old bugger died. The last thing Darcy wanted was to be like the old man.

"Let us strike a bargain," he said.

She folded her jeweled fingers. "Yes?"

"You receive Mrs. Fox, and I will do something of a similar nature for you."

That gave her pause and she arched a brow. "No complaints?"

Darcy cringed. There was only one thing his mother could be thinking of and it fair sent his balls crawling north. "No complaints," he gritted.

"I will receive this woman, if you will call on Lady Cordelia for no shorter than an hour."

Yes, yes his balls were definitely moving north. Elegant, well bred, and rich, Lady Cordelia was the perfect choice for a wife…if one discounted her Quakerish ways. The woman pressed her nose into a book and never looked up. Which was hardly a bad quality, but when one combined it with grey clothes and a sense of humility so vast, Darcy felt the need to apologize for sneezing. It did not bode well for the propagation of the Chase line.

Even so, his mother and Lady Cordelia's family kept hoping that his lecherous ways might tempt her from the path of Charity, Faith, and Hope. A rather odd desire for parents, but so it was.

"Do you agree?" his mother asked, her lips curling into a wicked smile.

Had she deliberately shoved him into this corner? Of course she had. His mother was a master at getting what she wanted through artful design. As was he. Father had created that necessity.

"Yes," he ground out. "I agree."

"Well, you needn't sound as if it's a death sentence. The girl is quite pretty."

"Mmm." And she'd lecture on the virtue of one's fellow man until one turned blue.

"Now, when shall this actress person arrive?"

"Soon." And God's teeth, he hoped it would be any moment because if she didn't, he just might gouge his eye out with his fork.

A melia shoved her brother's note into her small pelisse with more force than necessary. The parchment crumpled into a ball. Whipping the drawstring mouth shut, she looked out the window of the Earl of Chase's coach. They were fast approaching the most cherished addresses of London.

Groaning, Amelia placed a hand to her stomach. She felt ill. Her brother was up to his neck in something. She could sense it and these little notes he kept sending did not set her heart to ease. Only yesterday, he'd said he would not see her for some time, and now he wanted to meet her at Colton's print shop tomorrow afternoon.

On top of that, she'd been foolishly seduced into seeing Lord Chase out of teacher student capacity by the promise of a glimpse at a Folio.

Good Lord, what had she been thinking? The man had the devil's tongue. With words. Just with words. Her cheeks heated at the memory of his kiss and she had to admit that no, he had the devil's tongue in that regard as well.

The luxurious coach with its velvet seats and gilt leather walls was a heady reminder that Lord Chase was a very wealthy man. A lord. He was the kind of man her father would have hated.

They turned down a wider avenue that lined St. James' Park. Tall, stately homes built of brick and mortar towered above the street. Some stood freely on their own while others were attached, neatly in a row.

Only the wealthiest and titled families owned the free standing mansions along the streets and squares. Her father had tried to drive those titles into a place of insignificance. And while she might agree with the thought, his methods had been cruel and barbaric.

When the coach pulled up to one such place along the river, Amelia's stomach flopped. She shouldn't have been surprised that Lord Chase did not own one of the slightly less impressive edifices. Oh no, this house was five stories high with impressive windows and a wide set of double doors.

For some reason, she found the place more intimidating than the palace. But then, the king loved the arts, and actors and actresses. Many of the old guard nobles did not share his enthusiasm for welcoming players into Court life.

A footman hurried down the wide walk and opened the coach door. Amelia took his gloved hand and stepped down onto the ornately pebbled ground. She took one look up at the house before girding her nerves. Though she had been raised a daughter of a Puritan Parliamentarian at the head of Cromwell's army, she would not allow herself to feel intimidated by the Countess of Chase or her fine home.

When she stepped into the entryway, she was struck

by its elegant simplicity. A mosaic floor of blue and white marble formed a circular pattern in the round room. A statue of Venus stood at the center. The nude would have sent her father into fits of apoplexy.

The butler, in pale green edged in gold, stepped forward. "Your belongings, madam."

She handed him her China silk shawl and reticule.

He passed them off to a footman and gestured for her to follow him. "Lord and Lady Chase await you in the Orangerie."

They strode slowly down a wide hall, its walls hung with what appeared to be family paintings. She barely caught a glimpse at them before the butler opened a door to their left and stepped in, announcing her name.

After a moment, she followed. She smoothed her hands along the front of her dark blue dress and lifted her chin.

The high glass ceiling let in the late morning light, and for a moment, Amelia's eyes burned as they adjusted from the darker hall.

Tropical plants of every shape and size lined the walls. Their leafy branches bent in gentle grace, and low porcelain urns bore flowers of deep reds, purples, and white. In the center were a small table and four chairs.

The countess and Lord Chase were already standing to greet her.

His mother stood with the dignity of a queen, her dark green gown in the finest silks and lace, bringing out the blond in her curled silver hair and the gold flecks in her chocolate eyes.

The woman looked Amelia over from the top of her curled head to the hem of her gown, and she could have sworn her eyes shone with a touch of approval. Yet, the woman's haughty demeanor increased as she stated, "Mrs. Fox, you are a very pretty person. It must aide you in your profession."

Lord Chase's smile froze, giving him an almost comical air of frustration.

Amelia swallowed back a hasty retort. The old dragon was right, even if she was rude. "Yes, your ladyship, I am very fortunate. Though, I have learned that prettiness is valued in almost every aspect of society."

"How true." Lady Chase held her slender hand out toward one of the empty chairs. "Please, do be seated."

Amelia made her way to the chair and gave Chase a tight smile. The bastard had made it sound like his mother would be more than pleased to see her.

The harridan, albeit beautiful harridan, was about as pleased to have her in the house as a mangy alley cat. Amelia lowered herself into the seat. "Your son tells me you are a devotee of the theater."

Lady Chase frowned as she picked up the silver teapot from the table between them. "Hardly a devotee. However, I took great pleasure in court theater."

"Ah. As does your son."

The earl suddenly shifted in his chair and glared at Amelia, his eyes filled with warning. "I used to dabble, Mrs. Fox, but I have not been involved in court theater for years."

Amelia took the offered tea cup from Lady Chase, making sure not to grip the china too hard, lest she break it. For she had a most suspicious feeling that she'd been truly duped. "But you are eager to return to the boards, are you not my lord?"

She smiled sweetly at him.

"What's this, Darcy?" demanded Lady Chase, as she poured out another cup of tea.

"Just one sugar mother."

Amelia did not miss the three heaping spoonfuls that the countess poured into his cup.

The sight of the large man, perched on the delicate chair, clutching a tea cup was enough to alleviate some of Amelia's irritation. He scowled into his tea, took a sip, and winced. "It is nothing. Just a small pageant the king is putting up."

Lady Chase's face illuminated in a surprising smile. She beamed proudly on her son. "My son is actually quite the talented actor."

Amelia smiled back at her Ladyship then turned a withering glare on Lord Chase. "I am beginning realize that."

To her shock, Darcy's lips parted in a dangerous grin, as if he had sensed an invisible gauntlet being flung down and was clearly ready for the battle. What exactly had she gotten herself into? Whatever it was, she didn't understand it, for there was a hint of the hunter glimmering in Lord Chase's eyes.

Amelia lifted her cup in a small salute. If he thought her easy prey, he was very, very mistaken. If he wished a challenge, she would give it to him.

Chapter Nine

His mother was behaving surprising well… And yet things were getting out of hand. As he looked from his razor sharp mother to Mrs. Fox, he realized he may have made a severe tactical error.

It had not occurred to him to warn Mrs. Fox not to mention their professional relationship, which now struck him as extremely dense. All he'd wanted was to get her to himself again, and he'd been willing to say anything…

Except the important things apparently.

Darcy put his tea-cup down. "Mother, Mrs. Fox deals in the theater all day long. We should not bore her with it."

"And yet you brought her here to see Shakespeare's Folio. Yes. Very untheatrical."

Mrs. Fox covered her mouth with her hand and cleared her throat. "Pardon me, I have a tickle in my throat," she murmured.

Her eyes twinkled with clear amusement at his predicament. Right. Time to get the women apart. "Speaking of Shakespeare."

He stood and offered Mrs. Fox his hand. "Shall we?"

Nodding, she put her cup down then took his hand as she stood.

"Good day, Mother," said Darcy.

The twinkle had gone from her eye and she tugged her fingers from his grasp. "Are you not coming with us, Countess?"

"No. I am going into the City this morning." She rang the small silver bell next to the tea tray. "My son will show you the folio. It was a pleasure. Good day."

Mrs. Fox bobbed a small curtsy and flashed her an unconvincing smile. "Good day."

Darcy waited for Mrs. Fox to go to the door and followed. As soon as they stood out in the hall, the door shut behind him, she poked him in the chest. "You misled me," she hissed.

Certainly, but in which way? "How so?"

"You told me your mother would be here."

"So she was. I cannot always know her comings and goings."

"Perhaps I, too, should go."

"And not see the folio?"

She nibbled her lower lip, clearly torn. "I shall see it. But only for just a moment."

"Shall we not have our lesson, as well?" Now that his mother was going to be out of the house, and he could have Mrs. Fox alone in the library, he wanted to spend as much time with her as possible. A little easy conversation might make her tongue loose. In more ways than one.

"Perhaps. We shall see."

"Come with me." He headed off down the hall, keeping his steps smaller to accommodate her shorter stature and skirts.

Silence fell between them, and Darcy found himself missing their conversation…even if it was shoving him into corners and throwing him over fires he'd created for himself. He turned down the hall, which led to the east wing. "Did you have an uneventful evening?"

"Yes. But after the night with your highwayman friend several weeks ago, almost anything would seem uneventful."

Stopping in front of the library's arched doorway, he looked down at her. "I thought you wished to forget that night."

She blinked. "I have. 'Tis completely forgotten."

"You're certain?"

"I—" She scowled at him as she realized he was deliberately goading her. "Quite."

Darcy laughed softly. She was quite a sight, her cheeks pink with embarrassment and indignation. Yet, he had to remind himself she was no school room miss, but an accomplished pretender. He pushed open the doors and waited for her to go inside.

She quickly stepped in, her skirts rustling against the wood floor. She barely made it a few paces before stopping.

Darcy crossed to her side and looked at her awestruck face. Her green eyes widened with wonder and her pink lips parted. She stood with her head slightly tilted back as she took in the room.

He turned his gaze to the library and tried to look at it through her eyes, with her wonder, which struck a chord inside him. It was a mammoth room, designed by his grandfather, who had had a passion for books. The massive fireplace, high enough for a Highland Scot to stand in and wide enough for him to lie down in, dominated the far end of the room. Two hardback chairs were placed before it. Other chairs and leather couches were scattered over the artfully placed woven rugs.

In the center of the room stood a glass case with some of his grandfather's, his father's, and his own most prized literary treasures. It truly was an amazing sight, even if he had grown accustomed to it. "You like it?"

"Like it?" she breathed, her tone as reverent as a monk at prayer. "*Like* is not the word. I have never seen so many books in one place, nor on such display. I—" She placed a hand on his forearm and whispered, "Thank you."

Darcy's breath hitched in his throat. He'd never heard such genuine gratitude or wonder in something so simple. He'd given women jewels to ransom a prince and their response could never have matched Mrs. Fox's. He placed his free hand over hers, savoring the gentle warmth of her skin. "It is my pleasure."

Her eyes lifted to his, gazing up at him through long, black lashes. Their gazes held for a moment, and the room seemed to vanish around them.

Drawing in a shaky breath, she pulled back from him, and said brightly, "Will you show me the Folio?"

The moment gone, he shoved back a sharp sense of disappointment at its loss. He strode to the glass case. "Certainly." He easily swung up the heavy front panel. Reverently, he reached for it, grasped the Folio only by its edges, and retrieved it. Carefully, as though it were a newborn child, he placed it on the glass.

"May I?" she asked as she came up to stand beside him.

"Yes. But be very careful and touch it as little as possible."

Shaking her head in wonder, Mrs. Fox tentatively

reached out and opened the cover. Her eyes wandered over the page, searching over the dark ink.

Had he ever felt so passionate about anything? Certainly, he'd desired women, the restoration of his king, and even wealth, but he couldn't recall a time when he'd felt such child-like wonder.

The purity of her love for the Folio clenched his heart. What would he give for someone to look at him like that? He glanced down at her.

She stood with her head tilted down, the gentle curve of her neck exposed. A few tendrils of her black hair caressed her skin, and he wanted to brush them aside and replace them with his lips. Later. Now he needed to take advantage of her distraction. "Will you pardon me? There is something I must see to."

"You will leave me with it?"

"Are you intending to abscond with it?"

Laughing, she stole a glimpse at him, a surprisingly seductive little glance. "Perhaps you should not trust me."

"Perhaps I don't."

Her smile dimmed.

"Not with something you love so much," he said lightly. "You might try to sneak it under your skirts, and then I shall be forced to reclaim it."

She scowled at him, but a playful spark warmed her green eyes again. "You, sir, are incorrigible."

"So my nanny used to tell me. My mother also, come to think of it."

"And no doubt a vast many other women."

"No. Just you."

"Just me?"

"Mmm." And suddenly Darcy couldn't resist. He knew what he *should* do. He should go and search her reticule immediately, but it could wait. So, he slipped his arm around her waist and pulled her against him. This was what he *had* to do.

She let out a murmur of protest, but did not push him away. Slipping a hand into the soft folds of her hair, he tilted her head, readying her for his kiss.

Amelia held her hands out to shove the earl back as he pulled her against his chest. Instead of pushing, her traitorous hands clasped the softness of his jacket and yanked him towards her.

The long, hard length of his body pressed into hers and Amelia felt as if every inch of her skin had come alive. His mouth came down on hers.

She expected the kiss to be bold, but instead it stole her breath with its seductive gentleness. His lips caressed hers in heady strokes and his hands roamed to her hips. Slowly, he pulled her up to cradle her against the hard length of his cock. His heat and hardness pressed through the folds of her skirts and she moaned against his mouth.

She'd been kissed many times, had even allowed herself to go beyond, but she'd never allowed herself to give in. Always, she'd pulled back. But now, she wanted to let go. She was well aware that pleasure existed between men and women, even if she had no experience of the happenings between the sexes.

Shivering at the evidence of his need, Amelia stroked

her hands up his muscled arms to his shoulders. His tongue licked the line of her lips and she opened to him, letting him stroke the inside of her mouth in strong, spine tingling thrusts.

Suddenly, he was lifting her and she was suspended in his embrace. After a few floating moments, he gently put her down onto one of the hard wooden tables by the fireplace. Her feet dangled off the ground and she shifted, adjusting to the new position.

Reason was slipping farther and farther into the back of her mind at his sensual onslaught. Vaguely, she remembered that they were in his family house, and that servants lurked in the halls, that she was throwing her own set of rules away, but the urge to give into his touch drove the thought away.

He broke the kiss and stroked her neck with his strong fingers. "My God, you are beautiful," he breathed then pressed a kiss to the side of her throat.

Amelia sucked in a sharp breath and dropped her head back to give him better access. As his mouth descended, she felt his other hand sliding her heavy skirts up her thighs. The feel of the fabric slipping along her skin was erotic and shocking.

A moment of alarm shot through her when the skirts were bunched at her hips. She'd never let a man do this, but she wanted the earl and felt safe with him. Weeks of wanting him had driven her to this madness.

Slowly, he lowered himself to his knees and pushed her thighs apart. She tensed, and he cupped her cheek, locking gazes with her. "Let me please you."

He loved the word pleasure. She'd noticed how often he used it, but she'd avoided it for so long. Too long. Perhaps that had been a mistake. Because just this simple taste had her greedy for more. To know what came next. Oh, she knew the physical part, but she didn't know how it would *feel*.

Biting her lip, she looked down at him, unsure.

"Trust me," he breathed.

The urge to finally trust someone, to trust him, conquered the last of her reason and she nodded.

His lips curled in a wolfish smile and then he leaned down to her thigh, gently taking it in his big hands. His fingers worked in soft circles starting at her knee, caressing her through her silk stocking, and then his lips followed.

Amelia swallowed as she looked at him between her thighs. Tentatively, she wove a hand into his long dark hair, and felt him laugh softly against her thigh. The muscles between her legs tensed.

Kissing and nipping his way up her legs, he took his time, until Amelia was desperate with growing need.

"Patience, love," he murmured against the upper most part of her thigh, and then his mouth was on her. At that place she barely ever touched herself. A kiss so soft at first she wasn't certain he'd actually touched her. Then he used his tongue, caressing the tight little spot. An intense shock of pleasure at his touch caused her to cry out.

Amelia braced herself with one hand on the table, the other still entwined in his hair.

His hands held her thighs, keeping her open to him as his tongue swirled and licked.

It seemed impossible that she was allowing this to happen. But she was and she could barely take the sensations washing over her.

Tension coiled in her lower body, driving her closer

and closer to something. She panted for breath struggling towards it.

He sucked and caressed her with his mouth and tongue. Then he slipped a finger inside her and she moaned. As he kissed the delicate flesh between her legs, he stroked her inside, finding a spot that had Amelia thrusting her hips up towards him.

Darcy didn't relent, but quickened the pace.

Her muscles tightened and the world exploded in wave after wave of shining stars and a pleasure so intense she cried out. Instead of stopping, Darcy slid his finger farther into her body and traced his tongue over her delicate folds, hitting the most sensitive spot again and again.

Her body wouldn't stop shuddering with it.

When the last ripples faded away, her body relaxed, her mind dazed.

Darcy leaned back, gently stroking her legs.

They were both quiet, locked in what had just happened.

Amelia swallowed as reason flooded to the front of her mind. The library came back into focus, and she very nearly lost her grip on the table. She'd made a very serious mistake. A fascinatingly beautiful error. "We've definitely broken my rules now."

"Rules are made to be broken, love."

But not these she wanted to retort. How could she have gotten herself into this mess?

He stared up at her with eyes so dark they were almost black with unfulfilled desire. Clearly, he had not experienced any release. A little voice somewhere in the back of her head urged to help him. To finally allow herself the full measure of a man. "My lord—"

"Surely, you may call me Darcy now," he whispered, not moving.

She laughed nervously. "Yes. I suppose. Darcy. This... What we've done." Gad, she couldn't think with him between her legs. Her skin flushed red and she gripped her skirts, desperately wanting to tug them down.

"Is exactly what we should have done." Slowly, he stood, letting her skirts slip back around her legs. Pressing a kiss to her lips, he twirled his fingers around one of her dark curls.

The kiss was gentle. Unlike the others that had so burned her body with need, this one was soft and languid. Almost reverent.

He pulled back, caressing the lock of hair between his fingers. "And it is just the beginning."

"But—"

"Are you going to deny how much you want me?" He took one of her hands and pressed it to the hard length of his cock. "There is how much I want you."

Amelia's breath caught in her throat at the feel of him. He was so big and even through his breeches she could feel it pulse with need. Deny the way her body so evidently loved his? How could she? But that didn't mean she should yield to it again.

Was she willing to be just another lord's mistress? Granted, a very powerful and wealthy lord, but a mistress just the same. She pulled her hand back and looked away. "Darcy, it was beautiful, but I—"

"Shh. Don't decide now. Decide tonight."

Wonderful. Amelia nearly growled in frustration. He wanted her to decide when the sun had set and he was at his best and one with the night?

A smile played at his lips. "I don't suppose we shall have a lesson today?"

She arched a brow at him and with as much dignity as she could manage pushed herself down from the table. "No. Not today. I think I should go."

He caught her hand and held it gently. "Amelia," he said firmly, "this isn't merely a flirtation. You understand that, do you not?"

Her heart slammed in her ribs. What in the devil did he mean? She couldn't allow herself to think he might have feelings for her. Not like her own feelings, which she couldn't deny were growing with each day that passed. "A man such as you only has flirtations with women such as me."

"Not this man," he whispered.

God help her, she nearly melted on the spot. Did he always say the right thing to make a woman want to give herself without a thought for the consequences? But there seemed such truth in his dark eyes and strong face.

Amelia folded her hands before her and squared her shoulders. This had to end. She'd worked too hard to risk it all for a man. "Thank you for allowing me to see the Folio. I must return to the theater for a fitting."

He stepped back, inclining his head, but he could not hide his air of disappointment. "Certainly. I will see you at the king's mask tonight, in any case, but first you must look longer at the Folio."

Amelia frowned. "How do you know I'm attending?"

"Oh, Pepys can never keep information to himself."

Of course. He knew Samuel Pepys. Who did not? Still, she felt a tugging of some dark emotion in her stomach. But she was being foolish. Too many years in Cromwell's reach had made her too suspicious. "Yes. I suppose you shall then."

He held out his hand, and Amelia took it, trying to appear calm as their skin met.

"Forgive me for not escorting you out," he said softly, "but there is something I must attend to. Stay as long as you can with Mr. Shakespeare."

She stared, almost uncomprehending, as he slipped out of the room.

Yes, he was right, there was something between them that was more than a flirtation. And it was dangerous. Because like any wild flame eventually, it would burn everything within its reach.

Darcy stood in the small cloak room off his entrance hall and swallowed. He'd left Amelia in with the folio. But of course, he'd needed to search her belongings. It was his duty, but at this moment, his duty was making him ill.

And not just because he was spying upon her after sharing such intimacy, but because he had found something.

He handed Amelia's reticule to Williams. "Take these to Mrs. Fox and mention that I look forward to our next meeting."

The butler bowed and took Mrs. Fox's small purse as well as her cloak.

Darcy waited several moments until he was certain she had left. At the present moment, she clearly had no suspicion of his role in her life, and he was struck again with the thought that perhaps she truly was an innocent bystander in all this mess. For if she had any skills about her in such actions, she never would kept such a damning letter on her person.

But it didn't matter if she was a bystander. The king would never forgive treason, even if a person had done it unwittingly.

Leaning against the wall, Darcy recalled the words he had committed quickly to memory.

> *Sister,*
>
> *Please meet me tomorrow morning at Colter's Print Shop. Tell no one that you have received this or that you shall be seeing me. Come through the back alley for safety's sake.*
>
> *Your Brother ever in faith and love*

Darcy stared blindly. It was time to stop lying to himself. Somewhere along the way he'd crossed a very serious line. He liked the lady in question. Not just lusted after her, but genuinely liked her.

He blew out a heavy breath. It mattered not. Bystander or not, Mrs. Fox was involved in something dangerous. And one thing was clear, she was knowingly aiding her brother. In *what* was what he had to discover.

Duty called him and it was time to harden his heart. A heart which he feared had begun to soften. A man of honor would go straight to the king and Darcy Blake, Earl of Chase, was nothing if not a man of honor.

Wasn't he?

Chapter Ten

The young reverend glanced over his shoulder, the expression on his pale face worried as he searched for a follower. He sighed then slipped into the crowded meeting hall that the boy had frequented to hear more radical teachings.

A place he had originally introduced to the boy. It had been so easy to open the fool's ears to the sick teachings the boy's murdering father had embraced so well.

He'd watched. For weeks. All he had been doing was watching. He'd pushed the pieces. He'd maneuvered the board as best he thought he might. Now, he was not so sure he had given it enough force, because as far as he could tell the Fox siblings were no closer to the gallows than they had been months before.

He had held back from further action because Winters followed the boy often. Chase? The man was with the boy's sister many times a week for weeks. And still, nothing.

Neither Winters nor Chase had reported their findings to the king, although it was apparent they had been charged to spy for Charles.

The two were still free. Still blissfully happy. Unlike himself or his dead family.

Rain began to fall, splattering his cloak and hat. It was time to act. If Chase and Winters wouldn't see that the Foxes should hang for treason, he would make them see. And soon.

"Ned, my life is in a shambles," moaned Amelia as she wiped the last of her makeup from her face. She'd been a spinning bustle of repressed nerves since this afternoon. Tonight, she'd nearly fumbled her lines three times. Even worse, she'd nearly missed an entrance, an act so feared by every actor, that sometimes they lurked like over-painted ghosts in the wings of the theater, keeping a beady eye on the performance, instead of waiting in the retiring room.

"Save your theatrics for the stage, my dear." Ned eyed himself in his mirror then patted his already firm cheeks. "Do you think I am beginning to sag?"

"Ned!" Amelia growled, tugging at her thin linen robe. "You aren't listening."

She slapped her hand down on her dressing table, hoping that might gain the vain actor's attention. "I am in a great deal of trouble."

"I am listening," insisted Ned, though he kept eying his own reflection, like bloody Narcissus at the lake. "A good actor always listens." He pressed his firm lips together, angled his face right to left then let out a tragic sigh. "It is I who am in trouble. Soon, I shall only be able to play grandfathers."

Amelia picked up her makeup rag and threw it at him. "And you accuse *me* of theatrics?"

He caught the rag and placed it gently on the table. "You're in a fine temper. Whatever has got your garters in a snit?"

She rolled her eyes.

"No. Truly, is all well?"

Amelia paused. She had been rather down in the mouth this evening. But with damn good reason. "I need your advice."

Ned's mouth dropped open and he fluttered his eye-lined lids. "I beg your pardon? What did you just request of me?"

Gritting her teeth, she fought the temptation to throw her rouge pot at her mentor. After throwing the rag, it would be far too dramatic, and she refused to be a prima donna. "I. Need. Your. Advice," she gritted, each admitted word almost as painful as tooth drawing.

A beatific smile lit his features as he combed his fingers through his closely cut black hair. "Such sweeter words I have not heard since that lovely young porter offered to su—"

Amelia snapped up her hand. "I don't wish to know, Ned."

"Yes, you do, my pet," he cooed. "Lord knows, you've no amours of your own."

Blinking, she shifted in her wooden chair. Suddenly, its hardness seemed too uncomfortable to bear.

Ned's eyes flared and he spun in his chair to face her. "Good God, Amelia, you lied. You did have an assignation today!"

Not daring to meet his gaze, she stared into her own mirror and focused on re-curling her hair with her fingers. "That's not *exactly* true."

"Stop prevaricating. You lost me ten pounds. I had to pay for Pepys's dinner and his entertainments and you know how that man can eat... Food and flesh. Food and flesh. That's all he ever—"

"Don't be vulgar."

"Please my dear, you've said worse, you've heard worse, you've simply never *done* worse." He leaned forward, staring intently at her. "Nor do I think you've even done the deed itself." Shaking his head pityingly, he stood and pulled on his long, peacock colored robe.

Amelia glanced over at him. How could she make him understand her predicament? Ned had lost his virtue long ago, and now made a professional habit of helping others throw theirs away. "I'm asking for advice, not accusations."

Ignoring her, he walked over to their clothes rack, pulled off his leather breeches from the play, and picked up the silk ones he'd be wearing home. "It's a wonder your acting is as good as it is, having never experienced passion." He stuck his legs into the full, dark burgundy breeches then jumped, pulling them up. "Indeed my pet, I think you're in need of a truly good f—"

"Enough already," gritted Amelia, not wanting to hear that word and Lord Chase in the same sentence. "That is my dilemma."

He blew out a disparaging breath. "Getting someone to bed you? I hardly think so."

She fisted her hands, trying not to throttle the highest

paid male actor in London. Her employer, Betterton, would kill her if she did. "No, I am trying to get him to leave me be."

Turning back to her, Ned's hands paused at buttoning his breeches and he frowned. "Come again?"

"I—" She clamped her mouth shut. Now that she finally had to get to the point, she wasn't sure she wished to discuss it.

"I say, this *is* serious."

"So I've been trying to tell you"—she glared at him and pointed her finger—"these last ten minutes."

Buttoning the last black buttons, Ned strode over to her then pulled his chair close to hers. "Do tell. I love a tale dripping with juice."

Amelia narrowed her eyes. "You must promise to not breathe a word."

He nodded, pressing his animate features into a somber expression. "Consider me your Father Confessor. Feel free to divulge any sinful thoughts or deeds. It shall go no further than the dressing room, er, confessional."

"You're not Catholic," she hissed.

"But I've played the friar in Romeo and Juliet."

Her lips twitched, despite herself. "That does not qualify you to give absolution."

"You're deliberately avoiding the issue…which you brought up, I'll remind you."

"Right." She drew in a calming breath then stared down at her hands. "I've met a man."

"Just one?" he quipped.

Good god, could the man not go a moment without using that barbed tongue? She glared at him. "Don't be an ass."

"Apologies, my pet." He waved his hand in little circle. "Do carry on."

"He… We…" How exactly could she say this without linking her name to the lord? "Oh for goodness sake!" she exclaimed. "I've met a man I want to bed and it's a disaster. He's a lord, and he's exceptionally skilled with women."

Ned cocked his head to the side then rubbed his chin. "I don't follow." He rolled his eyes to the right as if contemplating some great question. "Wherein lies the problem?"

It was just like him to make light of her predicament, but he was the only one she could talk to. After the ordeal of changing her last name and the danger of being linked to her father, she had very few close acquaintances. "Suffice it to say, it is impossible for me to avoid him, and each time I have been in his presence I have been beyond tempted."

He grinned, a kind, knowing smile and placed his hand on her shoulder. "Pet, it is perfectly normal to be tempted. In our field, we are even allowed to give in from time to time."

Amelia resisted the urge to fling off his well meaning hand. This was not the advice she wished. She needed to stand firm to her convictions. "Not me. I cannot."

"Why?"

"My father, he—" Amelia bit her lip and looked away. She could not repeat the things he had said of actors. Of women. But despite how foolish she knew the old man to be, she couldn't quite shake his words from her mind. She wanted to prove she could be an actress without giving up her body in trade. And the last thing she wanted was to be named some man's mistress. It was hard enough surviving the taunts of men at the playhouse.

Ned stroked her shoulder gently not pushing for further details. "We cannot live our lives according to the mistakes of our parents."

Tears stung the corners of her eyes and she nodded. "Yes, I know. I see it in my brother. He cannot shake off how badly our father was disappointed in him."

"So you see? You should pay no heed to the old man's railings."

Amelia plunked her elbows onto her dressing table and cradled her face in her hands. "I know you are right, but I... I simply can't."

Very gently, he asked, "Well, then, what can I do to help?"

She turned and looked him in the eyes. "How do I make this lord stop trying to seduce me?"

"I take it you absolutely must continue to see him?"

"Absolutely." Risking the king's displeasure was extremely foolish, not to mention dangerous.

Ned leaned back then folded his arms over his broad chest. "Am I to take it he holds the upper hand?"

Amelia frowned. "I don't—"

"Meaning he controls the seduction. You are at his mercy when it comes to the physical aspects of your meetings."

Heat flushed her cheeks. Every time, it had been he who had initiated the intense intimacy between them. "Yes."

He shrugged as if the answer was perfectly obvious. "It is clear what you must do."

"What?" If it came so easily to Ned, perhaps she wasn't in so much trouble.

As if he was the most intelligent creature in creation, he announced, "You must seize the upper hand. Become the seducer and take hold of the situation."

She lifted her face from her hands. "The seducer? I have no intenti—"

"This is sheer wisdom. From one former woman to you my sweet. By controlling him, he will do as you wish, and you in turn will dangle him from your little finger."

Dangle Darcy from her finger? Now there was a tantalizing thought. Amelia stared at herself in the mirror, a smile playing at her lips. "You are serious?"

"As serious as I can ever be."

She leaned in, eager to learn. "So how do I lead this lord about?"

"Fuck me, my lord," purred the young, pink cheeked lady as she trailed her hand down the slightly unlaced bodice of her pale yellow gown. A matching gold domino hid the upper half of her face, blending into her corn blond hair that glowed like a halo in the candlelight that lit up all of Banquet House that night.

Darcy bit back a sigh. If only those words had come from Mrs. Fox. But alas, no. He doubted she'd ever utter such words, let alone in a public setting.

The court was always debauched, but masks turned it into a free for all. Even the most prudish of Charles's courtiers frolicked in the decadently decorated ballroom.

Still, when the woman smiled temptingly and attempted to give his cock a quick stroke, Darcy cleared his throat and backed away. "Not tonight, my lady," he said as he removed the delicate hand of the young voluptuary. "I am saving myself for a particular lady."

Her red painted lips pouted beneath her gold mask and she flounced away, into the raucous crowd of debauched nobles.

Winters strode up, eyeing the floating barges of nymphs in the reflecting pool the king had set up for the mask. He looked like a walking glacier in his ice blue costume and glittering white mask. "You may turn down as many wenches as you please, Chase, but you might ask me if I'm interested before you send them packing."

The full orchestra could barely compete with the laughter and loud conversation of the massive crowd dancing, running, and gossiping in every corner of the room. Each courtier was resplendent, everyone in their most ornate costume.

Glancing at the feast of bare flesh that lounged on the soft cushions on the ornate floating islands towards the back of the ballroom, Darcy smiled. "Face it, Winters, the chit wasn't interested in y—" but before he could finish the sentence, two young women, one in a peacock mask and the other in a Venetian carnival domino, descended on his friend.

Their white hands fluttered over his pale blue, silk coat. They giggled to each other, clearly friends, as they fingered the diamonds and sapphires embroidered into the fabric.

Winters wet his lips as he looked from behind his half white mask at the peacock then to the Venetian. "Whatever can I do for you, beauties?"

The peacock pushed herself up on tiptoe, cupped her hand to Winters's ear, and whispered.

Laughter burst from his throat. "Tragically my sweet, I am presently occupied. But later perhaps? The center island, you and your friend?"

The girls smiled, trailed their hands suggestively down

Winters's chest, then the Venetian threw an inviting glance at Darcy. "Bring him."

Winters pouted exaggeratedly. "Alas, he has taken Holy Orders."

"Holy Orders?" murmured the Venetian, her voice as intoxicating as a fine port. "Perhaps I should then kneel before you?" She bit her lower lip thoughtfully and then released it. "Will you help me find grace?" Her voice hummed with promise.

Despite himself, Darcy laughed then pointed at his friend. "Apply to him, for he has a fondness for devotion."

The two women linked arms then hurried over to a group of young men all preparing to enter a floating barge. Darcy let his gaze wander over the laughing crowd and dancers on the ball floor. "Have you seen Mrs. Fox?"

Winters shook his head. "You seem quite smitten. Should I be concerned?"

"She is my mission."

"Yet your usual detachment seems to have worn thin."

"She's a skirt with information. An extremely lush skirt." The lie passed easily over his lips, as all lies did these days. He only prayed Winters didn't guess that the lust Darcy felt was far more powerful than a passing interest for a bit of muslin. He looked toward the immense, gold covered doors at the end of the massive hall. "Is Warrington here tonight?"

"He's none of your affair, but Warrington is over there," Winters murmured. "The green devil mask."

Darcy spotted the tall wigged lord standing just on the edge of the dance floor. He stood alone, his arms crossed over his emerald green coat, which was embroidered with silver thread and encrusted with heavy silver scales. With the sharp features of the devil mask, he appeared to be straight out of Eden, ready to tempt Eve with the apple.

Narrowing his eyes behind his mask, Darcy tried to determine what the lord was staring at. When he shifted his gaze a little to the left he spotted her.

Darcy homed his gaze on Mrs. Fox. The scarlet red of her elaborate gown stood out as if she was the most exotic flower in paradise. Her entire gown shimmered, shot through with gold thread. Jewels encrusted the front of her gown, and matching rubies and diamonds hung from her slender neck with a finial cross nestling just above the swells of her mouth watering breasts.

A red and gold mask hid half her face and her black hair, studded with diamond stars, spilled over her shoulders and down her back in thick curls.

Darcy let out a slow breath. "There she is."

Winters turned sharply towards him. "Where?"

He fisted his thin gloved hands. "She's standing not ten feet from Warrington, and he's staring at her like she's a bloody Christmas dinner after the banns are lifted."

"Jesus, she's a sight." Winter's whistled low. "How did we miss her come in?"

"Have you discovered any evidence against Warrington?"

"Early days. But he does seem to favor dark corners with the wrong sorts. Traitor, he very well may be. Let's hope your Mrs. Fox doesn't turn out to be the wrong sort."

Darcy glanced from Warrington to Mrs. Fox as Winters spoke. He had a serious problem. Because if Warrington was a serpent, Darcy had a very bad feeling that Mrs. Fox was the fruit. And someone had to play God. That someone was going to be him.

Chapter Eleven

Amelia gasped as a hand boldly caressed her waist, pulling her back against a hard body. A man whispered against her neck, "May I have this dance?"

His rich voice evoked shivers of excitement, and she found herself losing track of thought.

Darcy.

Time to let the dangling begin.

"No, you may not," she teased. And she started to walk away.

His grip on her waist tightened, pressing through her corset.

A brief thrill raced down her spine, but she squelched it. He was no longer in control. She was. "Since, you are to be a woman, I shall take the man's part and I do not currently wish to dance."

He laughed softly. "I think you lack the man's part."

Amelia's eyes widened at his repartee, but she refused to give in. "Ah, but you follow my instruction nonetheless?"

"I do," he murmured, his lips dangerously close to the soft skin of her neck.

"And you must learn to be a woman?"

"Yes," he whispered, and his breath caressed warm and soft against her skin.

"So, I shall teach you something new," she murmured. "As any good woman, you must learn the art of distracting a man. Allow me to demonstrate." Boldly, she slightly rocked her hips back against his. He let out the barest moan. While he was still distracted, Amelia pulled free of his grip.

He hissed out a breath then said to her back. "A very clever lesson. Should I now practice it on you?"

She turned to face him about to deliver a piece of clever repartee. It died on her lips. Death stared back at her and it was the most erotic thing she had ever seen in her life.

He towered above most of the other nobles around him, and instead of the typical painted peacock beauty of the males of Charles's court, Darcy's robust soldier's strength was undeniably inspiring. He wore nothing but black silk. From his high boots, which stopped just above his knees, to his shockingly tight breeches, she just could not tear her eyes away. He did not wear a coat, but rather sported a fine silk shirt and a black velvet cape. He'd left his long black hair unbound. It spilled in shiny blue black waves over his broad shoulders. His mask, black satin, clung to his strong face, emphasizing the strength of his jaw. He was raw strength and power with no silly trappings of wealth.

A small group of women, fans wagging like eager dog tails, gawked at him. They were practically panting as they eyed him.

A sharp jolt of anger at the silly twits flared in her

blood. The women were watching him from behind their masks, most likely desperately hoping that he would turn his attention on them. To her shock, she did not like it. Not at all. Impulsively, she held out her hand. "Ask me to dance again," she purred. "Very nicely."

He took her hand in his gloved one then turned it so it was palm up. With agonizing slowness, he lifted it to his mouth and pressed a kiss to it. A collective sigh went up around them, and Amelia had to bite back a laugh. The man was a master, and she was dancing too close to the fire. But so far, everything he'd had said was true. As of this moment, he was doing everything she wanted him to.

"My lady," he murmured, glancing at her through the slits of his mask "I beg you to bestow a moment of your time upon me, so I might worship your body…in dance."

She inclined her head, and he led her onto the floor. As they promenaded forward behind another couple, they remained silent. But finally, she couldn't resist. "Shall we practice vocal tone in your next lesson?"

His gaze trailed to her breasts. "Only if you promise to make me moan."

"I'm sure I could manage that."

"How so?" he asked, his voice low.

"I'll bring you a corset," she quipped.

"How disappointing."

"Acting is a road full of much rejection, my lord."

"It is fortunate, then, that I am not overly familiar with it." He squeezed her hand, caressing it with his thumb as he guided her round the floor into position across from him.

She smiled, allowing a faint element of warning to barb her voice. "I should be delighted to acquaint you with it."

"Are you deliberately playing with me, madam?" he whispered as they stepped towards each other.

"Playing?" she shook her head, pouting her lips. "Certainly not. I am merely giving you a taste of your own tongue."

He took her hand leading her after the line of couples marching towards the orchestra. "Something I have no wish to taste… But yours? I like its taste very much."

"No." She forced herself to laugh, even as her breath hitched in her chest.

"What if I asked *very nicely*?"

She arched a brow at him and smiled. "No."

The music came to a quick crescendo, and disappointment tugged at her. They were both fighting for control in a battle of sensual wills, and he had far more experience.

He led her from the floor. "Your dismissal is so cruel. What has caused your words to contradict your actions?"

At that moment another man approached. He was tall, but not quite as tall as Darcy. His deep green costume was almost vulgar next to the earl's elegant masculinity. He bowed. "I should like to dance, madam."

Darcy cut in, tsking. "Sir, you must ask her *very nicely*, or the lady shall have none of it."

Amelia glared at Darcy then turned her attention to the newcomer. If she could leave the earl gaping after her, she would be extremely pleased.

"Some men are foolish enough to ask," said the green devil. "But I am more than happy to take." He took Amelia's hand. "What does my lady say?"

She looked him in his dark blue eyes and felt a moment of trepidation, but then recalled Darcy. "Who could refuse the devil?"

With that, she let the green devil lead her onto the floor. Amelia glanced at Darcy from the corner of her eye. She couldn't stop the pleased smile from tilting her lips. He stood staring, his sensual mouth pressed into a tight line.

Just as her partner began to turn her in a slow circle, their hands twining between them, Amelia spotted an ice masked man approaching the earl. Before she could get a good look at him, she and the green devil were promenading across the floor.

"Red is a becoming color on you, madam."

Amelia forced herself to focus on the man dancing with her. His movements were more graceful than Darcy's, almost sinuous as he easily moved her in the slow turning steps of the dance. "Red is becoming for many women."

"Hmmm." His voice hummed low in his throat like rich melted honey. "Indeed, but I think it is *your* color."

"Why is that?"

"It is the color of the temptress."

She tensed. He gripped her hands tightly and pulled her closer than the dance called for. "Then you are mistaken, for I am hardly that," she snapped.

He tilted his head and with the candlelight, bizarre shadows highlighted his mask. The thing virtually came alive, and she half expected him to hiss. Instead, he whispered, "If you are not now, you will be."

She narrowed her eyes. What in God's name was he talking about? "Sir, let me go. I am tired of your conversation."

"Ask very nicely." He held tightly to her hands, but his body remained at ease, as if nothing was wrong.

Amelia swallowed, suddenly unease making her ill. "No."

Slowly, he circled them, their hands clasped, creating

a small round space between them. He looked her in the eyes, and they smoldered. Not with lust, but something else. Dangerous ambition.

The music came to a halt, and she breathed a sigh of relief. She'd made her point with Chase, but she had paid for it dearly with this strange man.

"Thank you," she drawled, ready to turn on her heel.

"You will come with me now." His hands tightened as he led her off the floor and kept walking.

His grip bit into her skin. Wincing, Amelia, tried to pull without making it too obvious. She couldn't create a scene for all London to talk about. Pushing or slapping him certainly would do just that. "You have grown over-presumptuous sir. I have the ear of the king and will use it if you don't desist."

He stopped, but kept a strong hold on her hand. He looked down at her, the part of his face she could see, as hard as stone. "Please do go to the king." Suddenly, he began pulling her behind him, toward the red and gold dais at the opposite end of the opulent hall. "Because when you are done, I shall mention your brother."

Amelia dug her feet in, her heart suddenly cold. "What about my brother?" she whispered.

"You must come with me to find out."

She glanced around the masked faces, desperate for some sort of aid. But there was none. None of these people could help her. And if her brother was in trouble, it must be kept a secret. She'd seen too many men lose their heads to not take this seriously.

"Wait!"

He stopped, easing his grip ever so slightly.

She looked up at him, hardly able to believe this was

happening to her. But it was, and she would not allow herself to risk her brother. "I will go with you, sir."

"W hat the blazes is she doing?" Darcy couldn't believe his eyes as Amelia followed Warrington out of the hall.

"It's rather obvious," drawled Winters. "She's going off with our wolf in sheep's clothing."

Yes, but something wasn't right. "She doesn't appear all too happy about it."

"Most likely she doesn't want anyone to see them together. Conspirers rarely like to be conspicuous."

Conspirer. The word dried his mouth and chilled his skin. He'd known she might be a traitor, hell that's what he was supposed to determine for certain. But now, confronted with the cold hard truth, he felt ill because he couldn't banish the vision of Mrs. Fox swinging from her neck at Tyburn.

"Are you all right, man?" Winters clasped him on the shoulder. "You look as if you're about to chomp someone's flesh."

Darcy didn't reply, anger pumping though his veins. Why would she put herself at such risk? At the king's palace? Amelia had never struck him as the idiotic sort. And for Christ sake, why would such an acclaimed actress throw all her successes for a Protestant revolution?

"You can't follow her." Winters pinned him with a hard stare. "You'll overplay your hand."

"We can't just let them go off—"

"I'll follow Warrington. The man won't suspect me if I

accost him with wine and the promise of women. I've been drinking a good deal with him as of late."

Darcy gave a sharp nod then strode towards the fountains of champagne. He bloody needed a drink. A large drink. When he reached the table, he took one of the chilled glasses in his hand tossed the bubbling liquid down his throat and then grabbed another one. Just as he was about to make short work of its contents he stopped. What the hell was he doing?

He wasn't just going to sit and wait. Even if he should. He wanted to see for himself. He needed to see for himself if she was playing a dangerous game, and how better to determine her guilt than to witness her in the act of treason?

"You will do what I ask you to."

Trepidation squeezed Amelia's stomach. Even with her mask, this man seemed to know exactly who she was. "You will have to be a great deal more specific with your threats. How do I know my brother has truly done anything?"

"A few well placed words from a man such as myself, and your brother will have his guts pulled from his body before he's hanged. As a traitor. Besides…you know he's been acting suspiciously. It's why you came along with me, is it not?"

Her stomach heaved, and she thought back to her conversation with her brother just this morning. Oh dear God, what had he gotten himself involved in?

One needn't hard proof if the accusation was treason.

There were still many secret Puritans and Protestants planning to cause revolution if Charles had no son. "What do you want? Funds?"

"Wealth is not what I seek." He crossed to the marble mantle fireplace and leaned against it, the lace on his wide cuffs falling artistically about his strong wrists. "No. What I need from you is different. A few moments of your precious time."

Amelia ground her teeth together. She wanted to spit in his face and tell him to go to the deuce. Instead, she lifted her chin, keeping what little power she could. "Be plain. What do you want?"

He laughed, but no amusement lit his eyes. He strode towards her, his walk smooth and powerful.

Standing her ground, she stared straight ahead. All her life, she had worked not to be viewed as a temptress. Being attractive was beneficial to her profession, but she had never purposefully led a man on until this night and Chase. And that had only been to serve him his own desserts.

He lifted his gloved hand and trailed his forefinger along her cheek. "A man would have to be castrated not to respond to your kind of beauty."

"Please don't touch me," she said flatly. "It makes my flesh crawl."

The calm demeanor of her blackmailer disappeared, replaced by a scalding anger as his body tensed. He grabbed her chin in his gloved hand. His fingers bit into her flesh. "I don't think you quite understand the precariousness of your position." He leaned into her until his lips were a mere inch from her face. And if anyone should make a person's flesh crawl, it is you. If they knew anything about your family."

Amelia winced, but held still. She would not risk her brother's life just to speak a few pride soothing words. She lifted her hands to his wrists and gently pulled. "I am listening."

He didn't let go, but dug his fingers harder into her skin. Her eyes watered and she pressed her lips together to keep from crying out. He tilted his head to the side.

Pulling back a step, he cleared his throat and slipped a small bunch of folded papers from his coat pocket. A white ribbon fluttered around it, binding the pages together. "You will deliver this to a man at Colter's Print Shop. A Mr. Sharpton."

Amelia shook her head as her mouth dried. She'd heard of Sharpton. The man was notorious for his support of the extreme Protestant regime. The regime that supported The Duke of Monmouth's rise to the throne, even though he was Charles's bastard son. After all, to these men, any king was better than the Catholic James, Charles's brother.

A flash of her father and the last days of Cromwell's regime pushed in on her. Everyone who had served the Lord High Protector had lived in fear, knowing the monarch was about to return. She would not return to that life. "I cannot."

He held the papers out to her. "You can and you will. Your brother's life depends on it."

"Go to hell," she growled. She froze as the words left her lips, half expecting him to hit her.

Instead, his deep blue eyes darkened with pain and he smiled ruefully. "Madam, as you can see, I'm already there. Now, you will deliver these, and you will assist your brother in whatever plots he has embroiled himself. Or I will see to it that your brother is exposed to the king."

Amelia stared at the papers, feeling frozen, but somehow, she managed to take the sheafs. She tucked them into a hidden fold of her skirt. Confusion sent her thoughts rioting. "Why would you have me—"

"You have no need to know to understand my motives. Now, will you protect your brother and aid him as I say or no?"

She swallowed then nodded.

"Warrington!" a deep voice called from down the long corridor.

Tensing, the man in the devil mask turned. "Winters?"

Amelia held still, wishing for escape, praying this man would leave her alone. *Warrington*. She'd never heard the name before.

"You promised to join me in a drink," the earl drawled, lingering in the half-light of the candelabras.

A muscle tightened in Warrington's jaw, just below his mask. He looked down at her. "Do not forget and do not fail. Now, go."

Taking in slow calming breaths, Amelia turned and hurried away. As soon as she was down the narrow hall, she stopped and pressed a hand to her breasts. Her corset was too tight and she couldn't breathe.

This couldn't be happening. It just couldn't. When Charles had returned, and her father had died, she'd been certain that she'd never know another day of intrigue.

But now, she'd been thrown right into the bloody crush of lies and deceit. Chase's strong handsome face came unbidden to her mind. What would he think of all this?

She could never tell him. Never. He was a loyal man who had served the king. No doubt, he would consider it his duty to go straight to the government with information of her brother's foolishness.

She wished that this was some vast misunderstanding, but when she'd looked into her brother's eyes this morning, she'd seen that he'd involved himself with dangerous men. She'd simply not realized how dangerous. And now, she was involved, too.

Amelia braced her hands against her straining ribs. Could she do it? Her jaw throbbed from Warrington's hard grasp. Her brother was the last of her family, and if she didn't do as commanded, his life would be forfeit. So, the answer was quite simple. Yes, she could.

Chapter Twelve

Chase strode down another hall only to find it empty and silent, save the sound of his own boots on the polished wood. "God's teeth!" he growled.

Had Winters found them? He half hoped his friend hadn't. The last thing Darcy wished was for his friend to overhear incriminating discourse.

He stopped in the middle of a long hall, its hardwood floor reflecting the light of several lit candelabras. He had not just thought that previous thought. If she was a traitor, she deserved a traitor's death.

Hell, she was an actress, and he'd spent very little time with her. But despite that, he'd begun to feel as if he knew her. The kind of knowing that did not require words or time.

It bloody terrified him.

Darcy fisted his hands. He was being a fool. For, he knew firsthand how easy it was to hide one's true feelings and identity. She'd made a profession out of it. So had he. But she seemed to lack pretense.

In fact, she seemed filled with nothing but candor.

He blew out a harsh breath, taking a moment before resuming his search. Winters was right, of course.

To allow himself, a king's man, to be blinded was an unforgivable crime.

Though his family had been vastly rewarded for their loyalty, they'd given up a great deal to see the monarchy returned to England. England would not revert to a society that didn't follow the laws of monarchy. Not while he still drew breath.

"Focus on the task at hand man. Focus." He pressed his mask a little tighter to his face, savoring its anonymity, then strode down the hall and turned right.

There she was.

The candlelight flickered over her, sparking golden hues in her jeweled hair and gown. Darcy stopped in his tracks, still struck by the fact that he'd been highly concerned for her.

He remained silent.

She'd wrapped her arms around her slender middle and her head was bowed. The thick curtain of her curled black hair hid her face.

Though he could not see her expression, he could sense her distress. That a woman such as Amelia Fox could ever not stand proud seemed remarkably wrong. His chest tightened. What had happened between her and Warrington? What were the two to each other? He started towards her. "Amelia?"

Her head snapped up and she whipped towards him. The single glisten of a tear slipped from the corner of her mask, and she dashed it away. "L-lord Chase. I…"

She looked away, letting her words fade quietly.

The sight of that tear stabbed him right through the heart, a region he'd long thought dead to such emotions. He crossed the distance between them and stood before her. God, he wanted to ease whatever suffering she felt, but he couldn't allow himself to feel such sympathy. "What has happened?"

"Nothing," she said too quickly, flashing him a brittle smile.

"Nothing?" he echoed as he spotted light bruising on her skin. Anger flared in his chest.

Red marks ruddied her cheeks and chin. Finger marks. Darcy's heart pounded. The bastard had manhandled her.

Gently, he reached towards her mask. He moved carefully, expecting her to yank back. Instead she stood very still, not meeting his eyes.

He stepped closer, the soft warmth of her body caressing him through his thin shirt as he reached around and pulled the velvet ties at the back of her head. He slipped the leather mask away and looked down at her face.

The soft skin just beneath her eyes was damp, but she showed no other signs of tears. Even so, Darcy reached up and smoothed the tears from under her eyes. "How can this be nothing?"

She grabbed his hand and flicked her eyes to his. "I am merely tired. Too little sleep and too many hours at the playhouse. Then there is, of course, my difficult student."

He cupped her cheek in his palm, feeling a potent urge to cradle her in his arms. "Yes, but I am not usually given to evoking tears."

They stood silently for a moment. How the hell was he supposed to comfort her? He shouldn't even be trying to. Rather, he should be pushing her for information. "Shall I take you home?"

"Mr. Pepys—"

"Is no doubt scribbling down the witty remarks of Rochester and George Villiers. I shall send a footman to tell him of your whereabouts and take you home."

To his complete surprise, she wet her lips and placed her hand on his. "In truth, at this moment…" She looked up, her face pale and her gaze vulnerable. "I don't wish to be alone."

Darcy looked down at her small hand resting on his large one then nodded. Something had changed. He had no idea what it was, but he wasn't going to challenge it. Not now. "As you wish."

Amelia took one last look at the white walls and the towering windows of Banquet Hall before she climbed into Lord Chase's coach. It was a defining moment, a point of no return. By getting into his coach, she was making a choice. She was breaking a vow, because she could no longer bear to be so utterly alone. And tonight, she'd realized just how alone she was.

Both of her parents were long gone and her own brother had forced her into a terrible position. One in which she was putting herself at extreme risk. And if she was going to live with so much fear, she needed some comfort.

Darcy's genuine concern at her distress had touched her heart. She couldn't lie to herself anymore. She liked the man.

Too much for her own good. He seemed to see her in a way that no one ever had before.

And it thrilled her. She needed that. His admiration.

As she settled against the soft velvet seats, he climbed in and sat across from her. The footman closed the door with a quiet click, and they rattled down the cobblestone road.

The carriage was dark save for the golden glow of a small torch flickering in a lantern attached to the carriage wall.

Silently, Darcy removed his mask. In the faint light, most of his body was bathed in darkness but his eyes reflected the candle's flame.

He placed his mask beside him then tugged the delicate rope that bound his cloak. The fabric slid from his broad shoulders, and he was nothing more than a hard silhouette in the faint light.

Leaning forward, he set his eyes roaming over her, lingering on her mouth. Amelia's body turned languid, as if he'd actually touched her. It didn't feel real, the fact that she was here. With him.

Her blood was warm with wine and her nerves were frayed. All she wanted was someone to hold her close and tell her everything would be well. If that person were Chase, she would not protest. In fact, she longed for it to be him.

Deliberately, he tugged his gloves from his hands, then took her hand in his. Amelia waited for him to pull her onto his lap as she had seen so many men do to the other actresses. Their slaking of lust had been quick and powerful. Over in a few brief moments.

But after this morning's slow seductions, she should not have been surprised when he lifted her hand towards his mouth, turning it over. Just as he had done in the ballroom.

Gently, he bit the fleshy part of her palm. Amelia sucked in a soft breath. The sharp nipping of his teeth was quick yet soft. To her distress, she wanted him to bite a little harder.

"Amelia," he breathed against her skin as he pressed a kiss against her palm. He paused and looked up into her eyes. Slowly, he slid his hand along her forearm then over her shoulders and up to her chin. He cupped her cheek, tilting it.

The sound of her name on his lips and the touch of his skin shot shivers of anticipation down her spine.

"Kiss me," she whispered.

"Whatever the lady commands." His mouth covered hers, gentle, moving in heady touches so slight she wanted to beg him to kiss her harder.

She lifted her hands to his shoulders, savoring the hardness of his muscles. God, she wanted those arms wrapped around her. She opened her mouth and tentatively touched his lips with her tongue.

He moaned and gently sucked her tongue into his mouth. Amelia nearly melted at the sensation. The delicious taste of him sent a jolt of pure want to the sensitive spot between her thighs.

He sucked and licked her tongue until she could bear it no more. She was a wanton creature for desiring this. But this was for herself and no one else.

Ned was right. She was allowed to be tempted. According to the Puritans, she was going to burn in hell in any case. So, she might as well light the biggest blaze she could.

He moved his lips from hers and she panted trying to catch her breath. The movement of her breasts rising up and down clearly distracted him. Before she could protest, his lips were caressing the tops of her breasts, pressing feather light open mouthed kisses.

She bit her lip, biting back a moan. She entwined her fingers in his hair, pressing him closer as she leaned back.

He laughed, a deep rumble, against her chest. "You like that, love?"

"Mmm." She couldn't seem to think of a word to express how it felt and how much she enjoyed it. She simply wanted more.

"What wouldn't I give to get this gown off you."

Amelia swallowed. The dress was an elaborate affair, but the very thought of her skin pressing against his would be worth it.

Right now, she wanted something else. She trailed her gaze over his strong shoulders and smiled. "You first."

His lips parted in a wolfish grin. For a moment she thought he was going to leap on her and eat her up. Instead, he took her hand and led it to the loosely tied knot at his throat. "Consider me your present. Unwrap me."

Amelia giggled at the idea of him wrapped up like a Christmas present.

Boldly, she tugged on the soft material and unwound it from his neck. He waited patiently, his fingers gripping his thighs until she reached the lacings of his shirt. She tugged but it refused to come free. She growled in frustration, and suddenly he was wrenching the shirt over his head.

She dug her fingers into the folds of her skirts. She'd seen countless naked men in the playhouse. Some were quite comely, but not one could hold a candle to the pure beauty of Darcy.

The soft glow of light warmed his skin the hue of alabaster. The muscles in his hard chest shifted and rippled as he leaned back.

Bone and muscle worked together like music as he moved. The chiseled lines descended into several ridges along his stomach and then to twin chords that ventured into his black breeches. A soft line of black hair started at his navel and headed downward.

He stared at her, his lips slightly parted and his hands gripping his knees. "Go ahead. Take."

She swallowed at his commanding words. He was offering himself up to her, and from the straining muscles of his torso, she sensed that it was no sacrifice. She inched forward on the brocade covered bench and let her eyes roam over his hard body.

Every Puritan in London would be condemning her, Ned would be applauding her, but she didn't care. This one moment was for her. For all the pain and fear that had been in her life. Tonight, she would live like there was no tomorrow.

Chapter Thirteen

Swallowing at her audacity, Amelia tried not to think about the fact that she was in a moving carriage. With servants outside. She'd never done anything this bold and she found it oddly thrilling.

Tentatively, she reached out and stroked her fingers over Darcy's heart. He was warm velvet and flexing muscles. Somehow, he managed to sit still, though she could feel his eyes locked on her as she trailed her hands over his body. The skin seemed to barely contain his strength and vitality.

And she wanted a taste.

Bracing herself with a gentle grasp on his arms, Amelia leaned forward and pressed a kiss to his collarbone. Sweet and slightly salty. She glanced up into his eyes and froze. Her heart slammed. A fierce need mixed with a possessive protection tightened his features. What would it be like to belong to so strong a man?

She broke the gaze and returned her attention to the

ridges of his chest. She flicked her tongue over his nipple. He tensed.

She was a virgin, it was true, but she'd heard so much in the playhouse. Now, she could do whatever she had imagined with no hesitation. It was heaven.

At last, she moved her fingers to the waist of his breeches. She wanted to see him and return the pleasure he had given her in the library. Even now she could recall its intensity. Would it be like that again?

He lifted her to his lap. Her bum rested on his long, strong legs, and through the folds of clothing and underskirts, the hard heat of his cock pressed against her. Gently, she slid her leg against it. He hissed and captured her face with his big hands. "Not yet," he whispered. He lowered his mouth back to hers.

This time there was no gentleness in his kiss, only wild need. Amelia tried to circle her arms around his neck, but the tight strictures of her dress prevented the movement. She grabbed his hard upper arms to steady herself. They flexed beneath her fingers and she gasped into his mouth.

He took the opportunity to thrust his tongue deeper. She opened her mouth to him, welcoming the heady feel of his wet heat. Their tongues met, caressing, stroking moving back and forth in give and take. He mimicked a rhythm that tingled through her entire body.

"Darcy, I want—" She panted, not quite able to form a sentence.

"I want, too, love."

The carriage rolled to a stop. He tensed. The sound of booted feet hitting the cobbled road filtered through the coach walls.

Amelia's breath came in short gasps, her eyes widening. Though her mind was hazy, she had no wish to get caught by a footman. "What do we do?"

"Leave this to me." He whipped his cloak around his shoulders. He reached forward and adjusted the folds of her cloak to cover her breasts then pulled up her hood so it hid her face. "That'll do."

Just as he finished speaking, the door swung open. Darcy jumped down and turned, lifting his hand to her. Amelia hesitated for a moment. Though her body was tight with anticipation her stomach swirled with a hint of nerves. What in God's name was she doing?

She could still stop this.

Before she could argue any further with herself, Darcy's hand swallowed hers. Warm. Waiting. Eagerly, she squeezed it. There was no turning back now.

She stepped down from the carriage and paused, looking around. "This is not my home," she whispered.

"Here no one will know you and your reputation will not be sullied. If we went to your dwelling, the gossips would see a man entering your house," he explained softly.

This was oddly touching, even if it did make her feel like a foregone conclusion.

"Take me into your lair then," she teased, her voice more confident than she felt. With her hand in his, she felt safe and comforted. Something, in her tumultuous life, she had not truly ever felt.

Although the house was smaller than his family home by the river, it was nonetheless immense. A good four stories of sprawling splendor. Amelia let out a shaky breath and followed him up the carved steps and through the ornate, heavy door.

The butler stood waiting. He bowed his wigged head. His blue and silver livery sparkled under the beeswax candles glowing in the candelabras along the walls. "Good evening, my lord."

The older man's eyes shifted to her. Though his nose raised the barest hint, his voice and eyes did not betray his surprise. "Madam, may I take your belongings?"

"No, Benson." Darcy shook his head. "Thank you."

The butler nodded wordlessly as Darcy hastily led her towards the wide stairs.

She'd been in so many beautiful houses throughout the years, but there was something about being in *his* house.

She trailed her hand along the swirling gold gilt railing as he guided her up toward the west wing. Her foot caught the hem of her skirt, and she nearly tripped. Darcy caught her. Their bodies melded together for a moment.

He smiled down at her, "Feeling tired?"

"Not at—"

He swept her into his arms and cradled her against his broad chest before she could complete her sentence.

"That is not necessary," she protested, though she loved being surrounded by his strong body and spicy scent.

"Not necessary, but enjoyable. It allows me to feel like some sort of knight."

"Am I now a damsel in distress?" she quipped.

"Never fear, milady, you are safe with me," he whispered.

God, how she wanted it to be true. She shook the painful thought away.

As he strode down the hall, holding her with her legs hooked over one arm and the other easily holding her back, she felt as though she weighed nothing. She'd never felt helpless before. But right now, the feeling overwhelmed her.

Finally he came to a door. He stopped and stared at it. "As tempting as it is to kick the thing in, I should like to be able to close it again."

Amelia laughed. "Very wise. I think I can manage." She leaned towards the panel and turned the handle. It swung open silently and she smiled up at him. "Triumph."

"Indeed." He crossed the threshold then kicked it shut with its booted foot.

She gaped at the enormity of the room. It was half the size of her house. With a towering ceiling painted with glorious mythological events and green and gold silk walls, it was a bedroom fit for a king.

Or so she imagined.

"You like it?" he breathed, a half smile on his lips.

"Yes."

He walked farther into the room, toward the great fire-place with its carved marble mantelpiece. Candles already lit the room on tall gold candelabras placed strategically to give the most light. Her eyes fell upon the bed and she swallowed. The tall four poster was swathed in forest green velvet, gold tasseling, and a lighter sea green silk. Six people could have slept in it at least, and steps led up to the mattress.

He followed her gaze. "We'll get there eventually."

"Eventually?" she echoed.

He lowered her, letting her slide down his body. "First," he murmured, pulling her close. "Let us get your gown off."

"Do you need help? It is very diffi—"

His hands deftly slid to her back and unworked the lacing. The bodice came free in his hands and he slowly slipped the soft fabric down her arms then dropped it to the floor. Baring only her corset.

The gown had cost a fortune, but right now she didn't care that he'd simply tossed it aside. It showed that she was the only thing he was thinking of at this moment.

She yanked the tie of his cloak, and it fell from his shoulders. "Tit for tat," she said.

"Mmmm," he murmured. "But I feel a trifle more exposed than you."

He kissed the side of her neck. His fingers went to her corset.

Amelia grabbed his forearms, halting him. "If you take it off, I shan't be able to put it on again… Without help."

He pulled the string, untying the base knot. "I make a surprisingly good lady's maid."

The deftness of his fingers as he gently loosened the tight crisscrossed ribbon certainly supported his claim. As the restrictive clothing was released, Amelia drew in a deep, luxurious breath.

"Poor little prisoner," he said softly as he slipped her free of the brocade corset, tossing it toward her bodice.

The skin along her breasts and stomach that had been so encased by her undergarment shivered with extra sensitivity. His fingers stroked her through her thin chemise. Hypnotically, he trailed his fingers from her lower back to her sides and up to her ribcage. His hands paused. She leaned toward him, desperate for the feel of him.

He caressed the undersides of her breasts with the back of his hands and she swayed into his touch. Chuckling softly, he lowered his head to her breast. Despite the chemise, he pressed a kiss to her already taut nipple and flicked his tongue over her sensitive flesh.

Amelia cried out and cradled his head closer to her bosom. He worked the nipple with seductive swirls of his tongue then he sucked it into his mouth, dampening the fabric.

Her knees shook at the delicious feel, and when he pulled back she moaned, "No."

Shaking his head, with a patient smile that belied the wild need in his eyes he said, "You're not quite free yet."

He reached around to untie her skirts. Darcy's finger shook a little at the tight bow, and she reached back and undid it herself. It fell, and she stepped free of the folds of the skirts around her ankles.

The smile left his face, and his mouth opened while his dark eyes roamed over her body. The desire in his glance heated her body as much as the soft glow of the fire.

Silently, he lowered himself to his knees.

Reverence softened his hard features.

He caught the hem of her shift and slid his hands beneath it. He clasped her ankles. The roughness of his hands was smoothed by her stockings as he traced them up to her calves and squeezed.

Though her ribcage had been freed, she couldn't take another deep breath. Her legs were so seldom touched, she could hardly believe the intensity of the feeling. He started to caress the backs of her knees, but then paused.

"I want to see all of you." He took the shift in his hand and slowly, like raising a curtain, he pushed it up her legs, past her knees, and then to the apex of her thighs, baring the triangle of soft, dark hair between her legs.

Amelia stood motionless, shocked, yet excited, knowing that pleasure was soon to be hers.

"Take it off," he said as he passed the fabric into her hands.

She took the fabric from him. Before she could think, she whipped it over her head and let it whisper to the floor.

Her shoulders back and her arms at her sides, she stood proudly as she waited in nothing but her stockings and slippers.

His shuddering breath told her all she needed to know. He grabbed her hands and tugged her down into his arms. They tumbled to the rug before the fire. "You are—" his voice broke off.

Gently, he laid her on her back and took her shoes from her feet. She started to untie her red garters, but he stilled her hand. "Leave them on."

Amelia blushed, somehow feeling a trifle more wicked with them on. "You know, I believe I am the one who is now more exposed."

"So you are."

Her hands trembled as she reached for the tie at the back of his breeches. She tugged it free then gripped the soft fabric in her hands and urged it down. The hard, big length of his cock sprang free. Her breath caught in her throat.

She'd seen many men. It was the nature of the playhouse, and she'd known what to expect. But—

"Love?"

"You're very…"

He pushed a lock of her hair behind her ear. "Very what?"

"Large," she breathed.

"All the better to please you." At her words, he seemed to grow larger, if such a thing were possible. Quickly, he tugged his breeches, socks and shoes off and cast them aside.

Please her? She wasn't so certain.

Darcy leaned over her and kissed her abdomen, then nibbled the flesh.

Amelia jolted under the delightful touch and she dug her fingers into the rug.

"Hmm. Where shall I venture next?" Caressing her breasts with his big hands, he kissed her mouth, his tongue working languidly.

She could feel herself relaxing, yet tightening with need. When he finally stroked his hands along her hips, she tilted them up, her body crying out for him.

He needed no more urging, but kissed his way down to her hips, licking the curves of her body. Amelia tossed her head to the side as he parted her thighs and moved back to rest between them.

He gave her a tiger's smile, then he cupped her bum in his palms and tilted her up to his mouth.

She'd felt this before, knew what to expect, but somehow that made it worse. Her body was wet for him, muscles already desperate for his body. While his tongue licked and caressed her, she seized his hair, twisting it a little. When he tangled his tongue against hers, she moaned and her body tightened into spiraling waves of pleasure.

As Amelia came under his ministrations, Darcy savored the delicious taste of her hunger for him. He'd never known anything quite like her.

The ferocity of her coming hardened his cock, urging him to immediately thrust into her sweet core. But she was surprisingly tight around his fingers. And he wanted her ready for him. The shudders of her body calmed, and she relaxed the grip on his hair, which had stung but been more than worth it.

The wildness with which she responded to his touch without a hint of artifice was a heady aphrodisiac. He braced himself on his palms, his body so tight it almost pained him. But he wanted her to ask for it, so there would be no mistaking later. He paused at her breast and took a nipple into his mouth, loving its sweetness as he toyed over the hardness with his teeth and tongue. Her back arched towards him, and his cock bobbed in response. God, he couldn't wait any longer.

"Amelia, do you want me?"

"Mmm," she moaned, lost in her boneless pleasure. She lifted her hands to his back, pulling him. "I want... I feel empty," she whimpered.

"I'll fill you, love." The muscles in his chest and jaw tightened as he positioned himself between her thighs. He caressed his cock against her opening and her most sensitive spot, readying her. She rocked towards him, and that was all the encouragement he needed.

He thrust into her wet, hot flesh. Her core squeezed him with intense pleasure and Darcy's fingers curled against the rug. The intensity of her tightness had him seeing white and he wasn't even close to coming yet.

It took a moment for him to realize she'd gone completely still beneath him. Suddenly, he was struck by an impossible thought. His lust filled brain balked at the ridiculousness of it.

But she was so tight, and now, her body resisted him. He looked into her eyes, and instead of welcoming desire, her green eyes shone with pain and a hint of fear.

Bloody hell.

Chapter Fourteen

The lovely feel of his body against hers vanished at his invasion. Amelia dug her fingers into his back, and she wiggled underneath him, trying to get away from the growing pressure. She bit her lower lip trying to accommodate the size of him, but her body refused to cooperate.

"Is there something you wish to tell me?" he asked. His voice strained right along with his muscles as he held back.

She looked into his shocked eyes. "I've never done this before."

"So I gather."

"It's-It's not exactly pleasant," she panted.

"I wish you had told me," he said softly. "But I shall make it better."

That hardly seemed possible. He was so big and he'd barely entered her as far as she could surmise. He gently stroked the sides of her face and kissed her. As his mouth teased hers, he remained still, not venturing any further inside her.

Loving the feel of his lips moving over hers and his tongue caressing her, Amelia relaxed a little. She responded to the kiss, sliding her hands up his back. Hypnotized by the heat of his mouth, she didn't hesitate when he moved a hand between their bodies and stroked her between her thighs.

Despite the discomfort of his largeness, the touch of his hand over her sensitive spot unarmed her, sending a wave of pleasure through her body. Slowly, he thrust deeper and this time it did not hurt quite as much. But he was still too large.

He broke the kiss. "Amelia, it will hurt, but only for a moment." His dark eyes glowed with a tender fire as he spoke and she believed him.

"I trust you."

Returning his mouth to hers, he rested a hand on her hip then thrust forward in one swift motion. His mouth swallowed her short cry as he held his body absolutely still.

After a moment, the pain disappeared and she was distracted by the sudden fullness of her body and how strange and wonderful it felt. Slowly, she hooked a leg over his hip and pulled him against her.

The soft feel of their skin moving together thrilled her and he moaned. Taking up a slow rhythm, Darcy lifted his lips from hers and interlaced their fingers above her head. He looked down into her eyes, and Amelia couldn't believe the care in them.

As his hips moved in varying patterns, thrusting then circling against her, she met his rhythm, never looking away from his intoxicating gaze.

Unlike before, her body rushed with a wild anticipation that paled her earlier pleasure. The feel of him inside her was maddening. His pace quickened, and she lifted her other leg locking her ankles around his waist, wanting all of him.

She came in a sudden rush and she cried out his name as showers of stars blinded her. Gripping his hands until it stung, she gasped as pulse after pulse shimmied out from her core, bathing her in a perfect glow.

D arcy couldn't believe the intensity of her and the way she had so accepted him. It was terrifying and damned amazing as her muscles tightened around his cock. He thrust deep inside her, unable to hold back. "Amelia," he growled possessively as he came.

The ferocity of the pleasure tore through his body in intense ripples and he couldn't breathe or think. He doubted he'd ever be able to think again. But as her tight wetness gripped him, and he began to spiral back to himself, he was able to draw in a ragged breath.

He collapsed, bracing himself on his forearms, so he wouldn't crush her with his weight. Stunned by how spent he felt, he rested his head on the rug above her shoulder. He nuzzled her long dark hair, drinking in its clean, soft scent.

The wildness in his blood calmed a little and he rolled to the side, pulling her into the shelter of his chest and arm. This had been pure, unadulterated passion in which he had felt as if he'd somehow slipped inside her skin and she in his. "Are you well?"

She nodded her head against his chest. "A little sore, but yes." She was quiet for a moment, then said, "It was wonderful."

Yes. Yes it was. Gently, he stroked her hair. "You are wonderful."

She tilted her head up and smiled at him. "Thank you."

He hesitated, unsure how to broach the subject of her innocence. But it mystified him on many levels. How had she kept it, and why had she decided to gift him with it? "Amelia, you were a virgin."

"I believe we've established that," she said saucily.

"Yes, but I could have been gentler." He pulled her tighter to him. "Forgive me for asking, but how did you keep your innocence? That is no mean feat for the playhouse."

She shrugged. "It wasn't easy and there were a few times when I almost lost it. Men have trouble with the word no."

Darcy froze as her words sunk in. "Pardon?"

"It happens to almost all the girls."

"What happens?" he asked

"Men think that we should give ourselves just because we are actresses. Even the girls who liberally give themselves have been in dangerous situations. Why is that?" she asked, her eyes wide and determined. "Why do men think if you give yourself to one and are not married you should have no right to say no?"

His chest clenched as fury flashed through him. "I don't know," he gritted. She apparently hadn't been raped, but there were things almost as bad. "Did someone…hurt you?"

She looked away. "Not really. Why do you ask?"

"Because the idea of anyone ever harming you…" His mouth dried. God, she probably had to contend with such danger every day. No wonder she carried a dagger. "No one will ever hurt you again, Amelia. I swear it."

Darcy closed his eyes, anger at himself burning his chest.

He'd just made a promise that he might not be able to keep. Even he couldn't fully protect her from the king. Swallowing back the sudden thought that she could die, depending on what he found out about her actions, he took slow breaths.

It was a harrowing thing, knowing that she had given him her innocence, and yet he might prove her downfall.

She hugged him tighter, and the feel of her body curved against his filled him with a bitter sweetness.

It was so tempting to just ask her if she was doing things she should not, but then he'd have to explain why he was inquiring. And he was not about to tell her that he'd been following her, working his way into her trust for the king.

Somehow, his world had gone from simple to very complicated in a few short days. Part of him loved it. The other part of him was scared as hell. Because he was losing his heart. Bit by bit. And that was the one thing he couldn't afford to give. For all of him belonged to the king.

Chapter Fifteen

Amelia's eyes flickered open as she stretched in extreme contentment. She felt warm and safe.

Her eyes widened as she took in her surroundings. She tensed. Oh good lord.

At some point in the night he'd carried her to the bed and made slow, gentle love to her. Again. Now, Darcy's arm and thigh were draped over her, possessively.

She closed her eyes. The safe feeling dissipated as she remembered the night before. Slowly the fear of the man in the devil mask weighed her heart. All because Edward was a fool.

Her eyes flew open. Edward!

Gads, she was supposed to meet him this morning. Inching out from Darcy's embrace, she slipped her legs over the side of the bed and crept down the high steps. Standing naked beside the bed she caught a glimpse of herself in a tall mirror on the far side of the room.

Her skin glowed, and there was a radiance in her eyes

she'd never seen before. Dark clouds of hair floated about her shoulders, tousled from its perfect coif. Her gaze fell to her clothes on the floor. How in God's name was she going to get dressed? She couldn't lace her own corset on and if she didn't, neither her bodice nor skirt could be fastened at her waist.

So, she just wouldn't.

Quietly, Amelia tiptoed to her shift and pulled it on over her head. She stared at the heavy folds of her skirts thinking of the papers tucked in them. Wincing, she crouched down and fished them out. The parchment crumpled under her fingers. How had her life turned so drastically in such a short period?

But she couldn't dwell on it. Not while her brother was waiting. Besides, he had to have answers to all her questions.

She slipped her feet into her shoes and picked up her long cloak. Combing her fingers through her hair, she shoved it behind her shoulders.

After pulling the folds of the dark cloak around her body, Amelia stared at her prized wine and jeweled gown. She'd just have to send a footman around for it. Her cheeks heated.

If she was lucky, word wouldn't carry. If she was unlucky, word would spread like wildfire through the chain of servant's information.

She took one last glance at Darcy. He lay with his arms sprawled, one hand above his head and the other over where her body had been. His long dark hair spilled over the pillows. He looked like a well sated god.

Her heart tightened. He'd been so kind last night.

Shaking her head, Amelia forced herself to turn away. He'd comforted her when she needed it, but now she had to act alone.

Silently, she pulled the door open and slipped through it, heading out to face the light and reality of morning.

Darcy watched her through slitted eyes as she lingered by the doorway. She was sneaking out like a thief, but she clearly didn't wish to go. Something else was pressing her.

And if he had to guess, it was Warrington and her brother.

He forced his muscles to stay relaxed. She couldn't know he was watching her. She looked wistfully at him then hurried out of the room.

He silently cursed. He should have gotten up in the night and checked her gown for any hidden messages she might have received from Warrington. But his passion had made him blind to his duty.

After a moment, her footsteps vanished down the hall. Darcy swung his legs over the side of the bed. "Damn," he sighed.

Standing, he headed to his dressing room. After all, he needed to be clothed to follow her.

His eye suddenly caught a sparkle on the floor at his feet. He knelt. A diamond star winked up at him. It must have fallen from her hair when they had made love last night. He scooped it up, stroking it with his fingertips. It was hard and cold to the touch. Nothing like her. And yet, it was something of hers. He fisted his hand around it and stood.

Whatever she was up to, he'd find out. He only hoped he would not have to choose between the woman who had so recently snuck into his heart and the honor that had lived within all his life.

Chapter Sixteen

Colter's Print Shop, like many other shops in London, had a disgusting little alley behind it. Amelia scowled and stepped over the dead rat floating with its toes up in a slimy green puddle.

Lifting her plain green skirts higher, she said a silent prayer of thanks that she had worn serviceable knee high leather boots for this meeting. Said boots squelched in ankle deep mud mixed with last night's chamber pot disposal.

She was going to kill her brother. She really was… That is if Lord Devil Man didn't get to him first.

Amelia stopped before the narrow, paint chipped door and knocked her gloved hand softly against it. Biting her lip, she waited for several moments, her stomach rolling considerably, before the blasted thing cracked open. A tall, thin man with as many wrinkles as a basset hound peered out at her. He blinked pale blue eyes. As he took in her feathered hat and green dress, his upper lips curled in disdain.

Puritans. To him, she no doubt looked like the world's worst sinner.

"Let me in," she hissed. It wasn't as if she was a biblical temptress come to lead him astray. But the little man blocked the entrance as if he was baring her from the pearled gates.

"Paul?" her brother's voice filtered out from down the hall. "Is that Amelia?"

"Yes, Edward," she called, not letting her voice get too loud.

"Let her in," Edward said gently.

Paul grumbled but backed away from the door, giving way to a slight, whitewashed passage way. She hurried in, and Paul latched the door behind them.

Relieved to finally be out of the grim little alley, Amelia shook out her dress and took in an odor free breath of air.

Edward took her hand and pulled her down the narrow hall and into the small printing room. Immediately, the scent of paper and ink surrounded her, and her eyes stung from the strong chemicals. Light filtered in from a small skylight and a lantern swung from a hook in the corner illuminating a giant metal printing press.

A lumbering, marvelous invention.

An invention that had gotten many a man hanged.

She looked at her brother, unable to keep her suspicions from her voice. "What have you done?" she whispered.

"Pardon?" he asked, his own voice defensive.

She flung her reticule down on one of the wide wood tables covered with printing utensils. "Don't *pardon* me. This is twice in three days that we have met in secret—"

"I have an explanation."

Amelia folded her arms and waited.

The silence hung between them as Edward's eyes darted to the side. "I-I think I'm being watched."

She almost laughed. God, if he only knew. "And so you involve me?"

"I had no one else to turn to."

"What cause do they have to watch you?"

He rubbed his hands together. "I've been doing some writing."

"Not poetry, I take it?"

He gave out a little, strangled laugh. "Hardly. No. Um. Father's journals. I read them." Edward took a few quick little breaths and his skin paled. The boy looked like he was about to be sick. "I wanted to give him a memorial. So, I..."

"Oh God, Edward." She groaned. "You didn't."

"I wrote a pamphlet," he rushed.

"Just one?" she demanded.

"Ten."

Amelia dropped her hands to her sides and stared at her brother, shock leaving her speechless. Swallowing, she gathered her thoughts. "Do you know what you've done?" His silence only maddened her. "Do you?" she demanded.

"I just thought it would be a way of honoring him," he said quietly.

His gentle tone nearly broke her heart. Had he forgotten the way their father had treated them? The punishments for the slightest transgression? "He doesn't deserve to be remembered, let alone honored."

"He was our father," he snapped.

She drew in a deep breath and crossed the room, taking her brother's arms in her hands. "Yes, but only in blood. He was a horrible man. Cruel and unhappy."

"We should have tried harder to please him."

Her eyes stung with tears. "We did try." And they had. Every day had been a struggle not to anger their father or break his long list of rules. Their mother had tried, too, until one day she could not take it anymore. And disappeared, leaving them to battle their fierce and cold father on their own.

No matter how she wanted to, Amelia could not blame her mother for abandoning them to the heartless man.

Edward closed his eyes and his body tensed. "I did what I did. I cannot go back now."

It was true. There was no going back, but that didn't make her feel any less sick. "The pamphlets? Were they treasonous?"

Edward's pained expressions revealed a good deal too much. "Not exactly. I did not call for sedition as father did, but I questioned certain things."

"Like what?"

"The authority and morality of the king and his brother's right to inherit."

She closed her eyes, not sure she could take her brother's idiocy. "Oh my God."

"It was a mistake," he lamented. "I know it. But this man came to me and he told me to make my father proud. He was so artful that I thought it was my idea."

Amelia tightened her grip on his arms. "What man?"

He shook his head and shrugged. "He called himself Mister… Mr. Warrens."

For a few seconds she couldn't breathe. "Was he tall and dark haired?"

"Yes. How do you know?"

Amelia grabbed her reticule and yanked the blasted thing open. As she fished for the papers inside, she snapped,

"Because last night, he talked to *me*."

His pale face turned white and he blinked. "'Tis not possible."

"I don't understand how or why, but you are being set up for treason."

Edward pulled back from her, wiping a hand over his forehead. "What did he say?"

"He gave me this. I haven't read them. I don't want to know. I'm praying that my ignorance of it will keep me free of treason." She handed over the white ribboned stack, and her brother reached out tentatively as if the bunch might bite him.

He quickly pulled the ribbon and unfolded the first parchment. His lips moved as he read and then he stopped. He blanched. "I must tell you, I am not the only one being set up for treason."

She shook her head. "What do you mean?"

"This is pure treason. It calls for a return of the Republic."

Her mouth dried and she fisted her hands. "Edward?"

He folded it, crossed to the small fireplace, and tossed the bundle into the flames. The paper curled and blackened. "If anyone had caught you with that…" Edward shoved a hand through his dark hair. "You'd be in prison before you could say Cromwell."

"Why would anyone wish that?" she demanded.

"I don't know. What else did Warrens say?"

Should she tell him? The urge to protect her brother from the frightening words was tempting, but it would not serve him. Or her, it seemed. He needed to fully understand what a mess he hadn't gotten them into. "He said, if I did not do as he instructed, he would turn you in to the king for treason. That you would die. And then he gave me these papers to take to you."

"I am so sorry,"

"We need to tell someone," she snapped. "Now, lest it go too far."

His mouth hardened into a line. "You can't do it. I'll hang first."

"Perhaps not," she cried. "If you turn evidence against this man then—"

"I've gone too far already."

She swallowed. She believed him.

"Edward," she whispered, "We have made it through a revolution and the first years of restoration. You are my only family and I will not let you die over this." She folded her hands so she wouldn't fidget with them. "I think we should leave. Perhaps to France."

He gaped with horror. "The country is ruled by Papists."

"Do you hear yourself?" The men he'd been involved with had turned him into a judgmental idiot. "Better alive in a Catholic country, than dead in this one, don't you think?"

He drew in a deep breath and he paled. "What's happening? I feel as if we've been walled in again. Just like—"

He stopped before he could say the words she already knew. Just like when their father had lived.

Her very good and very naive brother had been swayed by powerful voices. And it needed to stop. "First, you must stop coming to this place. It is barely a secret what transpires here."

His face creased with indecision. "There is something else." He smiled wanly, desperately. "Only, you must not be angry."

She resisted the urge to throw up her hands and just give up. Hysterics would not do her or her brother any good. "What could be worse than how things are?"

"The money you've been giving me…"

Amelia closed her eyes, half knowing what he was about to say and wishing it wasn't true. She pressed a hand to her temple. "Edward?"

"I've been giving it to them."

Blowing out a harsh breath, Amelia opened her eyes. "It stops now. You admit that you have acted rashly?"

Licking his lips, he nodded. "That Mr. Warren, I've never heard anyone talk like him. Every time I had doubts he urged me on."

"I'm sure he did." Amelia picked up her reticule and twisted the silk tie about her wrist. Today she would keep her money lest her brother invest it in another damn treasonous cause. "You will come to the theater tonight and we will discuss what we are to do."

"I'm so sorry." Her brother looked at her with dark wounded eyes. Confusion filled their depths.

"I know. You only did what you thought right. I must go to the palace now." She had an appointment with Darcy, and though part of her thrilled to see him again, she was nervous as to how the meeting would go.

"Given the circumstances, do you think it wise?"

She bit her lip then forced a smile. "Tosh. Do you think anyone suspects an actress of Puritanism? Besides, how could I support a revolution that would shut the playhouses?"

Edward let out a pained laugh. "You've a point."

"And in truth, I think I must act as normal until we go. We mustn't arise more suspicion." He nodded.

Amelia pressed a light kiss to her brother's cheek. "Tonight then."

"Yes."

"Good." She headed for the door but paused in the frame. "Stay away from this place."

"I love you."

Amelia smiled at her brother, thankful to finally know the truth. "And I you."

A deep sigh of satisfaction escaped his lips. It was happening. It was finally happening. The letters had done the trick. Unaware, that he was being followed, Lord Chase stood in the shadows, his face grim as he stared as Mrs. Fox entering the bookshop, a decidedly guilty air about her appearance.

It would be only a matter of time before both brother and sister were behaving in such a guilty manner Chase and Winters could do nothing but accept that they belonged in hell.

He waited to feel the sweet taste of revenge. It didn't come. But of course, it wouldn't come. Not yet. Warrington knew he wouldn't finally feel that justice had been done until they were hanged.

"What news?" Winters dodged to the left, just escaping a solid right hook.

Darcy stepped in, keeping his hands tucked up near his face. "I don't want to discuss it."

"The lady is still proving elusive?"

Far from it. She wasn't nearly careful enough. Hell, he had enough information to bring both brother and sister in for questioning. Questioning which involved more than polite inquiries.

Winters's brow rose and he smiled, darting back and forth. "Ah… So you've tasted her charms."

"Go to hell." Darcy aimed a walloping blow at Winters's cheek. Throwing his weight in just enough not to lose his balance, he narrowly missed the man.

Winters twisted and jabbed his fist into Darcy's back. "Feeling touchy?"

Darcy shifted his weight and came around swiftly, his eyes locking with Winters's. "Sometimes the blithe Lord of Ice shite gets old."

"Really? Well, here's a little fire for you." Winters whipped to the side and landed another solid punch to Darcy's stomach.

Darcy's breath whooshed out of his lungs and he lifted his fists to prevent another blow. He was slipping, allowing his emotions to get in the way. A problem his friend didn't have. Of course, he hadn't just slept with a woman who was likely a traitor and developed protective feelings for her. Narrowing his eyes, Darcy found an opening in Winters's guard and let fly. His fist smacked Winters's jaw and the lord's chin snapped back.

Shaking his head, Winters pinned Darcy with an amused stare. "Not my pretty face," he mocked.

They circled each other. Darcy's blood pumped in his veins. This was good. He needed to work his problems out here. His body would have much preferred taking Amelia to bed, but that was clearly much too dangerous. He was learning that the hard way. "What news of Warrington?"

"Changing the subject, are we? Fine. He's getting himself in deep. He spends a great deal of time with Mrs. Fox's brother, Edward. And Edward writes seditious pamphlets, as you know. Warrington is also funneling funds into the young man's cause."

"Yes." He'd picked up a few this morning from Colter's, and he'd nearly choked at the high powered and dangerous words in the pamphlet. If the king saw it, heads would roll. Literally. Frankly, it was a miracle the young man wasn't dead.

Winters launched another punch towards Darcy's jaw, but he deflected it, and rammed an uppercut into his middle. Winters didn't even flinch, the bulk of his muscles absorbing the heavy blow. Even so, he took a step back. "Truce?"

Darcy nodded, sweat dripping down his chin. "Indeed."

Winters turned his back and walked over to a long marble table covered with a great silver urn. A decanter of wine and goblets rested just under it. After serving himself a stiff glass, Winters poured out another and offered it to Darcy.

Nodding his thanks, Darcy took it and crossed to the linens folded up on a high backed chair. He picked one up and wiped his chest down.

Winters took a long sip of wine. "So, I've told you what I've learned. What about you?"

Darcy gripped the glass tightly and took in a deep breath. "Not a great deal."

Silence filled the space between them for several seconds.

"She's very beautiful, is she not?" asked Winters softly

as he leveled Darcy with a hard stare.

"She is."

"Perhaps too beautiful?"

"Pardon? I don't gather your meaning."

"As a friend, I'm asking you to be careful," he warned. He tossed back the remaining contents of his wine. "Now, as I understand, you have a meeting with our dear Mrs. Fox."

Darcy nodded wordlessly. His mouth dry. Was it that obvious that he cared for her? Good God, did Winters know him that well, or was he losing his ability to hide his thoughts?

"Best not keep her waiting."

Darcy threw down his towel and turned his back.

"Good morning to you, then." Winters's footsteps echoed across the hardwood and then stopped at the door frame. "Oh, one last thing. In case, you weren't following her this morning... She was at Colter's. I followed her brother there."

Darcy didn't respond. At this point, he didn't have a good enough lie. And if Winters had seen Amelia, there was a good possibility he had seen that Darcy was there, too.

"Just thought you should know, old boy," Winters said casually.

"Winters," Darcy called, refusing to face to his friend. He swallowed down the foul taste in his mouth. And it wasn't the wine, but a sharp sense that no matter what choice he made, he would regret it. "Meet me tonight. We have a few things to discuss."

"Glad to hear it." His footsteps faded out into the hall.

Darcy drew in a deep breath but it wasn't enough, and his breathing grew ragged. Anger pumped through his veins and before he knew what was happening, he turned and hurled his glass to the floor.

It shattered, the crystal sparkling in the sunlight. Slender fingers of red wine snaked out along the floor.

What was he doing?

He was treading a very fine line. He understood his friend's subtle warning. If he wasn't careful, he, too, would be watched. No longer a trusted subject of the king, but a treasonous suspect.

Generations of Chase men had given their lives to the crown, his own father the most recent. Darcy closed his eyes. He could still see the old bastard. He'd been strong as a lion and cunning as a fox, teaching Darcy almost everything he knew about arms and the ways of war. Yes, he'd also tried to teach him that he was better than all the other people below him in rank, including his mother.

But even if his father was an ass, such a legacy could not be thrown away in a moment's fancy.

As Earl of Chase, it was his duty to protect the king and this land, not his own personal desires. That birthright could not be idly cast aside or ignored.

It mattered not if it broke his heart, it was time to start using his newfound closeness to Amelia. Because Darcy Blake, Earl of Chase, could not betray his king for a woman.

He was certain of it. Truly.

Chapter Seventeen

Amelia paced the bright reds and blues of the oriental carpet in the now familiar lesson room of Banquet House. Her stomach was tight and vague waves of nausea kept rolling over her.

Treason.

A word she'd never thought to hear again. Now, she could hear nothing else. Once, her father had been in danger of being a traitor until they'd cut off James I's head. And then he'd been a regicide and on the conquering side.

After her father's death, she had been sure that she and her brother would be free of such fears. It seemed that her father's hand had reached out from the grave to pull them back into his plots. Only this time, Edward was to blame.

And a Mr. Warrens, a lord if she had to guess from the way he had dressed and deported himself at that ball.

Aimlessly, Amelia wandered to the garment box she had brought with her then tugged it open. The corset, which had been designed for Ned's taller frame, nestled in soft folds of cotton, protecting the expensive garment.

Her lips curled in a temporary smile. Putting Darcy in a corset might bring her a moment's relief from her dark thoughts.

The door at the far side of the room swung in and he strode in.

At the sight of him and of his dark hair and passionate eyes, Amelia's breath caught in her throat. Would he be angry that she had crept from his bedchamber this morning without saying goodbye?

Silently, he crossed the room and pulled her gently into his arms then lowered a soft kiss to her lips. "I missed you this morning."

"I'm sorry. I had a previous engagement that could not be missed."

His eyes narrowed as he looked over her face. "Are you well? You look unusually pale."

"Do I?" Amelia pulled back. "I'm perfectly well. Only tired." She smiled and glanced at him from the corner of her eye. "I didn't sleep all that much."

He laughed softly. "No. Nor did I." He whipped off his cloak and flung it onto one of the low lying chairs. "What tortures do you plan for me today?"

Amelia smiled, but at the same time she couldn't help wondering at his bright mood. Shaking her head, she chastised herself. Just because her life was in shambles did not mean that everyone else would reflect her distress. She whipped out a fan. "The art of wig wearing."

She held the elaborately curled wig.

His eyed the thing as if it were a dead rat. "Surely not."

His reticence was quite silly, given almost the entirely of

the court wore wigs, and surely he'd have to wear one in a court performance.

"Darcy." She strode towards him. "Will you make this difficult?"

His eyes suddenly flashed with passion. "Difficult? I protest. I am the soul of affability."

"Then you shall don it without protest?"

He gave a suffering sigh then nodded.

"I think you should sit down for me to assist you with it."

Then she could catch her breath and try to get her riotous thoughts back in order.

"With pleasure." He strode to one of the long couches and lowered himself so he was at ease, an arm draped over the back and his legs sprawled slightly apart.

He looked like a famed pasha in a harem.

Despite herself, she found herself amused at his behavior. "You're incorrigible."

"So you've told me." His lashes lowered, hooding his eyes. "Now come here."

"I cannot think properly when you are sitting like that. And we are here for lessons."

"Well, there is something I should like to practice with you," he said, his voice low and promising.

What she wanted to do was to go over and nibble his delectable body. But that was over. Even though she had given herself to him last night, she was leaving. Sailing across a bloody ocean, and it was time to admit that whatever had passed between them was over. "We are here for lessons and that is all."

Darcy narrowed his eyes. "Do you regret what happened?"

She drew in a shaky breath. The last thing she wanted

was to hurt him. "No."

He lifted his hand, holding it out towards her. "Then come here."

Amelia's gaze fell to the growing hardness straining his breeches. Her skin tingled and she wet her lips. Would it be so bad to spend another few hours in his arms? Arms that made her feel safe? "They do say practice makes perfect."

"Mmmm. Now come here."

She let the wig slip from her fingers and slowly, she walked towards him. When she finally stood between his legs, she arched a brow. "Well?"

He took her hand. "Straddle my waist," he ordered softly.

She blinked then without question, lifted her skirts and placed a knee on either side of his hips. She lost her balance for a second and his hands grabbed her waist, steadying her.

Darcy lifted a hand and stroked the side of her face. "Amelia…"

Something haunted his eyes, just barely visible in the desire firing them.

"Yes?" she breathed.

He cupped her face in his hands and brushed a few tendrils of hair from her cheeks, gazing into her eyes. "What is this you do to me?" he whispered.

She smiled at him. "I have no idea, for you also do it to me," she confessed.

"Then God help us." His eyes so dark they were almost black, glowed with flecks of gold.

Slowly, it dawned on her that he was not smiling. That in fact, he was not relaxed at all. "What is wrong?"

He flashed her a quick smile. "What do you mean? All is well."

"You are a bad liar," she teased.

He shook his head, and said ruefully, "I'm not the actor you are, my sweet."

Amelia narrowed her eyes. "Do you mean anything by that?"

He dropped his head back to rest against the couch. "Pardon?"

"Do you think I lie to you?"

"That is not what I said."

"But is it what you meant?" she insisted softly.

"No." Even as he spoke, hesitation flickered through his eyes, belying his words.

Amelia pulled away, feeling sick. "It is. You think I lie to you." She wiped a hand over her face. "I suppose I understand."

He sighed and stood. "What do you understand?"

She turned away from him, and squeezed her eyes shut. She'd known full well when she'd given herself to him that he most likely just desired her body and nothing more. She hadn't minded then. Not much. But now… She was such a fool. She had no time for such things in any case. But that did not stop the pain in her chest.

"Amelia, what is wrong?"

"You think I'm a liar," she whispered, not trusting her voice.

He looked askance, the muscles in his throat working. When he looked back to her his eyes were surprisingly hard. "You're an actress."

His words cut through the air, and she winced as if she'd been slapped. "And the two are synonymous?" she said dully.

He shrugged. "Often, yes."

Why had he changed? Something had happened between last night and their present meeting. "You know what they also say about actresses…"

His eyes softened just a little. "Amelia, don't—"

She shook her head and flashed him a brittle smile. "They also say they are all whores," she said calmly. "Did you believe that about me? Or that now, since you've eased the way, it will be so?"

To her shock his face darkened with anger. She leaned back, surprised by the quick turn of his emotions.

He strode towards her but stopped a few feet away. A slow breath hissed out. "The idea of you with another man…"

Amelia swallowed. "*What*?"

"I don't like it." She had the strangest thought he might in fact kill any man that touched her. The thought wasn't upsetting. Actually, a small thrill of pleasure flashed through her.

"Indeed? What makes you say so?" she demanded. "You have not asked me to be yours," she said, to point out the absurdity of his claim.

"Not yet."

Amelia gasped. He couldn't mean that. It was far too tempting, especially when she was leaving. "Did you just hear yourself?"

"Yes. I can take care of you, Amelia. I could make you very comfortable and give you my protection."

Her mouth dried as the full weight of his words hit her. They didn't surprise her, but as their meaning dawned on her, it still hurt. That she would be no more than a mistress to a man like Lord Chase. And she wasn't prepared to discuss this. Especially not now. "I think perhaps this is best not discussed on the king's time."

He laughed.

The bastard actually laughed. Amelia narrowed her eyes. "Pray, tell me what amuses you, my lord?"

"The irony…" The laughter did not reach his eyes as he grabbed hold of her shoulders. "I care about you, and I don't want anything to happen to you."

Amelia held fast, leaning into his broad, protective chest. Lord, it was so tempting to tell him everything. About her brother and Mr. Warrens. Somehow, over the weeks, he'd found a place in her heart. But he could not protect her. He was a king's man and would no doubt be duty bound to turn her brother in.

Drawing in a deep breath, Amelia rested her hands on his. "I think it best we do not have our lesson today. I am not in the humor for play acting."

"Amelia…"

She smiled at him as best she could, wishing their last meeting had been kinder. Tonight, she and her brother would flee England. It was the only thing left to do, but nor did she wish him to feel as if she was bidding him goodbye.

"I shall consider your offer," she said softly. "It is a very tempting one."

He looked earnestly down into her eyes. "I did not mean to hurt you."

The truth of his words stabbed straight to her heart. He really did care about her. Yet, she had to leave him. "I know."

And she did. Darcy was a good man. And it was best she was out of his life as quickly as possible.

Chapter Eighteen

At last, Edward was here. Thank God. Amelia sighed in relief as she adjusted her long dark blue skirts and stood. She stepped forward as she heard footsteps coming through the velvet curtains. They had far too much to discuss.

Amelia froze, her hands gripping the folds of her skirts.

A half smile on his lips, Lord Chase strode through, his usually bright mood a trifle somber. Which matched his wardrobe, all blacks and dark burgundy. He bowed. "Amelia. I came across your brother. It is most odd to see him in a playhouse, given his garb."

Digging her nails into her skin, she forced herself to remain calm. Why was Darcy here? She and Edward were leaving tonight from the playhouse. Their luggage was here in her dressing room.

Her brother stepped in behind Darcy. "Your friend is very affable," he said hollowly.

"Thank you Mr. Fox," replied Darcy. "It's a pleasure to meet Mrs. Fox's family."

"Now, Edward, why ever are you here?" she asked with false cheer.

"I had a great longing to see you," he rushed. "A very hard day with my followers…" He stopped, his face paling.

Edward was a terrible liar.

The earl stood leaning one shoulder against the wall, quietly watching the scene between them. When she looked at him, she couldn't miss the strange expression on his face.

"My lord," she said, her voice rough, "My brother needs my company, so perhaps you could forgo the pleasure this night and leave us?"

Darcy's face darkened. "What is wrong?"

She shook her head and looked back to her brother who was suddenly looking at the wall. Drawing him into her brother's plots would only be cruel. "There is nothing—"

He took her chin between his thumb and forefinger and gently turned her face back to his. "You are perhaps not as skilled a liar as I supposed. You are distressed."

It was so tempting to lie further and insist he go. And that would be best. For he would leave. And she and Edward could escape without complications. She started to nod, but then she caught sight of his eyes. They glowed with concern. For her.

And the strength which she so relied slipped a little. How nice it would be to finally share her burden with someone.

He took her face gently in his hands and said, "Please don't pretend. Tell me."

Edward cleared his throat and stood from his chair. "Pardon, I'm going to fetch a glass of wine."

Amelia turned to him. "Do not go, Edward. I think you must stay for this."

His eyes widened but he stayed.

Tears stung her eyes and she looked down. "Oh, God. I want to tell you so much. But if I tell you, you could be implicated and I would never forgive myself."

Edward protested.

Darcy shook his head. "It doesn't matter. Whatever it is. I swear to you I will help you."

Should she tell him? Could she? Lord, she wanted to tell someone. She wanted to tell him, because he was the only person who made her feel safe. She glanced about. Most everyone had already gone for the night. It was late. Even the dressers for the actors had gone. "Promise me that I can trust you."

Softly, he whispered. "I promise."

She looked into Darcy's eyes unable to stop herself now from daring to hope. "Fox is not my real last name. It is Allworthy. Edward and I were the children of Cromwell's General Allworthy."

She felt his hands tense against her back, but then he stroked her comfortingly. "Is that all?" he said lightly.

Now that she had started, she wanted to tell him all, as though the words were rushing up like a great river of water. "And worse, my brother is in dire trouble."

Darcy glanced to Edward then back to Amelia.

"Tell me," he urged, his voice strong and reassuring. "I'll help you both."

Drawing in a steadying breath she curled her fingers into the folds of his coat. "A man came to him this fall and started telling him to print my father's journals. He played on Edward's troubled relationship with our father, convincing him it was the only way to atone for his failings in Father's life."

She hesitated and wished she didn't have to hurt her brother, but she needed to speak the truth. "Edward was never the son our father wished him to be, and he so desperately wanted his approval"

"What was his name?" Darcy gritted, turning to Edward.

"Pardon?" Edward replied

"The man?"

Edward looked terrified, like a small boy about to receive a beating "A Mr. Warrens."

"But it was the man from the ball," Amelia said quickly. "The man in the green devil mask. He threatened to expose Edward. And he gave me compromising papers. If I'd been caught, Edward and I would be in the tower."

Darcy's entire body tensed. He pulled back, grabbing her forearms. Gone was the gentle caring from his face. Instead he looked at her with an intensity that bordered on anger. "Your certain Lord Warrington sought your brother out and manipulated him? And your father was General Allworthy?"

Amelia swallowed, suddenly nervous. She'd never seen him like this. "Yes. Why?"

The muscles in Darcy's jaw tensed. His fingers tightened on her arms and she winced. He must have seen her discomfort because he loosened his grip a little. "Tell me everything." The gentleness had gone from his voice, but he gently stroked the side of her face. "I think you and your brother are in very serious danger."

"I already know it," she said.

Perhaps they could sort through this horrific mess. But perhaps not. She didn't wish any harm to befall Darcy. "I think you should go and allow me to take care of this myself."

"I am not leaving until you tell me all."

Amelia hesitated, but how could she deny such a heart touching request? Did he truly feel thusly? She nodded. "Edward and I will detail our encounters with Mr. Warrens."

She searched his face. He looked as if he were somewhere else. Her heart pounded. She was making the right choice by telling him. Yes, he was close to the king, but the way he looked at her... He truly cared. "Darcy?"

"Will you trust me in what I am to ask of you?" He searched her face as if making certain that she would not change her mind.

She shoved her hesitation aside. He was risking much by even listening to her story. "Yes, I trust you."

And she did. As she had never allowed herself to trust anyone.

Chapter Nineteen

"There is a hell of a lot more afoot here than we were led to believe," growled Darcy as he barged into Winters's candlelit bedroom at the man's London townhouse. The portraits shook on the walls and the candlelight wavered as he slammed the door shut behind him. He'd left Amelia not long before, and he was still shaking with his mixed feelings.

Winters jumped in front of the fire, and his grip on his glass loosened. Amber liquid sloshed out of it. Splashing him. "Well good evening to you, too," he drawled, clasping the empty glass as he brushed at a growing wet spot on the shoulder of his robe. "Must you make such sudden entrances? It is a waste of good brandy."

"Do forgive me," mocked Darcy as he strode farther into the room, circling the four poster to the massive fireplace. "I did not mean to disturb your beauty sleep."

Winters faced him; the flames illuminated his face.

"You're lucky I wasn't entertaining."

"It wouldn't have been anything I haven't seen before at court. And you're not listening."

"Well, if you keep rabbiting on without making sense —"

"She's not guilty."

That stopped Winters. The blond lord stared at him for a moment, all traces of humor vanishing from his icy blue eyes. He crossed to the small, ornately carved oak table by the window and placed his empty glass down.

"I see," he said as he tugged off his robe and then grabbed a pair of breeches and slid them on.

Darcy pulled the tie of his cloak and yanked it off. The damn thing was suffocating him. And Winters's mood was about as welcoming as his name. "You think I am partial to her."

Winters snorted as he searched for his cast aside stockings and shirt. "I *know* you are."

Darcy folded his cloak then tossed into onto Winters's big bed. "I like her. What of it. It changes nothing. I've done my duty"

"You're a Chase," said Winters dryly as he pulled his shirt over his head. "Of course you've done your duty."

"Then what is the issue?" demanded Darcy, sick of this. He'd always been a man of honor, and Scott knew that.

The muscles in Winters's jaw tightened, and he pinned Darcy with hard stare as he said quietly, "What concerns me is what you *will* do. Not what you have done. And frankly" — Winters shook his head — "she *is* guilty. An accomplice to sedition at the very least."

Darcy took in a slow breath. He would not validate Winters's accusation by raging like a furious lion. "The brother certainly is guilty of treason and sedition, though he was victim of severe manipulation. She is a victim. A person caught up in nothing of her making."

Winters cocked his head to the side. "So you admit Edward Fox—No, Fox, is guilty of treason."

Darcy hesitated. He didn't like this. Winters was a master of logic, and Darcy was in no mood to be cornered by words. "Yes. Did you know they were children of General Allworthy?"

"I confess not," Winters said, his stance growing tense. "How long has she known about her brother's treason?"

Darcy looked away.

Winters's lips curled in a cold smile. "There you have it. She is guilty of abetting a traitor. And her father should only convince you of her leanings."

Darcy stared blankly at his friend, unable to believe he had spoken so flatly. His own insides were clenching with anger. "You would see her swing?" he demanded, his voice harsh and low.

"She's a traitor by association."

"God's teeth man, do you hear yourself?"

"And you? Do you hear yourself?" snapped Winters. "I understand that you have come to like her but—"

Darcy stared at his friend. "This isn't like you."

"I have no wish to see my friend beheaded."

"The king would not—"

"Darcy," Winters said, his voice mocking. "Do you think he would jeopardize his throne? Even for you? I would hang Mrs. Fox myself if it meant we would not see a return of the bloody Civil War." Winters voice cut through the air, loud and brimming with ice. "Make no mistake. You helped the king back to his throne, but if you betray him for a woman—"

"You son of a bitch," he growled. "I serve the king above all else."

Winters bowed. "I am glad to hear it."

The conversation had grown too heated and he didn't think he was going to be able to make Winters listen. "I do not think the king knows all that is transpiring."

"What makes you say that?"

"The man that is manipulating the Foxes... The Allworthys."

"Yes?"

"It just so happens that he was at the Court Mask the other night."

Winters's closed his eyes for a moment. Opening them, he crossed to the sideboard and poured two sloshing glasses of scotch. "Warrington."

"At last you begin to see this as I do."

His friend handed him a glass of Scotch and headed to one of the tall chairs before the crackling fires. "Sit. Are you suggesting that Warrington's treason is because of what happened to his family and General Allworthy?"

Darcy stared at the amber liquid in his glass, savoring the cool feeling against his skin. He needed Winters. Yes, he could do this without him, but it would be damn nigh impossible. So, Darcy crossed to the chair just opposite his friend and lowered himself. He took a long swig of the slightly burning liquid. "Yes. I believe Warrington is seeking revenge for his family's murder by that general through destroying Allworthy's children, and I've come to ask you a favor."

Winters sat quietly, waiting.

"If I need your help, will you give it?"

"We have been brothers in arms these fifteen years. If you need me, I will be there."

"Even if—"

Winters shook his head. "You have risked your life on more than one occasion for my hide. Though I may not approve, and unless it is treason, I am your man."

Darcy nodded, relief easing the tenseness in his body. "Thank you."

"Don't be daft."

They sat in silence, drinking their brandy. Darcy couldn't believe the turn of events. Not a week ago, he'd been certain he would be turning in a pair of spies… Now, he was doing everything in his power to keep them from custody and safe. But at least, Edward was under his eye and not running around foolishly spouting treason and basically begging to be hanged.

After a few moments of silence, Winters took a long drink then held his glass towards the light, staring at it. "You know, I can see it in your eyes."

Darcy blinked, gripping his glass tight. "What?"

"That you're thinking about running with her. A last resort I'm sure, but nevertheless, I see it."

Darcy tightened his grip on the glass and tried to remain relaxed. "I would never leave the Chase title behind."

"Good."

Darcy forced a smile.

"If you do run," Winters said tightly, "the king will hunt you down and kill you both. Not even the Americas would be safe."

"I know." And he did. But it seemed almost impossible to believe that Scott had seen what Darcy had barely thought. Would he run to keep Amelia safe? Would he leave his mother, his land, and everything he had ever worked for?

If it came to it... Yes.

Because quite simply, he would never be able to stand by and watch her take the long road to Tyburn. He'd swing beside her first.

Chapter Twenty

"Why did you tell him? And why in God's name didn't we leave last night?"

Amelia rubbed her fingers over her temples and plunked her elbows down on her dressing room table. The room was dim, straining her eyes with naught but the light of a few candles. And Edward's railing didn't help. "First, *we* promised to meet him this evening. Secondly, I had no choice but to tell him."

"Yes," he retorted, his eyes wide and his voice high with disbelief. He paced away, giving her his back. "You did."

She dropped her hands with a smack to the table. "Fine then. I trust him, that's why."

Thrusting his hand through his blond hair, he glared at her. "With our lives?"

Amelia licked her lips. How could she tell her brother that Darcy and she had become close. Very close. "He's saved me before. Does that not prove he is trustworthy?"

"Well, after he tells the king, we'll see how safe you feel."

"He won't tell the king." She fisted her hands and stood.

He just shook his head with disgust. "His kind aren't to be trusted."

"And what kind is that?" Darcy drawled from the shadows of the doorway.

Edward jumped and his gaze skittered towards the lord.

She drew in a deep breath of relief and crossed over to Darcy. He pulled her into his arms and kissed her. The warm feel of his body and hungry mouth drove back her fear and surrounded her with peace. She pulled back after a moment, conscious of her brother's disapproving presence. "You must forgive Edward."

Darcy smiled. "I understand. And he is rightly suspicious. After all, trusting Warrens got him into this mess."

"Yes, yes," he grumped grudgingly. "Though don't mistake, I am grateful for your assistance."

"Gratitude is not necessary."

Amelia pulled him farther into the room. "What news have you?"

"It is not good, I admit. You are both suspects."

"*Both*?" Amelia echoed. "I don't understand."

She hadn't committed a treasonous act her whole life. And only she, Warrens, and Edward knew about the papers she had delivered.

Darcy's eyes flicked to Edward, and then back to Amelia. Emotion flitted through his eyes, but she couldn't quite read it. He was hiding something.

Her mouth dried. How bad could it be? "How do you know this?"

"I have friends. They've told me that your brother has

been connected with the pamphlets, and that you, Amelia, have been seen with Warrens, who is a traitor. You were also observed leaving Colter's Print shop. All this combined could be damning."

Amelia stared blankly. To be seen with someone. That alone could condemn her twisted her insides. "What course of action do we take?"

Darcy glanced at Edward. "You are not safe on your own now."

She shook her head. "You mean from Warrens?"

"From Warrens yes…" His lips pressed into a hard line. "And from the Crown."

Amelia pulled away from Darcy and crossed to the small window overlooking the street. Pressing her hand to her middle, she leaned her forehead against the cool glass. It was as if her childhood had returned. Whispers and rumors and plots. She'd rejected all of it, but apparently it hadn't been enough. As she spoke, she couldn't hide the unwilling resignation from her voice, "I think we should leave. Go to France. Edward and I will be safe there."

"Not yet," Darcy refuted. "If you run, your guilt will be confirmed by your actions. You will make yourself into an unquestioned traitor."

"Then I should go alone," said Edward softly.

She whipped around from the window. "No. We will see this through together."

Darcy's eyes lingered on her brother, and he folded his arms across his chest. "It might be for the best if Edward slipped out of the country—"

"But if he was caught?" hissed Amelia. "We must find a way to prove his innocence."

Darcy cocked his head to the side and his brows drew together. "Innocence, love? What innocence? He wrote treasonous documents that were distributed to the public."

Edward looked down, his shoulders slumping.

"He is not a traitor," said Amelia, her voice a hint too bright for her own ears. God, she could not allow her brother to be condemned. He was the only family she had. And this was about their father, not a desire to depose the king.

She stopped and took a breath. This time she said firmly, "Surely, the king would understand a young man manipulated and coerced by a man who wished the king harm."

Darcy narrowed his eyes and he lifted his hand. "What did you say?"

Amelia put her hands out, fingers spread in frustration. "He was manipulated. Used—"

"No," Darcy said, his voice low and dark. "The part about the king."

What in God's name was he going on about? Amelia blinked then folded her hands. She wouldn't lose her temper or her sense of reason because he was being a dolt. "Well, obviously this Warrens wished to hurt the king. After all, they convinced Edward to write seditious articles."

Darcy nodded slowly, his eyes glittered with hard calculation. "They convinced *Edward* to commit sedition."

"Exactly." Amelia stepped back as his words finally penetrated. "You think this is about Edward?"

"I do," Darcy said, "And you, Amelia."

Her mouth dried. Why would anyone wish to harm them?

Edward crossed to Amelia and took her hand in his.

"My lord, though I have behaved foolishly, and my sister has been kinder to me than she should, neither of us would see harm come to the king."

"I see that." Darcy rubbed his hand over his face and turned his back on them. "If Warrens wants you both and not the king then perhaps we have a few open doors yet."

"Why? What difference does that make?"

"Well, if we could prove this man had a personal motive for destroying both of you, then the king might be more understanding. But I must ask, is there anything that you two could have done to incur such vengeance?"

Amelia looked at Edward and was relieved to find only puzzlement on his young face. She drew in a soft breath and shook her head. "No. There is nothing."

"And your father? Could he have done something to Mr. Warrens?"

Amelia's mouth went dry. She nodded. "Anything is possible with my father."

Darcy gave a terse nod then pointed at Edward. "We will put you in hiding 'til we have need of you."

Edward opened his mouth to protest, but Amelia clasped his hand tightly. Darcy knew what he was doing. She could see it in the sheer determination written on his strong features. "He is right."

Edward clamped his mouth shut and nodded.

Darcy lowered his hand and turned to Amelia. "And you will live with me for the time being."

Chapter Twenty One

He was an ass among men. The lowest of the low. Actually, he was the scum beneath the scum of the Thames. Yet, Darcy still stood in Amelia's dressing room offering her his protection while he let lies spill from his lips like water. But right now, there was no other course of action.

But that didn't make him feel any less the bastard.

Granted, if he told her the truth, she would never trust him. And she needed to if he was going to help her. And help her he would. She was basically innocent. There was no question in his mind. The mention of the ridiculous coincidence of a Mr. Warrens and Warrington had convinced him.

Folding his arms across his chest, Darcy waited. Needing her to say yes, because if she didn't, he was going to take her captive and lock her in his attic 'til he could sort through this madness. And ensure her slender neck would not be stretched. "Amelia, what do you say?"

She looked from him to her brother, her face pale yet determined. "Edward, I think you should wait downstairs." Her lips tightened into a wry smile. "I'm sure a few of the actors would be glad to keep you company."

"No. This bastard wants to ruin your reputation—"

"For God's sake man," scoffed Darcy.

She leveled a hard stare at her brother. "If we are executed, I don't have a reputation to ruin, now do I?"

Edward's face drooped in resignation. He nodded. "I will wait in the theater." He shuffled out the door silently.

Darcy drew in a deep breath as he watched him go. He wanted to throttle the young man for putting Amelia in such a dangerous position. Did he not realize how valuable his sister was that he could risk her life?

She rubbed a hand over her face. She looked tired, with just a hint of shadow beneath her eyes. Yet, there was no sign of weakness in her. She stood with her shoulders back and her green eyes shining with resolution and courage. "My brother cares for me, and you must forgive his outburst."

He shook his head. Though Edward had behaved foolishly in the past, he was right to be so protective of her now. "There is nothing to forgive."

She dropped her hand to her side and closed her eyes. The muscles of her lids tensed and Darcy could have sworn she was fighting tears, but when she opened her eyes they were dry and filled with strength. "You do know what my staying with you means," he said gently, not wishing to hurt her any more than he had. If he had his way, nothing would ever hurt her.

Looking away, her face creased in a frown and she blew out a harsh breath. "I have worked so hard to keep my reputation. It is not easy to let it go so thoroughly."

He hated the resignation in her voice. And he wished that there was some other way to protect her. A way for her to keep what she valued so much: honor.

How he understood that need. Hadn't he acted on nothing but his vow to his king and the honor of his family his entire life? Wasn't he even now desperately clinging to it? The last thing he wanted was to take that from her.

She bit her lower lip then released it, shaking her head. "I am still not certain I like involving you in this." She looked back to him, her green eyes sparking with worry. "If we are caught, you will be implicated."

"I am protected largely by my title and…the king and I are friends."

If she was caught with him he would be perfectly safe. It galled him how simple it would be.

He could easily tell the king he had been seducing her for more information. He could even claim he was protecting Edward to encourage her trust. To his personal disgust, in some ways it was true. However, the boy had written outright sedition. Even so, Edward was young. Young men made the worst decisions.

"Why then are you helping us?" she asked softly.

Darcy's chest tightened as he looked on her, standing with her long black hair curling down her shoulders and back. She stared at him, her eyes slightly narrowed with confusion. Yet, she was confident.

He could not shake her strength and absolute conviction that she would help her brother. The women of his acquaintance would be in hysterics by now, begging him to protect them. Instead, she was worried about *his* safety.

Darcy swallowed, not sure how to say what he felt.

"In truth, I have come to care about you."

Her mouth opened slightly and she stepped forward. "You have?"

"Very much," he whispered. So, much he was breaking rules he wouldn't have even bent before her. Winters was right. His care for Amelia was leading him away from the loyalty his family had always given to the king. For now, Amelia was taking precedence.

And worse. He wanted it that way.

Her lips parted in a shy smile. "I have come to care for you, too, incorrigible though you are."

Trust her to bring humor to the situation. Darcy laughed, surprised at his own relief. She cared for him. The laughter died on his lips. If she cared for him and he for her, what was stopping him from the natural conclusion? A snap decision hit him as they stood there. There was one way he could truly protect her. And it was ridiculously appealing.

Still, it had never occurred to him to speak these words and suddenly he found himself nervous. "Amelia?"

"Yes?"

They stood silently for a moment while he got up the courage to actually say what he wanted. He drew in a steadying breath. "Marry me?"

She blinked. "What?"

Darcy strode towards her and gently grasped her upper arms. "Be my wife?"

He looked down into her shocked eyes, determined to convince her. Now that he'd said the words, he wanted it. Wanted it with a surprising need.

Not only would it bind her to him, it would keep her

safe. As safe as she could be, given the circumstances. "It is the best solution. The Crown will be far less likely to execute the wife of an earl, and if you marry me, you will keep your reputation."

"Darcy, I-I—" She stared up at him, and she smiled then frowned, emotions flitting over her face. "You've stunned me."

Was that a no? God, he hoped not. "So I surmise. I've never seen you at a loss for words."

She rested her hands on his waist then circled them toward his back. "Do you truly wish to marry me?"

"I would never be able to forgive myself if anything happened to you."

She tensed and as she looked up at him her eyes were sad. But her voice was firm as she said, "I will not have you sacrifice something so important for me. Though I value my own life, I will not marry you just to keep myself safe."

Damnation. What was he to say? He'd told her he cared for her. Darcy looked down on her with awe and a touch of self disgust. She was so good, and he was using that goodness. But all that would stop. The moment they were married and she was safe, he would tell her his role in this affair. "All I know is that the idea of you being harmed—" He could not even finish the though it so alarmed him. His throat tightened and he looked away from her.

What was this damn sensation? This all consuming need to keep her safe regardless of family and obligation. He knew with utter certainty that he would give his life for hers. What words did he use to tell her that?

Darcy froze. He knew the words, but had used them so infrequently that he hadn't even recognized what was happening to him. He looked back down at her, and gently cupped her cheek in his palm. "Amelia, if you will not marry me to keep yourself safe, marry me because I love you."

Her hands tightened at his back and she drew in a barely audible breath. "You love me?" she breathed, more to herself than to him, he realized.

"Yes."

Her eyes shone, and glowed as tears filled them. She did not cry, but smiled, her face glowing as she took in his words. After a moment, she tilted her head a little, resting her face in his palm. "I love you, too."

He let out a shaky breath. Surprised at how tense he had been waiting for her reaction to his admission, he smiled. "You've yet to answer my question."

She pulled herself tighter to him, linking her hands about his waist. "I will marry you."

The worst circumstances possible had brought them together. But none of that mattered now. He'd protect her. He'd find a way. Darcy leaned down and took her mouth with his, needing the taste of her more now than ever. He couldn't help feeling that she could slip away at any moment, and he must hold fast.

So, he pulled her tightly to his body and kissed her, claiming her.

Though it was the last thing he wanted, he pulled back. "We must take your brother to a safe place."

Her lips were parted and slightly swollen. She blinked several times then nodded. "You're right."

"We must go now. For, I shall not be content until you are my wife."

As reality came crashing back to them, she squeezed his

hands then went for her cloak. "Then let us go."

Darcy took her hand, and led her out into the receiving room. In this one evening, he'd made a choice that would completely alter everything he had ever known. But it was the right choice. The choice that would free them both.

Chapter Twenty Two

"I do not feel safe," groused Edward as he turned and looked about the room.

Amelia followed his gaze, taking in the plain austerity of the garret. The cream walls were bare and only a bed and a small table with a candle decorated the space. Not even a rug cheered the wood floor.

As the last rays of the sun disappeared, steel gray light filtered in through the windows, signifying dusk.

Amelia shot him a warning glance. Darcy was helping them, and the least her brother could do was not complain.

Darcy crossed to the window and yanked the tattered wool curtains shut. A sense of urgency surrounded him as he moved.

"You are safer here than anywhere else in London." Darcy turned to face them his strong face grim, yet determined. "A meal will be brought to you thrice times a day."

Edward stood in his simple black clothes and white

collar, yet he managed to look a lost sheep rather than a shepherd. "How long shall I remain here?"

"As long as necessary," said Amelia firmly. She would allow no risk to him, even if that meant he was cooped up and bored out of his wits.

"First, we must clear your sister and find out exactly what Warrington wants," Darcy pointed out. "Then, we can go to the king."

Edward's eyes widened. "The king?" He looked to Amelia, his pale face white. "This is a mistake. We should go. Now. Tonight."

The worry sharpening his voice chilled her, but she forced herself to remain calm. She would take care of him. As she had always done. "All will be well. Darcy is right. If we flee, we might be hunted down."

"We might also be free," he protested, crossing to her. He glanced at Darcy then back to Amelia. "Please, let us go."

Darcy strode forward, moving away from the curtained window. "That is folly. It is too soon for flight."

Though her insides were tense, she smiled reassuringly at her brother and put her hand on his shoulder. "Wait here. When we have solved this, I will come to you."

Edward glanced at Darcy then back to her. "If you are certain, I will trust him." He blew out a heavy breath. "Come as soon as you may."

She reached up on tiptoe and kissed his cheek. He would be safe here. "I shall."

Darcy looked to the door, shifting impatiently. "We must go. The bishop is waiting."

Edward pointed a finger at him and snapped. "Take care of my sister."

"That is without question," Darcy stated, as if his word was law.

Edward inclined his head. "Thank you. Go then. I shall be fine."

"Goodbye." Amelia hugged him then turned away. Before she could do something so foolish as cry, she hurried to the door.

Right behind her, Darcy followed her into the hall, and shut the door. "He will be well."

She smiled tightly. "Of course."

Taking her elbow in his warm grasp, he guided her quickly down the worn wood staircase and through the quiet little entry. As they hurried out onto the muddy street, he took her hand. "Are you glad to be wed to me soon?" he asked, as if checking her decision.

She felt herself relax a little at the sound of his voice and the mere thought of being his wife. It seemed impossible. A dream. And quite frankly, even with all the recent turmoil a part of her felt like floating. "Yes, I am. And you?"

They crossed so quickly to his coach her feet barely touched the ground.

He nodded. "The sooner we are wed, the happier I will be. I want you with me." He stopped and looked down at her, his gaze searching over her face.

She placed her hand on his arm, stroking him through his wool cloak. "Then let us go."

"Indeed."

She spared a last glance over her shoulder to the squat building hiding her brother. Hopefully, it would not be long till he could leave or until they had discovered what Lord Warrington wanted.

Silently, he helped her into his coach and he was in and closing the door before she had even adjusted her skirts. He knocked his fist against the roof and the crack of the whip cut through the night.

The carriage rattled down the road, causing the small lantern on the side of the wall to toss and shaking shadows over them. Darcy sat beside her, his hand wrapped around hers, but she could feel tension emanating from him.

He seemed worried, as if he would not be satisfied until she was married to him. Which was why they were headed directly for the Bishop of London.

Darkness descended outside and the only light came from the small lantern in the coach. Darcy turned to her, his face half bathed in shadow. "I've sent ahead for a friend of mine."

She frowned. His unease was rubbing off on her and she, too, wanted to be married as quickly as may be. "Why?"

"We need a witness."

She smiled, nearly laughing. She was so swept up, any thought of detail was out of her reach. She was going to marry this man and be his countess. "I had not even thought of that."

"I want nothing to go wrong," he said firmly. "Nothing to keep you from being my wife."

She rested her head against his shoulder, savoring the solid strength of his presence and the warmth of his body next to hers. "Nothing will. I promise to be your wife."

He tilted his head down, resting his cheek gently against hers. "I will hold you to that."

The coach rolled to a stop and the footman called, "We are here, my lord."

"Thank God," he breathed. He pulled away and she started to follow, but he shook his head. Stroking a lock of hair back from her face, he said, "Wait here. I wish to make certain that Winters has already arrived."

Amelia nodded, her stomach a mix of excitement and nerves. She could scarce believe she was uttering the words as she whispered, "I love you."

He smiled at her, his dark eyes, warm. "I love you, too." He kissed her softly on the mouth then climbed out of the coach.

Her heart slammed against her ribs. Suddenly it was all becoming real. Suddenly, she knew everything was going to work out as it should.

She folded her hands. Hating to wait. But it would be all right. Together, she and Darcy would make it all right.

D arcy climbed out of the coach onto the stone drive. The Bishop's courtyard glowed with the fires of multiple torches. His eyes adjusted and he searched the barely lit shadows for the figure of his friend.

Winters stood by the wide double door, reinforced with black iron. "I was beginning to think you'd changed your mind."

"No." Darcy walked through the empty courtyard, his boot steps echoing on the cobblestone. "You have the license?"

"Hmm." Winters strode forward to meet him in the center of the courtyard, his hand on his rapier. "They do say that marriage is a form of prison."

Darcy narrowed his eyes. "Hardly humorous, given the

circumstances."

"Too true. Forgive my gallows' humor."

Right now, mentions of prison and gallows grated him the wrong way. Darcy blew out a breath. "Well, shall we proceed?"

Winter's flicked his cloak back over his shoulders, freeing his hands, and the fabric rustled in the night breeze. "Yes. I am ready to be done with this."

A hint of suspicion tugging at him, Darcy's mouth went dry. "Winters?"

"I promised to help you. I did not promise to enjoy what must be done." Winters stepped forward, his boots thudding gently on the stone courtyard. "Call forth your lady."

With a tight nod, Darcy turned back to the coach. "Amelia," he called softly. He stopped just in front of the vehicle and waited.

His footman opened the door and handed her down. She stepped out into the shadowy light, her face hidden by her hood. She pulled it down and smiled at the two men. "Lord Winters, a pleasure."

Winters backed away a step. "I wish I could say the same, my dear."

Darcy's stiffened at his friend's coldness. "What—"

"King's men!" shouted Winters.

Soldiers ran into the courtyard, carrying torches. Their swords flashed in the light. They quickly surrounded the outskirts of the courtyard. Silent. Waiting. Ready.

Darcy's heart slammed in his ribs and he turned towards the soldiers. They wore the king's colors reds and yellow, and they stood at battle stance. Their swords drawn. He whipped his attention back to Amelia. She stood with eyes flared, panic and utter confusion written across her pale face. Dread socked him in his gut and slowly, he turned to his friend.

When his eyes fell on the pistol in Winters's hand, a pistol trained at Amelia, Darcy swallowed a strangled cry of rage. Winters looked at him, his eyes cold, calculating. "Thank you for apprehending Mrs. Fox. I shall take her into custody on behalf of the king."

"Darcy?" her voice rang through the cold air, a pained sound that sliced right to his heart.

"Winters?" growled Darcy. "What the bloody hell—"

"You wanted me to help you," the lord cut in, his voice hard and unyielding. Striding towards him, Winters kept the pistol aimed at Amelia. He leaned and whispered, "I am. And if you want her alive, you will play this scene out. Do you understand me?"

Acid burned the back of his throat as his gaze wandered over to Amelia. She'd backed up, her body pressed to the carriage as her eyes locked on him. Desperate for him to help her.

He flicked his gaze to Winters. "If you are lying to me, if you have truly betrayed her, I will kill you," he whispered so low, he almost couldn't hear himself.

Wordlessly, Winters nodded then took a step towards Amelia. "Madam, you are being arrested on charges of treason."

"Darcy?" she repeated, disbelief turning her voice to a whisper. She stepped forward, then stopped as her eyes switched to Winters and then the soldiers.

He could feel her fear. It was thick and it was killing him to behold.

Winters shook his head. "Do not turn to Lord Chase,

Mrs. Fox. He is the one who turned you in."

"You are a liar, sir," she stated, her voice hard with conviction.

Darcy stood, fisting his hands as he stared at the woman he'd come to love.

"Mrs. Fox, Lord Chase is a king's man. From your first meeting, his goal has been to expose you and your brother."

Amelia's whipped in Darcy's direction, ignoring the soldiers and their blades. She took a shaky step towards Darcy but stopped a few feet short and searched his face with her eyes.

"Why don't you deny it?" she demanded.

Darcy looked down into her wild eyes, which begged for him to explain, but he could not. Not here. Not now. And he could not lie to her any longer.

"I cannot deny what is true." The words sickened him, twisting his insides as they hung in the air between them.

She stared silently for a moment, then shook her head. Her hands pressed into the folds of her dark frock.

"I-I—" She sucked in a deep breath as her clear eyes glazed with tears. Her face contorted in pain. "It was all a lie?"

The desperate note in her voice that he refute his words gutted him. "No," he said. "It was not *all* a lie."

And it wasn't. But the sinking realization that she would never believe him was undeniable.

She swallowed and her eyes, which he so loved for their glowing passion, turned hard. Two flat pools of green acceptance. "And to think I was teaching *you* to act. My lord, you far surpass my talents."

"Amelia—"

She turned from him and looked at Winters. She held her head high and squared her shoulders. "Let us be done with this, my lord."

Winters nodded towards the soldiers, and two of them trotted forward and took her arms. She froze and turned towards Darcy. The defeat which had only just dulled her pain vanished as she locked eyes with Darcy.

A cry suddenly ripped from her.

"What have you done with Edward?" she yelled. Amelia struggled against the soldiers, kicking her feet out. "What have you done?" she growled. Her lips pulled back from her teeth in primal anger. "What have you done?"

Darcy fisted his hands and almost choked as he commanded, "Take her away." There was not a chance in hell he'd discuss her brother's whereabouts before all these soldiers. It was the only thing he could do for her at this moment.

"Bastard!" she screamed as the soldiers lifted her, carrying her like a sack between them. She kicked and yanked, twisting herself in their hold, but the soldiers kept their grip.

He dug his fingers into his palms so hard, his nails cut into his skin. He watched, forcing himself to stand silently as they bound her hands and feet. Anger pumped through him, demanding that he fight the bastards off her as they pushed her into the coach.

But that would not help her. Not in the end. The only way to save her now was the king. As she vanished into the black box of the plain coach, Darcy ground his teeth down.

She would hate him now. She would hate him for his lies. She would hate him for using her. She would hate him for gaining her trust while never trusting her in return. Hell, he hated himself.

Slowly, he sucked in a tight breath. He felt sick. So, sick, he thought he might vomit. Never in his life had he witnessed someone so shattered by treachery. The coachman cracked the whip and they raced off into the night. No doubt off to the Tower.

As it disappeared into the dark street, he knew she was not the traitor. *He* was. He had destroyed their love with lies.

Darcy charged at Winters and grabbed the pistol from his hand. He drove his knee into his groin. "You son of a bitch!" he roared.

Winter's moaned low in his throat and bent at the waist. His face darkened red. "God's blood," he gasped.

Cocking the pistol, Darcy aimed the mouth at Winters's head. "Tell me why I should not blow your brains our right now. Tell me how you have *helped* me."

Winters glanced up at him from the corner of his eye, his hands still cupping his balls. "You sodding bastard, I grant you have cause, but Christ," he panted.

"That is not a reason." Darcy planted the mouth of the pistol against the man's temple.

"Chase, There is much I must tell you."

"Damn right."

"I could do it better upright and without the pistol."

"Alas, you shall have to rise above it."

"I did help you."

Darcy growled disgustedly. "You have betrayed me. And more importantly her." Suddenly, Darcy's throat tightened. "Jesus you piece of filth. I came to you as a friend. You have condemned her to death—"

"I saved her life."

"Liar," Darcy hissed.

"Warrington. We must speak of him."

"Warrington?" Darcy echoed. "Do you want a quick route to hell, old man?" He lifted his hand, checking the pistol to see if it had been primed. The power was already pumped in. He pulled back the hammer.

Winters held up his hand, his face hard and earnest. "I've been watching you and Amelia all this time… Without your knowledge and Warrington's, too."

Darcy paused. "To the point now, or I will blow a hole in your head."

"Warrington wants her dead, and I know his plans. So, I can help you save her."

"I don't follow."

Winters's lips parted in a dry smile. "It's a rather elaborate affair."

Darcy lowered the pistol and glared.

Winters straightened slowly, keeping their gazed locked, just like in their fencing bouts. Clearly, the man was waiting for Darcy to strike.

He arched a brow, his old blasé demeanor back. "Let's just say, I'm full of surprises in how I've maneuvered Warrington and your lady love is one of them. I had to have her captured to redeem her and you for that matter. I *had* to."

Darcy nearly choked on his anger and shock. They had been friends since childhood for Christ sake. And all this time, Winters had been maneuvering him. "You've used me."

"Yes."

Darcy's hand gripped the pistol tightly. What he felt was only a pale reflection of what Amelia must feel. "I ought to kill you," he said, his voice quiet yet filled with warning.

"Kill me later. After we save the girl."

Darcy nodded. Winters would either follow through, or he would personally make the bastard eat his words, along with a mouthful of fired powder.

Chapter Twenty Three

The coach reeked of urine and vomit. Its intense odor only added to the sheer nausea rolling around her stomach. And for about the twentieth time, Amelia struggled against her bonds, tugging her wrists until her skin tore under the rough ropes. Tears stung her eyes, but she swallowed them back. She would not cry. She would not. Tears would not serve her now.

But how had she let herself be such a fool?

Trust me, he'd said. Over and over again. Twisting her wrists until the muscles in her shoulders felt like overused rope and her skin burned raw. She exhaled a shaky breath. He'd told her he loved her. She closed her eyes, trying to block the pain of his betrayal.

My God, he'd asked her to marry him. What a disgusting ruse. Had he needed to trick her so cruelly? It would have been far kinder to just drag her to prison.

She had trusted him. Trusted him with her body, her

life, and her love. He'd thrown all three away as if they had meant nothing to him.

Worse, she had trusted him with her brother's life, and now Edward was at the mercy of Darcy's false hands.

The coach jolted over a deep groove in the road and she bounced painfully on the rough seat. It was no fine coach like the Earl of Chase's, but a vehicle meant for transporting those the Crown wished secret. Men's fear stank up the small space and she huddled down, trying not to be overwhelmed by it. But the black wood walls closed in on her.

Why had Darcy done all this? Had he known all along that General Allworthy was her father? Had he known everything about her from the moment they met? Like a fool, she had told him her story. And he had listened so kindly. Amelia closed her eyes at her foolishness.

The coach slowed, grumbling to a stop and Amelia struggled not to slide forward and down to the floor. Were they at the prison already?

"Orders," called an articulate voice.

Amelia tensed trying to hear, but the exchange of dialogue between the messenger and soldiers was low.

"But my lord—"

"Silence!" the other man snapped. "You have your orders, now open the door."

Amelia's breath came in shallow gasps. Had Darcy somehow managed her freedom? Perhaps this was all some vast misunderstanding.

The coach door creaked open and a soldier stepped in. Amelia pulled into the back corner of the seat, but he reached forward with his big black gloved hands and grabbed her arms.

"Let me go," she cried, as he yanked her forward.

Her shoulders tightened at the pressure as he yanked her forward. She tried to move with the soldier so that he would not increase the pressure on her pinched muscles.

The soldier pulled her out of the coach, and she stumbled down the steps, her knee hitting the corner of the folding steps with a sharp whack. She winced and sucked in a sharp breath.

The soldier's torchlight bathed the road in a small pool of yellow light. But beyond that small circle she could not see. Amelia blinked, her eyes trying to adjust to the light. She stepped back, her calves brushing the coach steps. "What's happening?"

"Quiet," snapped the soldier standing beside her.

"Your manners, sir, are appalling," she drawled with as much dignity as she could muster.

"Mrs. Fox," mocked the lord as he stepped from the shadows and into the torchlight. "You are hardly in the position to be giving advice."

As he closed the distance between them, her heart plummeted as she realized that Darcy was not here.

But she should not have even entertained the foolish hope. He did not love her, never had. He loved his king first and foremost, as a true noble should. It didn't hurt any less knowing he had betrayed her for a king.

She forced herself to focus on the situation at hand.

The lord stood tall, only a few feet before her. His frame was clothed in a black coat with silver braiding and buttons. His long russet hair was tied behind his back and a simple black tricorn covered his head. The man was shockingly handsome, yet his face was tired. Small lines creased his golden eyes.

He was magnificent and terrifying in his austerity.

Amelia narrowed her eyes. "My lord—"

"Your silence is expected," his strong voice cracked through the air with the effect of a military command. He turned to the soldier standing to his right. "Captain, I am taking her into custody for questioning."

The captain unfurled a small parchment, glancing it over. "Lord Warrington, it appears you have the proper documentation, but Lord Winters and Lord Chase mentioned nothing of this."

Warrington nodded, his face calm and understanding. "They are not aware of the most recent evidence. And as you can see, this comes directly from the king."

The captain rolled the parchment and tucked it into his red coat. He gave a small salute. "As the king commands. Will you require a set of guards?"

"No. I can handle Mrs. Fox on my own." Warrington's smile was hard. "If you will escort her to my coach."

One of the soldiers took her by the arm and marched her toward a nondescript black coach. Something wasn't right. Truly not right. Who was this lord? What did he want? Darcy had suggested that perhaps he hated her and her brother for a specific reason. But why?

She forced her mind to think quickly as they headed to the coach. She didn't struggle, needing all her wits. Before she could protest, the soldier shoved her into the coach, and Lord Warrington climbed in behind her.

The door slammed shut and Amelia stared at the man sitting across from her. "Mr. Warrens or is it Lord Warrington?" she whispered.

"Both," he confirmed as he thumped his fist against the

roof. Their coach rolled down the street and Lord Warrington removed his gloves, flexing his fingers.

Amelia stared transfixed at his big hands. What did he intend? "Those weren't real orders from the king, were they?"

"I confess not."

Warrington. Warrington? Amelia stared at him; the small coach light threw just enough illumination for her to make out his features. She had heard that name before. "Why did you take me?"

"You're a very smart woman, Mrs. Fox. Would you care to venture a guess?"

Amelia ground her teeth, struggling with the need to slap him, but her bound hands prevented that. "Please. Do not force me to play games. What is it you want with me?"

Lord Warrington shook his head. "You move too quickly my dear. First you must tell me where your brother is."

At least, the bastard didn't know Edward's whereabouts. "Why did you go to so much trouble to condemn us?" she demanded.

"It doesn't matter, Amelia." He leaned forward, resting his forearms on his knees. "This is not how I wished to do things, and I've had to make hasty arrangements." A muscle in his cheek tightened, belying the formality of his words. "I'm a patient man, and you will tell me eventually."

"Why do you hate us so much?" she said softly.

He turned away from her, staring out the window. "Because once, I had a family."

Amelia's mouth opened slightly and her heart squeezed, moved by the sadness in his voice, but her stomach clenched in fear. Her breath hitched in her throat because truly, his words could mean only one thing. Darcy had supposed correctly. Her father had died, but the effects of his actions were still alive. And now, they'd come to haunt her.

"All this time, you have been spying upon us all?" Darcy couldn't believe it. The urge to pound his head against the Bishop of London's study wall was all consuming. Anything to thump the disbelief and pain from his skull. Instead, he rested a hand against the fireplace mantle and glared at Scott.

Amelia had no doubt reached the prison by now. She would be taken to a cold dark room, and there she'd sit and wait. And all he wanted was to go to her. But he needed answers first.

Winters looked down at his hands then sighed. "I would rather not discuss the details."

"I don't give a damn what you would rather. Your cloak and dagger machinations will result in her death."

"Point taken, but I do not believe her death is imminent."

"Your beliefs give me little comfort."

Winters crossed to the windows and pushed back the heavy curtains with one hand. "What I tell you now could bring my death, but I want you to understand. The king needed someone to do the things that no one else would. Or the things that could not be known. He needed someone who would not falter."

The heat of the fire warmed Darcy's back, but he felt cold on the inside. "And not faltering included using your friends?"

"Yes," Winters said plainly. "Though, you were never supposed to be caught up in this whole mess."

"Thank you," Darcy snapped. "Please. On to Mrs. Fox's fate."

"My God, man! When Charles chose you to watch her, neither of us could predict the effect she would have on you."

"Say her name," Darcy growled as he pushed away from the fire. "Say the name of the woman you have condemned."

Winters turned from the window, his face an unreadable slate. He crossed to his desk and planted his fists onto the polished dark wood. "You still don't understand."

What he couldn't understand was how anyone trusted a soul in this world, what with all the lies being thrown back and forth as truths.

"Warrington was going to kill her."

"I would have protected her," gritted Darcy.

Winters shook his head. "You were on the fast road to treason and execution. She would have been murdered if she wasn't brought in." Winters voice softened as he said, "She is safe in prison."

Darcy narrowed his eyes, not believing the words that had just passed the man's lips. "Safe?" he ground out.

Winters smiled dryly. "Safer. Safe from outright and imminent murder. Warrington won't be able to touch her."

"Others might touch her. Hurt her!" Darcy raged.

Winters stared.

Understanding of the whole damn mess seemed just within reach, but Darcy still didn't understand. "Why has he gone to such lengths to condemn them as traitors? If he hates them so, why not have them killed in the street. Make it look like a bit of violence?"

"Simple. He's acting out of vengeance and wants them to suffer. To go through the anguish of capture, imprisonment, and death."

"Vengeance against a minister and an actress?"

Winters folded his arms across his chest. "Think back. How did Warrington become the viscount?"

Darcy shook his head. He vaguely remembered the story. There were so many like it during Cromwell's power. "His family, all vocally loyal to the executed king, were killed while he was on the Continent serving Charles. The estate was destroyed, set on fire by one of Cromwell's men, was it not?"

"Yes," Winters said quietly as he lowered himself into the hard back chair behind his desk. He bridged the tip of his fingers. His blue eyes turned into rocks of hard ice. "His father, his mother, his young sister, and his brother, a mere babe, were rounded up. The man in charge ordered the house to be barred and they chained the doors and boarded the windows. All were killed in the fire. Given no chance to escape, you see."

"Christ," hissed Darcy. He'd heard these kinds of stories, but no matter how hard he tried, he could not grow hardened to them. "What does this have to do with Amelia?"

"General Allworthy, their father—"

"Fired the house," finished Darcy.

Winters nodded.

Darcy turned his attention to the fireplace as the enormity of the Warrington's circumstances hit him. The man had lost his entire family while he had been supporting the king on the Continent. God's blood, that certainly explained the man's actions. But it didn't excuse him. He was going to kill innocent people in his quest for revenge. "And you haven't immediately stopped him?"

"His cause is not entirely unjust. He served Charles and was repaid with the death of his entire family. Amelia's brother was also easily convinced to treason. Not so innocent, is he? Did you read the pamphlets he wrote?"

He nodded. They had been full of troubling suppositions. Young men were easily swayed to revolution and war. Edward was passionate and driven by a past that Darcy could never fully understand. "Then you made the king aware of his treason?"

Winters stared coldly. "You will go to the king—"

"You told me the king would not listen."

"That was before. Your involvement has changed things. I think the king may be sympathetic to you... Perhaps."

"Christ," rasped Darcy.

Winters ignored him, speaking with single minded determination. "What must be done, must be done. The king must be protected from a string of executions. So, if the Allworthys can be saved and simply banished... It might be a good thing. None of us wish there to be some sort of bloodbath, which will stain the king's reign.

Darcy searched Winters's hard face. The man had been his friend for most of their lives. Could he trust him? Darcy swallowed. He had no choice...just as Amelia had had no choice when she had trusted him. Darcy shoved the painful reminder of his betrayal aside. "What must I say to the king?"

Winters crossed around the desk and closed the distance between them. He looked into Darcy's eyes, his own gaze hard and unyielding. "If you truly care for her, you will offer the king anything, and I do mean anything, in exchange for her life."

Darcy nodded. After what he'd done, he owed her, whatever the king might request. "And her brother?"

Winters didn't even blink as he stated, "The brother is a traitor. There one can only hope the king will take mercy on a boy."

"There must be something…" Darcy looked away, seeing Amelia's face as she had screamed at him, demanding to know what he had done to her brother. "She will never forgive me if…Edward is condemned."

A solid knock pounded against the study door, and Winters backed away from Darcy. "Come."

The door opened and a young solider hurried through, his face red with exertion and his hat askew. He held out a parchment. "My lord, this just arrived. It is most urgent."

Winters took the missive and gestured the soldier out. Silently, he scanned the parchment.

Dread pooled deep in Darcy's stomach. "What is it?"

Winters looked up, his eyes hard. "Warrington. He came with forged orders and took Amelia."

Darcy fought the urge to grab Winters and slam him up against the wall.

"Safe, you said," taunted Darcy, his blood boiling. Slowly, he strode to Winters then grabbed his lapels. Shaking him, he growled. "Is this safe?"

Winters grabbed Darcy's wrists. "We must to the king."

"There is no time." He uncurled his fingers, tamping down the rage pounding at his head. "This time, we shall do things my way."

"As you will." Winters smoothed down the front of his

dark green coat. "But don't rush off like a mad man. I know where he is most likely taking her."

Darcy gave a tight nod. "Will he kill her?"

"No."

"Why?"

"He doesn't have her brother."

"Thank God for that." Darcy only prayed Amelia could keep from telling the bastard. If she did, she was dead. "Come. We must find someone."

"Who?"

Darcy ignored Winters as he charged through the door.

Winters ran after him, calling out, "Who?"

"The Cavalry, damn it." He was going to find Amelia then bloody kill Warrington for putting them all through this hell. And God help anyone who got in his way. He'd failed her once. It would never happen again, not if he had to tear all London apart to find her.

Chapter Twenty Four

"My arms hurt."

Warrington glared at the infuriating woman sitting across from him. "You'll just have to make do."

"I don't wish to *make do.*"

Warrington lifted his gloved hand and massaged his temples. Bloody hell, a normal killer would just box her and leave her quiet, but he couldn't do it. He wanted her dead, but he couldn't bring himself to outright assault her. "Madam, you will cease speaking or I shall be forced to gag you."

She managed to sit in silence for a moment and then she demanded, "Where are we going? Out of London? Why is it taking so long? I have a right to know where you are taking me."

"Christ, woman," he roared. "I've kidnapped you, and you know damn well what I'm capable of. Be quiet."

She stared back at him. The small lamp attached to the

wall glowed with gold light, bathing her in its soft color. If she was in the least bit afraid, she was hiding it remarkably well. She tilted her dark head to the side. "Actually, I don't know what you're capable of."

He sat silently. Maybe if he didn't speak, she'd desist.

"Are you going to rape me?" she asked quietly. Factually.

He sighed. "No." It bloody disturbed him how well she was taking this. He didn't know what he'd expected, but this calm inquisition was certainly not it. She wasn't even pleading for her freedom.

"Are you going to demand ransom?" she asked, as if she wanted to know whether he preferred coffee or tea.

"No."

The delicate muscles of her throat worked as she swallowed. "Are you going to kill me?"

This time he didn't reply. The silence stretched between them, and he leaned back the better to observe her reaction.

She looked away. "I see."

"I don't think you truly do." Warrington closed his eyes. He shouldn't be talking to her. Not like this. For God sake, this was Allworthy's daughter.

"Would you care to enlighten me?" she ventured, softly.

He blinked and caught her staring at him her gaze animated by curiosity and pride. "No."

"Is that your favorite word?" she asked dryly.

He couldn't stop the small twitch of his lips. "No."

"You frightened me, that night at the ball."

He inclined his head. "Then I succeeded."

"Yet you don't frighten me now."

Warrington stilled. Her noblesse oblige was worthy of any titled man. And though it galled him, he found himself admiring it. "Why is that?"

"I suppose I've had a very bad day."

"Indeed?"

She nodded tightly. Fidgeting on the seat, she grimaced. "Pardon, but I really am quite uncomfortable. My gown you see, it's not designed for my arms to be like this, and the rope is tight."

Warrington hesitated for a moment. Though he planned to kill her, that didn't mean he couldn't be civilized about it. "I will untie your hands, and then bind them before you."

"Thank you."

It was such an odd thing to be thanked for. "You're welcome." He reached forward and she turned her back to him.

"I have a pistol, so don't try anything clever," he warned.

"I wouldn't dare," she mocked.

"Has anyone ever told you you're either remarkably stupid or remarkably brave?"

"No. And I'd like to believe the latter, though recent events seem to suggest the former."

Warrington worked at the bonds. They'd been tied rather tight. His fingers dug into the tightly woven fibers of the coarse rope. Even in the dim light, as he pulled the bonds away, the dark splotches of blood on her wrists were visible. Welt marks and cuts circled her wrists.

The wounds disturbed him, and it dawned on him that he was not as pleased by this whole event as he had believed he would be. He had convinced himself that killing her would bring him some peace. But that peace was nowhere in sight.

Slipping the rope from her hands, he moved back and pulled the pistol from his pocket. "You're wrists are damaged. We'll let them have a rest before re-tying them."

She frowned as she slowly brought her arms around to her front. Her face tightened in pain as her shoulders stretched. "You're being rather noble under the circumstances."

Warrington snorted. "Comes with the blood line."

She gently rubbed her wrists. "I'm sorry but, do I know you?"

"You met me at the ball," he remarked dryly. The coach jolted over a deep rut in the road, and he grabbed hold of the seat with his free hand, keeping a grip on the pistol.

Swaying left and right, she lost her balance a little. She focused on the pistol. "You will make sure you don't shoot me too soon? I'd hate for it go off accidentally."

"Don't be afraid." The ridiculousness of his words rang hollow in his ears.

Her laugh was brittle. "Right." She readjusted herself on her bench-like seat so that she rested her back against the cushioned squabs. "Before the ball, did we meet?"

"I think that very unlikely."

"You never came to the theater?"

"No."

"Then why?"

Warrington looked away, swallowing. God, he needed to stop talking. If only he could just get this over with. He'd been seeking his revenge so long now. So long. All he needed was her to tell him where her brother was. But nothing was going according to his plan.

She was pretty. She was witty. And even worse, he liked her.

Which was certainly not part of the plan. Warrington fisted his hands. Damn it. She was a step in securing his family's rest. That was all. Was it not?

Warrington forced himself to look at her. His sister had black hair. Hair that floated like clouds around her pale face. Would she have grown up to be as beautiful as the woman before him?

Cocking his head to the side he said quietly. "Were you familiar with your father, General Allworthy's massacres?"

She stilled and her gasp was audible. "Yes."

Her reaction robbed him of a quick response. From the sudden lack of witty reply, her father was a sensitive subject. "And were you proud of the old man?"

She flinched. "No. And he was not proud of me."

Warrington narrowed his eyes. She was trying to identify with him, to win his sympathies. "Cease."

She shook her head. "Pardon?"

"You're a talented actress, I understand. But I won't be fooled by your attempts to soften my resolve."

"Whatever you believe, my lord, what I said was true." She looked down at her hands in her lap. "Whatever he did to you, I am very sorry and—"

"Don't," he growled.

She snapped her head up, her face pale.

Warrington leaned forward, aiming the pistol at her chest. He could do this. It was time to get it done. "Where is your brother?"

"Tell me what my father did to you," she insisted quietly. "I'll tell you anything I know, in exchange for my brother's life."

"You think to bargain for information?" he demanded, hardly believing his ears.

"I am not so foolish as to think I can bargain with you.

But you said something about your sister and brother. And I wish to know why you have condemned me. Is this about them?"

Warrington took in slow even breaths. He would remain calm. He would remain in control. "Yes."

To his shock, her eyes shone with tears. "Did my father kill them?" she whispered.

He tore his gaze away. He would not be fooled. "Yes. And my mother and my father." Drawing in a steadying breath, he looked her in the eyes, determined to convey the past. "He locked them in our house, and then he set it ablaze. They were defenseless, and he murdered them, tortured by fire."

"There are no words to say—"

"Then don't," he rasped. Glancing at her from the corner of his eye, his breath caught in his throat. Tears slipped down her cheeks. Warrington clenched his fists tighter. Damn it. Why did she cry for him, when she had not cried for herself? "Don't," he growled. "Don't cry. You don't mean it."

"I'm sorry. I can't help it." She reached up and smoothed the glistening tears from her cheeks. She took a shaky breath.

Did she actually feel remorse for her father's actions? Warrington ground his teeth as he stared at her pale face. Did it matter? All he wanted was to lay his family to rest. "I want you to tell me where your brother is. My sources tell me that Chase put him somewhere."

She tensed and her eyes flicked away. "I don't know."

"You expect me to believe that?" he bit out.

"If I told you," she snapped, "'t'would be no different than killing him myself."

"Damn it woman." He pulled the hammer back on the

pistol. If he could just get the information, he could collect her brother and then kill them both. And it would be done. At last. "Tell me."

She stared at the mouth of the pistol. Her hands gripped the seat cushions. Flicking her eyes to his, she asked, "Would you have done it?"

He blinked. "Done what?"

She shifted on the seat across from her, tilting her head to the right. "If in my position, would you have turned your brother over to my father? Even if your life depended on it?"

He stared blankly, almost not seeing for a moment. When he'd left home his brother had only taken his first steps. The babe had laughed at faces hidden behind hands. His little brother had delighted in senseless songs and stuffed animals. There wasn't any comparison between his brother and Edward Allworthy. "My brother was a mere babe."

"My brother was a babe once, too."

"Shut up," he roared. Anger shot straight through him. It was not the same. She was not the same. Warrington shook his head. He could not give up now. He couldn't.

"You're certain about this?"

Darcy leveled Tony, Duke of Haverston and irresponsible highwayman, with an I'm-going-to-pull-your-entrails-through-your-nose stare for asking such a foolish question.

Tony nodded, his red feathered hat bobbing in the night breeze. "You're certain."

"Are you?" returned Darcy.

"If I get caught thieving, I've already got a noose waiting to send me to the other side. This is a far nobler death. He that lay down his life for a friend and all that."

Darcy frowned reached up and adjusted his mask. "Tell me why I'm wearing this?"

"You said we were to be highwayman. The mask comes with the territory. I, for one, would prefer not to be identified."

"Point taken." Tony was risking a great deal to help him. "If we fail, will Winters arrive in time to save your lady love?"

Darcy gripped his reins tight. "We won't fail."

"Of course not." Tony pointed to the road, deeply grooved with mud and rainwater puddles. "Can you see the coach? It's just near that ledge."

Darcy narrowed his eyes. The moon beamed down in full silvery force, and in the countryside near Hampstead, he could see for miles under the clear sky. But he still couldn't see it. "No."

Tony pressed his mask against his face then took up his stallion's reins in one hand. "I suppose my eyes have accustomed themselves to this sort of thing. Over the years, I've gotten quite—"

"The bastard is going to kill her," Darcy growled.

"Right. Sorry." Tony pulled out his rapier, its long length glimmering in the moonlight. Never without cool noblesse oblige, he said coolly, "For England and St. George?"

Darcy pulled a pistol from his waistband. "No."

"Pardon?"

"For Amelia, damn it." With that, Darcy kicked his boot heels into his stallion's ribs and they were off racing across the field toward the road. He narrowed his eyes against the wind. The thunder of horse hooves rumbled around him but his mind kept repeating *Amelia, Amelia ,Amelia*.

This time he would not fail her.

At last, he spotted the outline of the coach hurrying down the road. But it struggled against the general bad state of the road and its deep grooves, making a slow pace.

Tony caught up and rode towards the front of the vehicle. He came up side by side with the driver and yelled, "Stand and deliver!"

Amelia refused to look at the pistol. Instead, she kept her eyes locked on Lord Warrington. Good Lord, she was going to die. Tonight. "I will not give him over to you."

"You know I'll find him."

Digging her fingertips into the cushioned seat, she leaned forward. "Which means you'd kill me anyway. This way, at least, I did not betray him."

"Noble words."

"It is not in my blood line, sir. But my brother is all I have ever had." Though, for a few brief hours she'd had Darcy. But he'd destroyed that fragile illusion. Swallowing back the growing lump in her throat, Amelia fought to remain calm. He wasn't a cold killer, not by nature. She could feel it. He was just a man who'd lived with his own pain far too long. "Please don't do this."

Warrington drew in a deep breath, and his eyes blinked slightly, as if he was steeling himself to the task. "Then I am sorry."

Amelia gasped and slowly leaned back. She wouldn't cower, but God help her, she didn't want to die like this. Not without her brother. And not while her heart still longed for Darcy. Forcing her eyes to remain open, Amelia braced herself. Waiting.

And waiting.

Warrington's hand shook. His entire body looked so tense that a blow might break him. His brows drew together then he blew out a disgusted sigh. "I can't do—"

"Stand and deliver!" a voice yelled from outside the coach.

Amelia froze. Could the night grow any more complicated?

The coach jolted as the driver pulled up the reins. Warrington glanced to the window, his body still tense. Amelia swiftly struck her hand out, shoving at his extended arm. The hand holding the pistol jerked towards the ceiling.

The pull of the trigger clicked through the chamber. And then the hissing of the powder lighting-flashed through space between them. The sound cracked through the coach, deafening her. Embers burst into the air as the pistol fired into the ceiling.

Wood splinters showered down on them.

A voice roared from outside, but she could not make it out.

The coach rolled to a complete stop. Warrington and Amelia sat sucking in sharp breaths as they stared at each other. He lowered his arm. He smiled weakly. "I'm sorry."

Amelia let her gaze drop to the fired pistol.

"Sod it," he rasped and tossed the useless weapon aside.

Before she could reply, the coach door flew off with such force it ripped the hinges. The coach lights poured in through the open door, temporarily blinding her. She blinked as a silhouette stood in the doorway.

Dressed in black from his feathered hat and black leather half mask, to his booted feet he aimed a pistol at Warrington. His gaze searched the inside of the coach and fell on Amelia.

Her breath caught in her throat. Though the top half of his face was hidden by his mask, she knew exactly who it was.

Darcy.

A mixture of relief and confusion churned inside her. What in God's name was he doing here?

Chapter Twenty Five

Darcy spotted Warrington, his hands fisted on his knees. He pointed his pistol at him and swung his gaze to the seat across from Warrington. His heart slammed in his chest. She sat in the shadows, and from her rapid breathing, she was alive. "Thank God," he rasped.

She leaned forward into the light. Her green eyes shone with excitement and a touch of fear. "Yes."

"You are unharmed?" Darcy repeated, unable to believe he'd been given a second chance.

"Yes."

He turned towards Warrington. "Get out."

"Bugger off." The man's face was hard and unyielding.

Darcy's blood simmered, threatening to boil at the man's nonchalance. "You bloody bastard, you were going to kill her."

"'Tis none of your affair."

Darcy gripped his pistol tighter, keeping his finger off the trigger lest he shoot the bastard in the head. "None of my affair?" he smiled dryly, a hint of anticipation humming through him. "Right." Reaching forward, he grabbed Warrington's cravat and whipped his cheek with the butt of his pistol. "I said get out."

Blinking at the hard hit, Warrington shoved back at Darcy. "I should kill you," he hissed.

"Pompous words for a man on the wrong side of a pistol," Darcy pointed out. But he backed away, allowing Warrington to climb down.

Tony was just a few feet behind him, rapier in hand. "Is this the rat bastard?"

"'Tis indeed."

Tony looked Warrington up and down as the lord descended from the Coach. "Hmm. Have you considered a madhouse, my lord? I do believe one might suit you."

"Hold him for a moment," said Darcy.

Extending his arm, Tony strode forward until the tip of his blade was a mere inch from Warrington's cravat. "With pleasure."

Darcy climbed the first coach step, lowering his pistol to his side. He leaned in and ran his eyes over Amelia. He wanted to pull her into his arms to ensure she was truly safe, but he had to deal with Warrington first. "I want you to stay in the coach."

"Why?"

"There are things that must be done." He reached out with his free hand and stroked the side of her face. Though his fingers were gloved, the mere feel of her beneath his hand was a balm to his soul. He didn't know what he would have done if he'd lost her. "I don't want you seeing this."

She slowly pulled back from his hand. "Darcy, no."

Darcy stood with his hand cupping air as he mouthed, "No?"

"He was wanted revenge against *me*. Not you. This is my right."

He bit back an instant retort. She was right, and if he ever was to prove himself to her he had to utterly honest. Though he wanted her safe, he wouldn't keep things from her ever again. "If you wish. But you will stay close to Tony. Do you understand?"

"Darcy?"

He took her hand, ready to help her down. "Yes?"

"Why are you wearing a mask?" she whispered.

"It's a highwayman thing."

"Oh." She frowned as she stood and climbed down. "But you're not a thief."

"Highwayman, love," cut in Tony. "Highwayman. Thief is such a disheartening word."

Warrington's eyes widened and he broadened his stance, despite the rapier pointed at his throat. "What the hell is this?"

"It's justice coming full circle," said Darcy, his voice dripping with anger.

"You're not a highwayman," said Warrington softly, more to himself than to him.

"Ah. Point to Warrington. He figured us out, Chase," drawled Tony.

"Take off your mask," bit out Warrington.

Tony tsked as he twisted his wrist a little. His rapier caught the moonlight and he extended his reach a breath closer to Warrington's throat. "Now why does everyone always ask me to do that?"

Warrington threw Tony a killing stare then focused on Darcy. "Take it off," he bit out. "I want to see your face."

"Happily." Darcy yanked off the black leather piece.

The air around Warrington seemed to deflate as he took in Darcy. "This isn't about you, Chase," he said softly.

"When you made it about her, it became about me." Darcy felt Amelia stiffen behind him. He only hoped that one day she would understand what he had done and that now, everything he did was for her.

"This is revenge," Warrington stated.

"Well, it bloody well isn't justice," snapped Tony.

"You're a thief," retorted Warrington, his eyes wide with disbelief.

"Highwayman," quipped Tony with a dangerous smile as he very slowly pinned the first fold of Warrington's cravat with his rapier.

Warrington didn't flinch or pull back, but stood steady, his eyes hard.

And for a moment, Darcy wondered if the lord hadn't grown a shade mad in his quest for revenge. "Warrington, you're a coward, but you're a dangerous coward."

"I am not a coward," Warrington said levelly.

"What do you call killing Amelia?"

"Revenge."

"And you would be no better than her father?"

To Darcy's shock, Warrington flinched. But he recovered and glared at Darcy. "Go to the devil. If you think me a coward fight me. Here and now."

Darcy cocked his head to the side. "A duel?"

"Yes."

God's teeth, he longed to fight the bastard. To feel his

flesh give and break against his fists, but this was about keeping Amelia safe. "No. I will bring you to the king's justice."

Suddenly, Warrington dropped to the ground. Out of reach now from Tony's rapier, he tumbled to the right. As he sprang to his booted feet, he whipped a long dagger from his hip.

What the hell was the bastard doing? Darcy pointed his pistol at Warrington and gestured for Amelia to get behind Tony.

Warrington lunged forward. Darcy aimed at his arm and pulled the trigger. It fired. Sparks flew into the night air, and Warrington staggered. His face whitened as a dark spot spread over his dark jacket along his upper arm. He fell to his knees and the blade dropped from his hand.

Tony stepped forward, his blade still at the ready, and picked up Warrington's dagger. "And just what did you hope to accomplish, mate?"

"I am not going to die in prison." Warrington's face tightened with strain as he pushed his hand against the bloody tear in his coat. "Not when I have failed."

"Well, then perhaps you'll die right here." Darcy flung his spent pistol to the ground. It landed with a dull thud. He grabbed the jeweled hilt of his rapier and slipped it free from its scabbard in a smooth arc.

"Don't!" shouted Amelia as she ran from behind Darcy and Tony.

All three men stopped and stared at her.

"Don't," she said again, her voice firm. She gently placed her hand on Darcy's arm. "He wanted to kill me, but he couldn't do it. He has suffered enough at the hands of my family. I do not wish his death."

Darcy couldn't believe the words coming out of her mouth. "But—"

Amelia looked down at Warrington. "My lord, I cannot return your family to you, but I can return your life to you. Will that be enough?"

The thunder of horse hooves pounded through the night, rushing over the plain. Darcy narrowed his eyes, knowing what the approaching sound meant.

Scott was about to arrive, the king's soldiers in tow. And with them their justice. He was going to lose Amelia. Again.

Chapter Twenty Six

Soldiers grabbed Warrington's arms and hauled him to his feet.

Amelia fisted her hands in her skirts as she stood to the side. Warrington glanced at her, his strong face a mix of confusion and sadness. As the soldiers roughly pulled him away, she forced herself to watch. He wasn't a good man, but he wasn't a bad one either. Not truly.

She'd lost her mother years ago and the pain of it had eaten her heart, but beyond that she'd only ever had her brother. What would it be like to have your entire family brutally killed? She couldn't even imagine.

Darcy strode towards Warrington and the soldiers. Above the din of horses, she heard him demand a tourniquet for Warrington's arm.

When the two soldiers had Warrington bandaged and tied up they mounted him onto one of the horses. Darcy turned to her. His long dark hair was tied behind his back.

He'd pulled his coat off, leaving him in his black breeches and black linen shirt. Her breath hitched in her throat as their eyes met. He looked like a Highwayman, but he was worse than a thief. He was a liar. A liar who had stolen her heart.

As he slowly approached, she stood frozen.

"Amelia?" his deep voice surrounded her in its warm embrace.

She folded her arms just under her breasts and looked at the ground. "I suppose I should thank you for saving me for the gallows."

"Please—" His pained voice broke off and he reached out, taking her arms in his large hands. He pulled her closer.

The hard planes of his body pressed against her front, enveloping her in his spicy scent. She longed to wrap her arms around him and tilt her head back for his kiss. Lord help her, why did her body not understand what her heart and mind did?

When she did not return his embrace, he pulled her tighter to him as if somehow that could make her accept him. "Amelia, I need to tell you…"

Remaining stiff in his arms, she hardened her heart. She would not hope to find love in his voice. She'd proven a fool to his ways before, but she would not again. Clearing her throat, she looked up at him. "Yes, my lord?"

Silence hung between them and she struggled at the pain lodged in her throat.

Once, he had made her feel so safe. So safe, she had betrayed herself by trusting him. Because of him, she would never feel safe again. The Earl of Chase had offered love and trust then he had ripped them both away. In fact, she didn't think he had ever truly given them. They had only been a lie.

His dark eyes searched over her face. "None of this was supposed to happen."

She dropped her arms to her side, standing like a stiff doll in his arms. "Excuses are not becoming, and I don't wish to hear more lies."

"I—"

"What have you done with my brother?" she demanded. "Can you tell me true that you have not jeopardized his life?"

"He is where we left him." He glanced towards Scott and Tony then whispered, "Lord Winters must bring him in as a traitor. But for you, I will do everything I can to let him slip away before the king's men come for him."

A small spark of hope flamed inside her, which she quickly squelched. He had called her a liar, but he was the true master. "Why should I believe you?"

Gently, he lifted his hand to stroke her face, and then faltered. He dropped his hand. "I don't expect you to ever forgive me, but it doesn't change the fact that I love you."

She tensed as if he'd slapped her. Tears stung her eyes and for the first time, she feared that she would truly become hysterical. Her throat burning and her body numb with anger, she glared at him and ground out, "You love me?"

He gazed down at her with such tenderness that for a second she almost believed him. But she'd seen that look before. Right before she'd found out he was a spy.

In one night he'd told her he loved her, asked for her hand in marriage, and then turned her over as a traitor. Never again. "I don't even know you," she hissed.

His eyes widened in the torchlight.

She held her hand up between them. "And you certainly don't know me. Not after what you were capable of doing."

"Amelia?" he asked, his voice filled with confusion. He seemed truly lost. But if he now regretted on some small level what he had done, so be it.

Her throat tightened around her words. "I told you I loved you, but I was wrong."

He flinched. "You don't mean it."

"Unlike you, sir, I don't lie offstage. You seem to do nothing but."

Quietly, he stepped back, his face hard and drawn. "You're right, of course. And since you cannot trust me, there is nothing left to say."

She nodded. He was right, yet her heart cried out for him to protest how much he loved her. That he'd been a fool. That he'd come after her because he loved her.

Lord Winters crossed over to them, looking from one to the other. He held his hand out to Amelia. "My dear, if you please. I do believe we can do this without bonds."

"Certainly, my lord," she said, squaring her shoulders. She took Winters's gloved hand and tried to go without looking at Darcy. She couldn't do it. She glanced back over her shoulder. "Good-bye."

He stood still. The playful intelligence that always surrounded him had disappeared into a brooding quietness. "'Til we meet again, Amelia."

The question was, would that be in this life or the next? Perhaps she would see him at her trial. After all, as the man who had given evidence against her, he would have to be there.

Amelia followed Winters, her heart heavier with each

step. Would he tell them everything? Would he tell them how they had made love? How he had tricked her, or how she had been foolish enough to trust him with her brother's life?

She only prayed that Darcy had not lied about Edward. Perhaps he would be able to slip away. If he did, she'd gladly die in his stead.

Winters walked silently beside her until they reached his horse. "You shall have to ride with me."

"That's fine," she said dully.

Offering his hands to help her mount, Amelia pulled up, sitting sideways on the saddle. As he swung up behind her, he whispered, "The fool does love you, Mrs. Fox."

"Lord Winters, you are not any more trustworthy than he is."

Winters laughed softly. "You are very perceptive, but in this, madam, my word is true."

He flicked his reins and the stallion charged off down the plain, heading back toward the spires of London.

If only it was true. But she knew better. Love was too high a price for a soldier and a spy to pay, whether they be Cromwell's men or the king's.

Chapter Twenty Seven

"She is a traitor, Chase," King Charles boomed as he strode into his receiving chamber. As he walked to one of the side tables housing designs for Christopher Wren's architectural designs, the courtiers present sunk into curtsies and bows.

Darcy followed him, doing his best to keep a respectful distance. At least the king had granted him an audience. But in truth, he wished to grab the monarch and shout at him to make up his bleeding mind. They'd been discussing her innocence for the last ten minutes.

He gripped his hat so hard the brim twisted into a lump of feathers and felt. Glancing over his shoulder at the curious courtiers, who remained distant yet observant, he whispered, "Sire, I ask for her life."

Charles turned, the long skirt tails of his black and gold coat spinning about his legs. He rested his hands on the table behind him. "That good was she?"

The courtiers tittered, their hissing whispers and laughter filling the air like bat wings. Darcy resisted the urge to throw the vultures a murderous stare. He needed to focus.

He ground his teeth, biting back an angry reply at the king's insinuation. One did not insult the king when one was trying to get in his good graces. Darcy inclined his head. "Your Majesty, she made foolish choices, but in no way did she ever plot sedition or rebellion."

Sunlight spilled in from the tall windows behind the king, bathing him an ironically saint-like glow. Charles smoothed his thin black mustache with a jeweled finger. "Chase, We are inclined to be moved, but she covered for her brother. That, in itself, can be construed as treason." He tilted his head to the side and the long curls of his black wig brushed his shoulders. "You know that."

God's teeth. If he could not convince the king now, he never would. And that left him one last means. Means that could get him beheaded. "Indeed, Your Majesty, but if *your* brother was doing something he should not…would you not protect him?" he whispered, not wanting the court to hear this particular tidbit.

Darcy held his breath.

The king's lips pursed and his eyes narrowed. He pushed away from the table and eyed his signet ring.

Darcy held still, not daring to back down. But he might have gone too far. For the king, indeed, protected his Catholic brother, James. A brother that most of England wanted dead, or at the least out on his ear.

"You are very bold, my lord." The king's strong voice cut through the air like a knife. "So, you ask for Mrs. Fox's life. Why should *We* give it to you?"

"Majesty. I do not merely ask for it." This time Darcy spoke loud enough for all the court to hear. His love for Amelia would never be a secret. That he would swear to. He lowered his eyes and knelt, a completely unfamiliar word about to pass his lips. "I *beg* for it."

A hushed silence fell over the court at seeing one of their most noble lords beg for an actress's life. Darcy kept his eyes to the king's feet. If this did not sway the king, nothing would.

Charles cleared his throat. "Get up, man. Get up."

"Majesty, I would prefer to remain at your feet whilst Mrs. Fox's life is in your hands."

"Well, Chase when We asked you to learn to be a woman, We did not expect you to gain the benefit of intercession."

"I have learned many things from Mrs. Fox."

"If she can bring you to your knees, We would not waste so talented a teacher." Charles snapped his fingers and a page hurried forward. He waved his hand as he said, "Arrange for Mrs. Fox to be freed. Chastened, of course, but free."

The page nodded and hurried away.

Darcy stood his heart hammering his chest. "Your Majesty is most gracious—"

"Oh for God sake, Chase, We've known you since you wet your knickers. This bizarre behavior can only mean one thing. You are in love with the woman."

"'Tis true." Darcy drew in a deep breath, wary to press his luck, but there was nothing for it. Scott had managed to imprison Edward Fox. "Sire, I must ask you one more favor."

Charles sighed. "Indeed? Your lady's life will not suffice?"

"If it so please you, Sire, no."

"And if it does not please Us?"

Then Darcy was royally sodded. "I must beg for the life of Edward Fox."

His voice echoed through the long hall, and belated, Darcy realized the courtiers were still listening in rapt attention.

"You reach too high, Chase," chastised the king. "Can you contest the man's treason?"

"No. Only he is even younger than Mrs. Fox and was swayed by those who wished him dire harm."

"Warrington?

"Yes, Majesty."

"Warrington's desire for revenge did surprise even Us. However, your young friend freely chose to write such dangerous material."

Darcy's throat tightened with dread. If Edward went to the gallows, Amelia would never forgive him; she would be stricken with grief and he had already caused her far too much pain. "I will do whatever is required to encourage your majesty to be lenient."

"Do you realize what you say?" the king asked softly.

Darcy inclined his head, ready to be sent to the farthest reaches of Russia. "I do."

"If We spare Edward Fox, he shall be sent to the Americas to help in the establishment of the new colonies."

Darcy drew in a deep breath. "Your Majesty is most kind—"

"Hold, Chase." The king folded his arms, his gold embroidered coat sleeves shining in the sunlight. "You said you would do what is required for what We assume is your lady's happiness."

The relief that had just flooded his blood died a hasty

death. The king's tone did not bode well. "I did."

"Then you shall give Us your title, your lands, and your manors, in exchange for Edward's and Amelia Fox's lives. We shall then banish you from this fair isle. Only then will We ensure what you have begged for."

Darcy stared at the king, trying to process what exactly he had said. He was the fifth Earl of Chase in a line of men who had given themselves over to the royal bloodline of England. For Amelia, the king was asking him to give that up, and there was not even any insurance that she would take him back.

"Do you love her my lord? Do you love her enough?"

So much he'd give his life for her. "I do."

Charles smiled. "Good, Chase. Then your requests are granted."

"Majesty—"

The king smiled a strangely pleased smile. "One should consider quitting while one is ahead. Besides, We don't believe you have anything left to bargain with."

But Darcy could not leave this be. If all his lands were seized— "My mother, Sire?"

"Ah. Lady Adelaide. We shall take her into our household and ensure her comfort. She will not be made to pay for the follies of her son."

Darcy nodded, relieved that his mother would not be overly sullied in this. "Thank you."

The king waved his hand, lace cuff fluttering. "Now, hurry from my sight lest We feel less generous."

Darcy bowed took several steps back then turned from the king. He faced the crowd of nobles who had no doubt overheard every word. News of his banishment and the stripping of his titles would spread like the Great Fire.

Staring straight ahead, he strode through them and out the tall double gilt doors at the back. He had made his choice. He had chosen Amelia. Even if she might never choose him.

Chapter Twenty Eight

The rattle of a key in the iron lock echoed through the damp stone chamber. Amelia turned from the small window overlooking the muddy parade ground and glanced toward the door.

Her throat tightened and she gripped her shawl tighter about her waist. There had to be worse prisons than the Tower, but it was certainly frightening enough.

The mammoth wood door swung inward in its black hinges and the warden stepped forward. His plain black attire suited the austerity of the stone walls. "Madam, you shall not go to trial."

Amelia stepped forward. "Have I been condemned? Without—"

The man's wrinkled face bunched into tight lines of contrition. "No, madam. You are to be set free. The king himself has arranged it so."

She dared not believe him. "In truth?"

He nodded. "Aye, in truth."

For the first time in days, she took a deep breath and didn't feel her lungs contract with dread. "And my brother? What of him?"

The warden's lips pursed down ward and he rubbed his hands together.

"Oh god," she breathed. Edward could not die whilst she lived. She would go to the king. She would—

"Your brother is to be sent to the Americas.

Amelia blinked. "Banished?"

"Aye."

Sighing out a heavy breath, Amelia smiled. She lifted a hand to her face and closed her eyes. Thank God. She lowered her hand and beamed at the older man. "Thank you. Thank you so much."

"Thank the king, madam. Parliament wanted your brother's head. Luckily, he's a Protestant. Any other religion, and it might have started a riot."

"Indeed." London was rife with fury these days over the lack of a Protestant heir for the throne of England.

"Since you don't have much to pack, shall I escort you out? Shall I send for a coach?"

"Oh. I-I don't know." And she didn't. She'd only been in the Tower a few days, but lord help her, she had not thought this far. Her thoughts had strayed too often to Darcy and the terrible risk she had taken in trusting him, and how she'd almost lost everything because of it. But now she was free. And her brother was as good as free, even if he had to leave the country.

Perhaps she would go with him. The only thing left to her in London was the theater. She did love it, but there were dark memories here. She turned her attention back to the warden. "Yes, I suppose I can simply leave."

"Right then, come with me."

"Is Edward freed, or must he remain here?"

"Your brother may go, accompanied by a guard so that he might collect his belongings. The next ship for the territories is not for another two weeks."

At least she'd have time to say goodbye to her brother and perhaps they could forgive each other for this nightmare. "Thank you."

She followed him out the door and out into the cold corridor. Amelia wrapped her shawl tightly around her fighting the cold. For a moment her thoughts wandered to Lord Warrington. "Wait."

The warden turned, his great furrowed brows drawing together. "Yes?"

"What of Lord Warrington? Has he been tried?"

"No. And will not likely be soon. Perhaps months. But given the circumstances, it is quite possible that he shall be beheaded."

"Truly?"

"Madam, did he not try to kill you?"

Amelia looked away. "Yes. Well, no. He intended to." Amelia pinned the warden with a determined stare. "I wish to see him."

"You what?"

"Lord Warrington. I wish to see him now."

"But—"

"My good man, I am a free woman now, and wish to visit a prisoner."

"This is most odd."

Well, she would hardly call herself normal. "Nevertheless, lead on."

He smiled, exposing two missing teeth. "His lordship resides on the same floor."

"Does he indeed?" That was rather funny. "All the better."

Shrugging, the warden fingered his large iron key ring and shuffled down the hall and stopped at the end. "He's got quite the good view of the river."

"I'm sure he finds that heartening," Amelia said with a false sense of cheer. If anything, it probably drove the man wild to distraction, the real world just outside his cell.

"I won't allow you to be alone with him."

"I understand."

After plugging one of the keys into the lock, he turned it and with a great heave, shoved the door open.

"Go to the bloody devil!" shouted the man inside. "Leave me be!"

Amelia stepped back at his growl. She didn't know what she'd expected, but when last she'd seen Warrington he'd seemed rather beaten.

"Are you certain, madam?" whispered the Warden, his face twisted with distaste.

Nodding, she stepped into the surprisingly large room lined with shelves and tables. Apparently, nobility warranted better accommodation. Warrington stood leaning against the stone wall staring out the window. His linen shirt hung loosely about his muscled frame, barely tucked into his breeches. "I've told you, I don't want a priest. I don't want a wench. So bloody sod off."

Amelia folded her hands in front of her and stepped a little farther into the room. "Well, I'm certainly not a priest, though I have been called a wench, which I took great umbrage to."

Warrington turned sharply. His eyes narrowed.

She half expected him to hiss *you*! He folded his arms across his chest.

"Why are you here?" he said flatly.

Amelia smiled tightly. "I'm not sure myself, but I couldn't leave without seeing you."

"Leave?" he asked dully.

"Yes. Edward and I have been pardoned."

"Foiled, eh?"

"For a man imprisoned, you've a particularly good sense of humor."

"It's the only thing left to me, Mrs. Fox. I forsook it sometime ago and am glad to have it back again."

Despite his many faults, she felt a strong sympathy for this man. "I am sorry."

"It is ironic that I strove so intently to place you and your brother in this prison, and now it is I who shall remain."

"It is."

He glanced at her, his eyes glimmering with a hint of respect. "I was mistaken in you."

"This was never about me."

"No." His jaw tensed and he let his arms fall to his sides. "I thought that by avenging my family it would lay them to rest. But I find all this time, it is I who am walking the earth looking for peace. They no doubt found theirs years ago."

The pain in his voice tore at her heart. "I am sorry," she said softly.

He lifted his brows ruefully as if amused, yet pained by his own folly. "Don't be. You could have let Chase kill me, but you did not. You proved yourself to be ten times my value and certainly nothing like your father. So, will you forgive me for so nearly destroying all that you hold dear?"

Amelia pressed her hands against her skirts. "I forgive you."

His lips parted into a small smile. A smile that seemed to convey some semblance of peace. "Thank you. Now, please go. I have many thoughts to put in order."

"Lord Warrington, the tragedy is that something so horrible happened to a man who is so clearly good. Sometimes in grief, we all are driven to madness."

He nodded, then turned from her, facing the window. "Goodbye, Mrs. Fox."

She hurried from the room, tears stinging her eyes. He'd threatened her, kidnapped her, and blackmailed her, but in the end far worse had happened to him. But his actions would haunt him… Right into a very early grave.

Moments later she was in a coach, riding back to the only stable place she had ever known. Her old life, her old world, her friend, the theater.

"Your alacrity for stupidity seems particularly poignant at this moment."

Darcy lifted his glass of brandy in salute to his mother. The glass had been married to his hand for a few days now. "Many thanks."

She arched a delicate brow at him, strode forward, her skirts rustling, and snatched the glass from his hand. "What in the blazes do you think you are doing?"

He frowned at her then reached for the decanter by his side. "I am getting sodding drunk."

"Luckily, my perceptions acquainted me with that much," she said dryly.

Darcy turned from her, twisting in the leather chair. His life had gone to hell and the last thing he needed was his mother twisting the damn knife in his wounds. Surely at some point he had walked through that door which said Abandon hope all ye who enter here. Yet, he could not recall it. "I don't wish to be lectured."

"You've thrown away your lands, your titles, and some are even saying your honor for this woman."

"God's teeth," Darcy cradled the decanter as if it was a beloved child.

"Do you love her?"

His mother's hard voice didn't jar him, but the words certainly did. "Haven't I proved it?"

She reached around and yanked the decanter from his grip. Stumbling back as it popped from his grasp. "Men will never learn. They are fools of the heart and not much better with the head."

Sighing, she placed the glass and decanter back down on the table beside him. He started to reach for them and she slapped his hand.

"Mother," he growled.

"Don't you *Mother* me." And then she did something incredible. She lowered herself to kneel by him. Gently, she cupped his chin and forced him to look at her. "You have always done your duty, and yet you turned your back on it for this woman. I ask you, do you love her?"

He yanked his chin away. "I have given up everything,

and she won't see me."

"Does she know it?"

His mouth opened and closed. "I don't know. But it matters not. I will not have her merely because she is grateful to me."

"Son, you have made a grand gesture. One that will change your life forever, but without her, it will be empty and meaningless. Your sacrifice is only proof of love if you go to her and tell her."

"She won't let me."

His mother rolled her eyes adjusting her skirts as settled back, still on her knees. "Now when did the word *let* mean anything to my clever son? You will find a way."

Darcy narrowed his eyes feeling a touch of suspicion. "Why are you suddenly so enthusiastic about Mrs. Fox?"

"I like her. She is intelligent, beautiful...for an actress," she teased. The playful light left her eyes. "I lived in a loveless marriage that united two powerful families, making a rich title richer. I would not visit such unhappiness upon my son."

Darcy looked at his mother and he felt an awe inspiring wave of love. "You always deserved more."

She laughed. "Oh, most certainly." She placed her hand on top of his. "Go and have what I could not."

He squeezed her delicate fingers. Then stood. "I've wasted time, haven't I?"

"Yes. What are you going to do?"

Darcy smiled. "Only a fool tries to fight alone."

And in this case, his compatriot had better be more helpful than he'd been in the past. But with Lord Winter's verbal skills, Darcy was sure the earl would get him an audience into Mrs. Fox's dressing room. Then it would be up him to find his way back into her heart.

Chapter Twenty Nine

"You're being a silly twit of a girl." Ned twisted in his chair and looked at her over his shoulder. "And I won't stand for it."

Amelia yanked off her bodice and flung it onto the small couch by the wall. "I am warning you. If you so much as say his name, I will tell the scandal sheets your true age."

Ned's mouth dropped in mock horror. "Not even you would be so cruel."

"I would, indeed."

"Whatever have you done with my dear girl? She's been replaced by a bitter old harridan… Whose acting happens to be off. The balcony scene was dreadful."

"Leave it to Betterton to choose Romeo and Juliet," gritted Amelia. "I am in no mood for romance."

"Yes, but you're an actress." Ned spoke slowly, gesturing with his hands as if he was talking to a small child. "That means even when you're not in the mood, you pretend to be.

It's what you're paid for, love."

Amelia narrowed her eyes. "Unless you wish me to replace Tybalt's sword with the real thing, you will stop it this moment."

"Hmm, well that certainly would add a large dose of realism to Mercutio's death scene. Though, if I must say so myself, it was quite good tonight."

"You always die beautifully. There's no question. But right now, I'd like you to choke. Very slowly. Somewhere far out of my hearing."

"Just because no one applauded tonight when you stabbed yourself—"

"Ned!"

"Well, you were dreadful. You were about in love with Romeo as much as a pox ridden sailor."

"Love can go to the devil." Amelia pulled at the ties in her skirt, but her fingers got caught and the dratted thing wouldn't loose. She sucked in a deep breath, but couldn't get enough air, her corset was so tight. Why did Ned always have to shove her problems right under her nose? All she wanted to do was forget Darcy.

"Darling, you look like the devil." He stood from his dressing chair and crossed to her. Gently, he unwound her hands from her skirt ties then pulled the ribbon free. "There you are."

As the skirt whooshed to the floor and she stood in her shift and corset, Amelia placed a hand over her middle. "I haven't been sleeping and frankly, I've not been feeling at all well."

Ned's usually mischievous face dimmed. "Truly."

"The whole thing just makes me sick. I mean how could

I have been so foolish?"

"At what time?"

Amelia rolled her eyes and sighed. What he on about? "I was foolish the whole time."

"No, love, I mean when are you sick? Generally or specifically?"

She shook her head, so tired she couldn't care less. "Oh, I don't know. I just can't get the man from my head."

"He did save you, my dear."

"Yes."

"And your brother."

"Apparently."

"And you haven't replied to any of his notes, and you won't admit him to the dressing room."

"Stop pointing out the obvious."

"I think he loves you."

Her face compressed into that horrible mass of wobbliness, which signified tears. "But how could I ever be sure? He lies as well as he tells the truth." To her horror, her last words went up a whole octave and hot tears filled her eyes.

"There, there." He pulled her against his slender chest and patted her back. "I'm going to ask you again. Are you generally sick or specifically?"

She frowned against his shoulder, tears slipping down her cheeks. "Wh-what?" she hiccupped.

"Amelia," Ned softly as he gently soothed her with his hands, stroking up and down her back. "You made love to him, did you not?"

She pulled back and wiped the tears from her eyes. "Ned Kynaston, that is none of your business."

"No but—"

The curtains at the end of the room swished open, and Lord Winters strode into the room, formidable in sapphire blue, which turned his eyes turquoise. He held his hat under his arm, but that was as gentlemanly as he looked.

The man positively glowered. "Madam, have you not heard?"

Amelia twisted out of Ned's grip. "There is so much to hear in London, my lord. But clearly *you* have not heard it is rude to enter without permission."

"Do not avoid the obvious," Lord Winters retorted, unshaken by her set down. "You and your brother are free. Do you not wonder why?"

She grabbed her dressing gown and pulled it over her shoulders. "I assume you and Lord Chase protested our freedom, which I thank you for."

Lord Winters snorted. "Not I. Though I did not wish your pretty neck stretched, it was not I who went to the king."

Amelia looked askance as she pulled her hair free of her dressing robe. "It was good of Lord Chase to ask for our lives."

"And yet you show him no gratitude."

"Gratitude?" she snapped.

Ned tentatively held up his hand. "Ah… Lord Winters, now is perhaps not the best time—"

"Save it, Kynaston."

Ned's eyes flared and he squared his shoulders. "I beg your pardon."

"I am here to make it clear that my friend is leaving for the Continent, the king is giving him just enough funds to abscond with his life, and the least this baggage could do is say goodbye."

The words pounded through her head, but she didn't fully comprehend them.

"He's what?" gasped Amelia.

Strangely, Lord Winters glanced towards the curtained door and scowled. "I suppose he has not told you."

"Told me what?" Amelia demanded. "He's told me nothing."

Lord Winters turned back to her and advanced a few steps. "How many times has he asked to see you?"

"I was freed only a few days ago, and I've avoided everyone I possibly can except for on stage."

"How many times, madam?"

"Several." Amelia bit the inside of her lip. How could she confess how much it hurt to even think of him, let alone face the idea of seeing him.

"Perhaps he would have told you, but he went to the king right before you were freed. He begged for you and your brother's life. And the king demanded a price."

Amelia stepped back, not sure she wanted to hear this.

"A price?" she echoed.

"He is to be banished from England."

Amelia shook her head. 'Twas not possible. "After restoring Charles to the throne?"

"You weren't exactly going to be executed for petty thievery. Your brother was even worse." Lord Winters's eyes glittered with astonishing honesty as he spoke, his words as powerful as daggers. "A slap on the wrist was not going to suffice."

If he was banished, she might never see him again. Which was what she wanted. Was it not? But that he had given up so much for her? "How long will he be gone?"

Lord Winters shrugged, though there was nothing careless about his stance. "As long as it pleases the king."

The room swam a bit and Amelia blinked furiously. "Good lord," she breathed. "He did that for my brother?"

Lord Winters snorted. "No, madam. He did it for you. And that is not all. I think I should sit."

But she couldn't move. Her feet were stuck to the floor as she waited for Lord Winters to speak. Amelia swallowed, almost not wanting to hear, yet she felt a strange thrill that Darcy had gone to such trouble to free her. She'd deliberately avoided any mention of him, any news because it had simply been too painful.

Lord Winters arched a blond brow. "In exchange for your brother's life, Lord Chase is Lord Chase no longer."

Ned gasped. "'Tis not possible."

She scowled at her friend. "Ned, don't be overly dramatic." Besides, if anyone was going to be emotional it was her. "I don't understand."

"The king has stripped him of his lands and titles."

Amelia gaped. She'd grown to dislike this man who had taken her into custody not once but twice and had deceived her right along with Darcy. But now, she believed him. It made perfect sense. "Oh, God."

"Exactly," stated Lord Winters. "He is to leave tomorrow."

This time, she managed to find her way to her dressing chair. She lowered herself into it. "Why would he do such a thing?"

Clearly annoyed it was taking them all so long to come to the correct conclusion, Lord Winters rolled his eyes. "Think very hard."

"He loves you Amelia!" shouted Ned. "He truly loves

you!"

Lord Winters winced. "Yes. Thank you."

Ned grabbed her hand and shook it till her whole arm jiggled. "You asked how you would ever know if he loved you? What other proof do you need?"

What had she been thinking? She'd been thinking with her head, because when he'd hurt her, she'd feared to think with her heart. But she could not let him leave like this.

"I need to go." She pulled free and headed for the door.

Lord Winters grabbed her shoulders. "That is not necessary."

She twisted her arm and glared up at the Lord. "Release me." She stomped on his foot. "I've waited too bloody long."

Lord Winters bent over, his face reddening. "That is not what I meant."

Ignoring him, she yanked the curtains back ready to head out into the streets to find Darcy. She yelped as she came face to face with him.

His lips twitched with amusement as he slowly took in her barely dressed state. "Were you really going to go out in a shift?"

Amelia stared up at him, her heart thudding and her body warm with hope. "Pardon?"

He pointed down to her waist and legs. She looked and gasped. Taking in her thin shift and corset, she laughed. "I suppose I was."

Darcy backed her into the dressing room, his gaze drinking her. "You don't mind me coming to see you?'

She shook her head. "Mind? No."

Ned scurried around them and grabbed Lord Winters's shoulder. "Come along. Don't linger."

"But there are things to discuss," pointed out Winters.

"Discussions are for later," Ned hissed. "Right now is for reconciliation and extremely good—"

"Ned," warned Amelia, shooting him a look from the corner of her eye.

"You see," said Ned, pushing Lord Winters ever so slightly towards the door. "We are not wanted."

"I wonder why?" Lord Winters drawled as he shoved his hat on his head and followed the actor out.

Darcy smiled at their retreating forms. But when he looked back to her, his smile dimmed. "Amelia, I am so sorry."

She stroked his shoulder, trying to reassure him. "'Tis I am who am sorry."

He tensed at her touch, but from the way his eyes lit, it was with pleasure. "No, you were right."

"But I should have listened."

"I shouldn't have lied."

She laughed softly. "You had your reasons."

"There is never a good reason to lie to you."

Amelia couldn't help herself. She smiled at him. "That is a very good reply."

"Do you forgive me?"

"After all that you have done for my brother—"

He lifted his hand and gently touched his fingers to her lips. "Do not mistake me. This was not for your brother." He slowly caressed her lower lip. "It was all for you."

Amelia half closed her eyes at his touch. It was so tempting.

"Kiss me," she whispered.

His eyes widened as if this was the last thing he'd expected to hear. But he didn't hesitate. Pulling her tightly against him, he lowered his lips to hers. The kiss stole her breath. His mouth moved over hers, branding her with his desire and need.

Amelia circled her arms around his back, hungrier for him than she'd ever been. When he thrust his tongue into her mouth, she welcomed him, caressing him back with tempting strokes.

He pulled back and brushed her curls back from her face. "I love you."

She stared silently up at him. She'd been such a fool. A practical fool, but a fool nonetheless. His eyes shone with love and the hope that she wouldn't tell him to go to the devil.

"I love you, too."

"Fancy running off to France?"

Amelia frowned for a moment, then glanced to her dressing room. This was the only life she'd ever loved. The theater.

He followed her glance and pulled back a little. "Forgive me. I shouldn't have asked."

Amelia gasped as she realized what he must think. She lightly punched his arm. "Don't you go and be a fool. I love the theater, but you are my life now… And as I understand there is very good theater in Paris."

He smiled. "So there is."

"I won't ever be able to repay you." He'd given up everything she'd never really had.

"I nearly got you executed."

"Yes, but you've given up your family, generations of history—"

"You are my family." He gently pressed a kiss to her forehead. "My history," he murmured as he kissed her cheek.

"My future," he whispered, barely kissing her lips. "And my wife?" His lips lingered just above hers.

"Do you think we'll make it to the church this time?" she teased.

He smiled as he hugged her so hard the air whooshed out her lungs. "Is that a yes?"

"Of course it's a yes."

"I've still got the license."

She tilted her head to the side. "I like a man who thinks ahead."

"I'm thinking very, very far ahead."

"And what do you see?"

"Us, Amelia. I see us."

Chapter Thirty

"Man and wife."

Her lips tilted in a perpetual smile that hadn't stopped for the few weeks since she'd learned the truth. Holding Darcy's hand, she turned to face her guests.

The small church was filled with the strangest collection of people. She couldn't fight a bemused laugh. The king himself was in attendance, which was quite a shock.

And she'd never expected to have guards at her wedding, but the king had been particularly magnanimous and allowed Edward to attend. Of course, he was being marched straight off to his ship as soon as the breakfast was over, but she was glad to see him here.

There was Lord Winters, standing stoic as ever. Right beside him, of all people, was Tony the highwayman. The cheeky man winked at her, his youthful smile broad and infectious.

Amelia did not miss that his dukely dress was much

more somber than his highwayman's costume. Why he wasn't married himself, she couldn't fathom.

"Kiss her then!" bellowed the king.

Darcy bowed. "As His Majesty commands." Grinning like an idiot, he pulled her against him, dipped her back, and kissed her so thoroughly the cherubs carved into the stone walls surely blushed. She certainly did. The heat bloomed in her cheeks…and right between her legs. But no one else needed to know that.

When he set her back to rights, Amelia laughed. Too her astonishment, the small crowd was applauding.

"Bravo!" shouted Ned.

As Amelia and Darcy walked down between the wooden pews, she couldn't stop looking at him. He was so handsome in his dark green coat, shot through with silver thread and black braiding, that set off his slightly dark skin, all she wanted was to take him into a hall and ravish him.

But she would have to wait.

After all, the king had come to her wedding. Why on earth, she was not sure… But Darcy had made clear that it was not to suddenly clap her and her brother in irons.

Charles swaggered forward, particularly resplendent in a big red velvet hat adorned with purple feathers and a gleaming diamond buckle. His long, wine red velvet coat was embroidered with gold flowers and his hand rested on a jeweled rapier. "My dear, what a beautiful bride you are."

Amelia curtsied. "You are too kind, Your Majesty."

He smiled, his white teeth gleaming under his mustache. "And We are about to be kinder."

All guests quieted, eager to hear whatever the king had to say.

He cleared his throat and looked from Darcy to Amelia. "We will give you one gift for your wedding, and it may be of your choosing."

Darcy squeezed her arm. "Go on, Amelia."

Amelia looked up at Darcy and smiled tentatively. He genuinely meant it. He would accept whatever she wanted. But what should she ask for? Her husband's titles? Should she request her brother be allowed to stay here? And what of Warrington?

She hesitated. *Warrington*. She'd given a great deal of thought to the lord since his imprisonment. "Majesty, there is something which darkens this day and…my heart."

The king opened his arms magnanimously, as if he were the sun itself. "Speak then. What can We do?"

"I ask for Lord Warrington's life."

The silence intensified around them, and the king's smile dimmed. He glanced toward Lord Winters, whose eyes were as wide as saucers. "My dear, surely you wish for something else. The man wanted to kill you and your brother."

Amelia cleared her throat, aware that she was on dangerous ground. "I do not ask that he go entirely free. But he has suffered so much, and as I understand, except for this, he has always been a most loyal subject."

"Good gad," Charles rolled his eyes with exaggeration as he glanced about at the company. "All anyone does these days is ask for lives to be spared. What say you, Chase… pardon, We mean Blake. It will take Us years to adjust to your name."

Darcy smiled. He looked down at her. "Is this truly what you wish? There is no guarantee that he will not try to harm you—"

"My father killed his entire family. I can never repair what was done, but I can plead for Lord Warrington's life."

The king folded his hands, an approving look warming his face. "You speak like a queen. As you request, Lord Warrington shall be spared." Charles shook his head. "It seems We are banishing everyone, but what can One do?" He glanced over at Lord Winters. "Find a unique place to send him."

"Yes, Majesty," said Lord Winters.

A self satisfied smile played at the king's lips. "Some place particularly hot, We think."

"With pleasure," agreed Lord Winters, with a wicked gleam in his eyes.

"Now, does that please you?"

"I can never thank you enough."

The king took Darcy's hand and Amelia's, joining them together. "Love each other with the power that We have seen between you. That is enough… Oh, and name the first boy after me. Charles is such a fine name, is it not?"

"Indeed, Your Majesty," said Darcy, grinning.

"Well then, We must be off. A country to rule, don't you know." Charles headed toward the end of the chapel, his guards in tow. He stopped at the entry. "You know, Darcy."

"Yes my lord?"

"We don't think We can take this new arrangement."

Darcy tensed beside his new wife. "Yes?"

"We think We shall have to go on calling you Chase after all. And We never did see you perform in that frock."

"Majesty?" Darcy asked.

"Oh God's blood, Lord Chase, you've proven your love to the lady, and besides, since she carries your firstborn, We think the child should be born on good English soil. Don't you agree?

Amelia blinked, gaping at the king. "How did you know, Your Majesty?"

Charles smiled. "We know everything, Lady Chase. We are the king." And with that, Charles whisked out of the room.

Darcy stood gaping. "First born? *Amelia?*"

She smiled tentatively at him. "I don't know how he knew, I only just found out myself."

"You're with child?" he asked, his voice barely more than a whisper.

"Yes. Are you pleased?"

Darcy blinked a few times. "I'm going to be a father."

She laughed. "Yes, yes you are."

"And you're to be a mother? I'm to be a husband and a father?"

She grinned up at him. "That is how it usually works."

"And no doubt, I'm about to behave like an idiot for several months."

"Which won't be anything new," drawled Lord Winters.

Tony strode forward and clapped Darcy on the back. "It's a good thing you two were wed then, don't you think."

Darcy grinned at Tony. "Yes. Very handy that she would have me, was it not?"

Epilogue

"It's a letter from the Americas!" exclaimed Amelia as she tore the wax from the parchment.

Darcy lay back against the pillows. "Your brother, I assume."

"'Tis not his hand writing." As always, a hint of trepidation tugged at Amelia's insides. Anything could happen to her brother out in the wilds, but from the one letter she'd received, he seemed to love it.

Opening the parchment, she took in the bold handwriting and lowered her gaze to the signature. "Good heaven."

Darcy looked at her through half lowered lids as he trailed his fingers to her large belly. His hand rested on the curve and he smiled. "Who is it then?"

"Lord Warrington."

His languid attitude vanished and he propped himself up on an elbow, taking care not to jostle her. "What the devil?"

"Shh. I'll read it aloud."

"I should think so."

She rolled her eyes at him. He could be so protective. It was truly endearing, except when he insisted on carrying her about. "Well, he says,

> *My dear Lady Chase,*
>
> *I know not how to begin, but feel I must thank you. It was my great surprise to learn that it was you who was the cause of my redemption. If not for you, my family would have died with me, ending my line. When I wished you harm, I believed it was a price worth paying. More fool I. Thank you for your understanding and forgiveness.*
>
> *You shall be surprised to hear that your brother and I were banished to the same colony and though only a few months have passed, he and I have actually become friends. Strange, I know, but we share a mutual interest in the customs of the native people. Oh, please tell Lord Winters and the king that the weather here is not in the least hot, but the winters can be the very deuce.*
>
> *Your humble servant,*
> *Lord Warrington.*

"I thought he was sent to the West Indies." Darcy took the letter from her limp grasp.

"So did I." Amelia stared ahead, trying to fathom the great wonders that led people into each other's lives. "Good lord, can you imagine Edward and he friends?"

"Not easily, no." Darcy read through the letter again. "Fascinating. It sounds as if he's found some sort of peace."

Amelia tilted her head and gazed on her husband. "Then I am happy for him.

Casting the letter aside, Darcy eased himself down next to her. "Everyone should know our peace." He kissed her softly, his mouth over hers working with a sweet, unhurried passion.

The babe inside her kicked and Amelia laughed against Darcy's mouth.

"Amusing, eh?"

"Always," she teased. She took his hand and guided it to her abdomen. "Feel."

The child kicked again and she winced a little, but savored the feeling of life inside her. Darcy's eyes widened and his face lit with awe. He looked down at her, a touch of hesitation in his eyes. "Do you miss it?"

She reached up and caressed his cheek. "Miss what?"

"The theater?"

"A little."

"Perhaps we could find a way around it," he suggested.

Lord, he loved her. It warmed her soul how much. Even now, he wanted her happiness, and was trying to find any way to make it possible. She smiled at him, a wicked thought coming to her. "How about our lessons?"

He scowled at her. "I seem to recall skirts and corsets."

"Let me wear the corset."

"And what shall I wear?"

"Oh, I think…nothing at all."

Other Books by Eva Devon

The Twelve Days of Seduction

About the Author

USA TODAY BESTSELLING AUTHOR, Eva Devon, was raised on literary fiction. Quite accidentally and thankfully, she was introduced to romance one Christmas by Johanna Lindsey's Mallory novella, *The Present*. A romance addict was born. She devoured every single Lindsey novel within a few months and moved on to contemporary and paranormal with gusto. Now, she loves to write her own roguish dukes, alpha males, and the heroines who tame them. She loves to hear from her readers. So please pen her a note! evadevonauthor@gmail.com